he brought back a book full of blank paper and two pencils. "Now mind," he told her, "leave my books alone."

WHERE WERE HER PARENTS?

On the wall of her bedroom. Her mother had made the drawing the day they got married. Helen, wearing a dress, the folds nicely shaded, was sitting in a chair; Teddy, in his Sunday suit, stood behind her, his left hand resting on her shoulder. Lizzie seldom glanced at them, but every morning she looked at the little white house with two red doors which had belonged to Helen and which stood on her chest of drawers. In fine weather the woman came out of her door; in bad weather the man emerged; sometimes each hovered on the threshold but they could never come out at the same time. Besides the weather house and the drawing, Lizzie had inherited her mother's border terrier, William, whom they buried in the apple orchard soon after her grandfather cut himself, and a handful of stories. Helen could undo any knot; she could imitate a thrush so that birds sang back; she had rescued a calf from drowning in the river; she was partial to gooseberry jam. About her father, she knew even less. Teddy had been a fisherman. His boat was named St. *Fillan* after the saint who had lived in a cave on the Fife coast and wrote by the light of his glowing left arm, but neither God nor St. Fillan had saved Teddy's boat when the fog rolled in one October day. Seven months later Lizzie was born; twelve months later Helen died. "Not because of you," Flora had said. "Pneumonia. Your father drowned in one way, your mother in another."

She had the ducks and the hens for company, the orphaned lambs and calves, but whenever she and Flora went to Langmuir notable events, besides her arrival, were the mild weather and the early harvest.

Her great-great-grandfather had bought the farm in 1807 with money he made in linen. The gently rolling land was two miles from the village of Langmuir; six miles from the market town of Cupar. He had put a new roof on the white harled farmhouse and planted the beech trees that cast too much shade in the garden. Next to the house was an apple orchard and beyond that a field where Acorn, the mare, and Ivanhoe and Rob Roy, the cart horses, grazed. The cows mostly stayed in a large field beside the farmyard. In the south corner of the field, near the gate, was the duck pond. In the north corner was a small circle of standing stones, two fallen. Down by the river Elder was the meadow where her grandfather had cut himself. Other fields, farther away, were used for turnips, potatoes, corn, barley, oats, and hay. The north pasture and the moorland belonged to the sheep.

It was her great-grandfather who had planted the rowan tree beside the door of the farmhouse to keep witches away and built the lean-to which sheltered the carts, the plough, and the harrow. The other buildings—the barn, the byre, the granary, the dairy, the henhouse, the stable, and the hayloft—were part of the original farm. Between the house and the farmyard, a track led south to the river, and north, past the lochan, to the village of Langmuir. As a child, Lizzie knew every stone and puddle and nettle. She spent her days with her grandmother, Flora, who was tall and blue-eyed and sometimes carried Lizzie on her shoulders when she went to fetch the cows. Lizzie would pat her golden knot of hair, inhale her comforting fragrance of green soap and tea. When she drew a cow in the back of *The Voyage of the Beagle*, Flora spanked her but kept the drawing. Next time her grandfather went to market in Cupar,

into the room, carrying a basket of potatoes. As he washed them
at the sink, she patted his legs, searching for the cut beneath the
rough fabric of his trousers. "What is it, Lizzie?" he said. "Do I
have mud on me?" She told him what she'd seen. "I'd have to be
gey clumsy," he said, "to cut myself digging tatties." She was still
wondering why she had seen a scythe, not a fork, why the sun had
been shining though the sky was grey, when her grandmother
returned and together they went to feed the hens. By the following
July when Neil, their neighbour, carried her grandfather home in a
wheelbarrow, she had forgotten the scene beneath the table. Only
as Dr. Murray made dark, untidy stitches in Rab's leg did she recall
her glimpse of the meadow months before.

She thought of them as pictures because she could see everything so clearly, as if she were standing nearby, although she never
saw herself. Sometimes she saw ordinary things: her grandmother
choosing which hen to kill; a cow stuck in the mud by the river.
She saw a picture of Nellie in a white dress at the front of the
church and three months later Nellie announced she was marrying Angus. "You could have knocked me down with a feather," her
grandmother said, reporting the news at supper. Lizzie started to
say she had known for weeks, but her grandfather was already talking about the sheep shearing.

All this happened at Belhaven Farm, which was in that part of
Scotland called the Kingdom of Fife, surrounded on three sides by
water: the Firth of Forth to the south, the North Sea to the east, the
Tay estuary to the north. Fife was known for its collieries, its fishing, and its university in St. Andrews, but the farm was inland, far
from the coal mines. The year of Lizzie's birth the explorer David
Livingstone died in Africa, the RMS *Atlantic* sank off Nova Scotia,
and the Scottish Rugby Union was founded. On the farm the most

I

The summer she was ten she learned not to speak of it. She told the hens, she told the cows, she told the pond at the bottom of the field and the ducks who swam there and her pet jackdaw, Alice, but she did not tell her grandparents, Rab and Flora, or Hugh, the farm boy, or Nellie, who had helped in the house when she, Lizzie, was learning to walk and whom they still saw every week at the kirk. The first picture came on a dreich November day. Her grandmother was in the dairy, skimming milk, her grandfather in the fields, digging potatoes. She was beneath the kitchen table, making scones for her doll—she must have been three or four—when the flagstone floor and her bowl and spoon disappeared. Instead she was watching her grandfather, his shirtsleeves rolled up, scything hay in the meadow by the river. He was working his way along the bank, cutting wide swathes; one moment the hay was upright, the next fallen. At the end of the row, he stopped to sharpen the scythe. She could see his shirt clinging to his back as he ran the whetstone back and forth. He was starting on the next row when the blade bit his calf.

She was still exclaiming "No," scrambling from beneath the table, when the kitchen door opened and her grandfather stepped

The
Road from
Belhaven

For Kirsty Shorter
1990–2023

By night and day we'll sport and we'll play
And delight as the dawn dances over the bay.
Sleep blows the breath of the morning away
And we follow the heron home.

"FOLLOW THE HERON HOME"
BY KARINE POLWART

THIS IS A BORZOI BOOK
PUBLISHED BY ALFRED A. KNOPF

Copyright © 2024 by Margot Livesey

All rights reserved. Published in the United States by Alfred A. Knopf,
a division of Penguin Random House LLC, New York, and distributed in
Canada by Penguin Random House Canada Limited, Toronto.

www.aaknopf.com

Knopf, Borzoi Books, and the colophon are registered
trademarks of Penguin Random House LLC.

Library of Congress Cataloging-in-Publication Data
Names: Livesey, Margot, author.
Title: The road from Belhaven : a novel / Margot Livesey.
Description: First Edition. | New York : Alfred A. Knopf, [2024] |
Identifiers: LCCN 2023008420 (print) | LCCN 2023008421 (ebook) |
  ISBN 9780593537046 (hardcover) | ISBN 9780593537053 (ebook)
Subjects: LCGFT: Gothic fiction. | Novels.
Classification: LCC PR9199.3.L563 R63 2024 (print) |
  LCC PR9199.3.L563 (ebook) | DDC 813/.54—dc23/eng/20230224
LC record available at https://lccn.loc.gov/2023008420
LC ebook record available at https://lccn.loc.gov/2023008421

"Follow the Heron Home" from the album *Scribbled in Chalk*
reprinted with the permission of Karine Polwart.

Jacket images: *Farm* (detail) by William George Gillies © Estate of
  William Gillies. All rights reserved 2023 / Bridgeman Images;
  Jackdaw by Magnus, Wilhelm and Ferdinand von Wright.
  Photo © Purix Verlag Volker Christen / Bridgeman Images
Jacket design by Kelly Blair

Manufactured in the United States of America
First Edition

The
Road from
Belhaven

*

Margot Livesey

ALFRED A. KNOPF
NEW YORK 2024

The
Road from
Belhaven

she gazed longingly at the girls in the school playground. At last, the August she was five, she set off to join them, wearing a clean pinafore, carrying a slice of bread and a piece of cheese for her lunch. She walked the first mile on her own, past their fields and the track that led to the lochan and Neil's fields. Then she knocked on Dr. Murray's door and walked the rest of the way with Morag, the oldest of his three girls. On that first day Morag hung back, afraid of the boys jostling in the playground, but Lizzie ran into the schoolroom eager to begin. The teacher, Miss Renfrew, put her in a desk next to Sarah, who lived in a house near the blacksmith's. Her milky skin was dotted with freckles that Lizzie kept trying to count.

She liked the morning hymn, she liked writing and counting and reading and reciting and she particularly liked lunchtime, when they were free to play for half an hour. She was good at catch, fast at running; soon she knew the skipping rhymes: "Down in the Valley," "Bluebells, Cockle Shells." After school she was meant to walk home with Morag, but one sunny afternoon she joined a group of girls playing hopscotch. How many times had the church bell struck before she heard a voice calling, "Lizzie Craig?" As they walked along the track, Lizzie skipping to keep up, her grandmother explained she couldn't stop and play whenever she liked. She had the hens to feed, the ducks to shut in for the night. "You've seen the foxes," Flora said, "sneaking under the gate at dusk."

She still enjoyed the games at lunch, but while she gathered the eggs she knew the other girls were whispering confidences, running in and out of one another's houses. She was the only pupil with no sisters, no brothers. Then, one January morning the spring she turned nine, Bob, the cowman, slipped in the first snow and decided he wanted to stay home. A week later her grandfather returned from Cupar with a wheaten-haired, lanky-limbed boy wearing too-short trousers and a too-large shirt. Her grandmother cut Hugh's hair, shortened his sleeves, and made him a bed in the seldom-used parlor. That night at supper he said cheerfully that he was the seventh of seven sons; his father, a tanner, referred to him as surplus labour. When he wasn't working with Rab, ploughing and harrowing, planting and sowing, Hugh helped Flora with the garden and took over the milking. He let Lizzie follow him around; he whittled her pencils and praised her drawings. The farm was no longer lonely.

In May, two days before her birthday, she came home to find a box in the kitchen. A small bird, its black feathers just beginning to bristle, stared up at her with blue-grey eyes. Hugh had found the jackdaw under an ash tree, no parents, no nest in sight. He showed her how to feed it worms and grubs. All evening she kept the bird on her lap, feeling the sharp prick of its claws, stroking its neck feathers.

"What will you call it?" said Hugh.

"Alice," she said. Last winter, they had taken turns reading *Alice's Adventures in Wonderland* aloud.

Alice's eyes lightened to the grey of the lochan on cloudy days. She learned to fly and accompanied Lizzie as she fed the hens and ducks. When she and her grandfather played cribbage, Alice tried to steal the wooden pegs. On her grandmother's birthday, Lizzie tied a little paper banner to Alice's leg: *Happy Birthday, Flora*. In the evenings, while Hugh milked the cows, Alice perched on a hayrack, chattering softly and ignoring the barn cats slinking around in the straw below. As soon as she had done her homework, Lizzie joined them. She told Hugh the news from school—an older boy had broken his arm and had to wear a sling; Miss Renfrew had set a surprise test on the kings and queens of England, and she had passed because he had made her recite the names so often. Hugh told her Neil was putting two of his hives in their orchard and would give them some of the honey. In the *Fife Herald* he had read they were building a railway bridge across the Firth of Forth. He and Lizzie both remembered the storm that had brought down the Tay Bridge. At Belhaven, they had lost a haystack and several trees.

Seated on a milking stool, Lizzie leaned her head against Viola's dusty flank, took hold of two teats, and tried to imitate Hugh's steady motions. Nothing happened; Viola shifted restlessly. "Why won't she milk for me?" she said.

"You have to squeeze and pull at the same time," Hugh said. "Like a calf needing its supper."

She was squeezing, pulling, when Viola and the empty pail vanished. Instead she was looking at the orchard, the apples still small and green, and there was Hugh standing beside one of Neil's hives. The bees were coming and going, their legs knobbly with pollen. Hugh was bending over a hive, lifting off the top, as she had often seen Neil do. Then he was lying on the grass while bees, too many to count, covered his face and arms. His lips were moving but there was no sound. She was wondering how the bees, with their tiny stings, could hurt Hugh, when Viola swished her tail, and the orchard was gone. A few drops of milk dribbled into the pail.

"Hugh," she said, "will you do anything with the bees?"

"No. They mind themselves. When it's time, Neil will show me how to get the honey."

"Promise you won't do it without me," she said, and he did.

After supper, in her room, she took out her sketch pad and drew what she'd seen: the apple trees with their fruit, the hive, and Hugh lying on the ground, covered with bees. She wrote the date at the bottom, *June 16th. 1882*, and slipped the drawing inside the copy of *Jane Eyre* she had won for attendance at Sunday school.

That summer she was tall enough to help with the shearing, guiding the sheep to the shearers, carrying the fleeces to the byre. For days afterwards, she found tufts of wool in her clothes and hair. School ended and the woman came out of the weather house every morning for a week. When Hugh finished the milking, they walked up to the lochan and, while Alice flitted among the birch trees, he taught her to swim. By the time the weather broke, she could breaststroke to the willows on the far side.

MAYBE IT WAS BECAUSE OF HUGH THAT SHE REMEMBERED everything about that year. They lost half a field of oats at harvest time and the snow came early. When it reached the top of her boots, she didn't have to go to school. In the long evenings, while her grandmother mended shirts and socks, she, Hugh, and her grandfather took turns reading *The Princess and the Goblin*. Lizzie imagined herself as the young princess, brave and truthful, and Hugh as Curdie, the miner's son, who defeats the goblins. Her grandmother was the princess's mysterious great-great-grandmother, tall and strong, with shining hair. And her grandfather was the king, on his white horse.

At Christmas Hugh said, if it was all right, he wouldn't go home. They ate one of the ducks, she tried not to think which one, and played Happy Families and whist. At Hogmanay, she and her grandmother cleaned the house from top to bottom, sweeping out the old year to make room for the new. She was allowed to stay up. When the grandfather clock struck midnight, the four of them held hands and sang "Auld Lang Syne." On Twelfth Night a blizzard orphaned two early lambs. She named them the White Queen and the Red Queen.

She was on her way to fetch their milk one wintry evening when she saw light spilling out of the byre. As an adult, she would try to draw the scene: her grandfather, holding a knife, bent over a sawhorse from which hung a small white body. Every spring he skinned the dead lambs and tied the skins onto the living orphans so they would be adopted. Stepping into the lantern light, she asked which lamb would get the skin.

"The White Queen," Rab said. "She's smaller."

"But the coat will be too big." Blood dripped onto the straw.

He said that didn't matter; ewes recognised their lambs by smell, not sight. In the kitchen she held the White Queen while he tied on the skin. It gaped around her shoulders, engulfed her tail, but in the morning, the ewe let her nurse.

On Burns Night she came home from school to find the haggis already made. She hurried through her chores and set the table. Neil and Dr. Murray and his wife came to supper. Hugh gave the "Address to a Haggis," and her grandfather recited "Tam o' Shanter." As he said the lines

> O Tam! Hadst thou but been sae wise
> As taen thy ain wife Kate's advice!
> She tauld thee weel thou was a skellum,
> A blethering, blustering, drunken bellum,

he eyed her grandmother in a way that made them all laugh. Then his voice grew serious as he recounted Tam's drunken ride, the witches and warlocks in fierce pursuit. Years later, when Lizzie found herself living at the Tam o' Shanter pub, she would think her grandfather had, unwittingly, led her there.

THAT SPRING HUGH SUGGESTED SHE TAKE ALICE DOWN to the meadow by the river. A flock of jackdaws was nesting in the pine trees; perhaps she might find a mate. Three Saturdays in a row Lizzie sat reading while Alice flew from tree to tree, playing in the wind. Sometimes she brought Lizzie a pine cone or a twig, but even when the wind took her near their nests she ignored the other birds. "Och, she's decided we're her family," Hugh said.

At school she overheard the girls talking about the hiring fair in Ceres; there would be music, peep shows, confectionery stands, races. After consulting Hugh, she cleaned the henhouse without being reminded and at supper asked could they please, please go to the fair. Her grandparents exchanged a glance.

"It'd be grand to have a day out," said Flora. "Can you manage that, Rab?"

Lizzie had been to Ceres only once, when her grandfather sold a cow to a farmer there. Now as the cart approached the village green, she stood up in her excitement; so many stalls and booths and nut barrows, people everywhere, some, like her family, in their Sunday best, some in their working clothes. There was a cattle competition which her grandfather claimed Viola would have won and a race for farm lads; Hugh came second and won a Kilmarnock bonnet. After the race, she was making her way from stall to stall when she spotted a small tent with a sign: *Madame Solange Will Read Your Future. Two pence.* She was searching her pocket for the sixpence Rab had given her when her grandmother appeared. "Lizzie, what are you doing?"

"I want to ask her if my drawing will win the school prize."

"Time will tell." Flora reached for her hand. "We all want to know the future, but only God can know what's coming. It's the devil tempting us when we try to find out. Besides, Madame Solange is probably some Edinburgh wifie who knows no more of the future than you or I. Let's try the pies."

While they ate slices of apple pie — "Not as good as yours," Lizzie said loyally — they watched a flock of bantams. She wanted to buy the little black rooster with his sharp spurs and feathery tail, but Flora said he'd be more trouble than he was worth. They moved on to the pigeons; Rab sometimes talked about building a dovecot. They were walking back to the cart when Lizzie glimpsed a woman, tall, thin, and dressed in black, slipping out of the back of Madame Solange's tent. She lifted her veil to reveal pale cheeks, lips red as apples. As she tilted her head to look at the sky, Lizzie was sure she heard her sigh.

SCHOOL ENDED; HER DRAWING WON THE PRIZE; THEY brought in the hay. The strawberries ripened, then the gooseberries, the black currants, the raspberries. Lizzie picked and picked. Alice came and went, occasionally tossing a berry into the air, mostly bored. While Flora washed the fruit and measured sugar, she washed the jars and set saucers of sugary froth on the windowsill to waylay the wasps. When the raspberry jam was finished, her grandfather said, "Red sky at night, shepherd's delight. Why don't you two go to the seaside tomorrow?" Her grandmother, before they married, had been a housemaid in St. Andrews and still missed the sea.

The next morning, as soon as the milking was done, she shut

Alice in the dairy and brought Acorn down to the farmyard. Hugh put the mare between the shafts and drove them as far as the hill known as Largo Law. In geography she had learned that it was an extinct volcano but now it was only a large, grassy mound dotted with sheep. Shining in the south was the blue-grey water of the Firth of Forth. "Bring me back some pretty shells," Hugh said. "I'll let Alice out as soon as I get home."

They walked the rest of the way, her grandmother carrying their picnic, while she carried a blanket and a towel. At the town of Lower Largo, they turned east along the path that followed the shore and climbed through the prickly grass down to the beach. They spread their blanket next to a tree trunk, silvery from being in the sea, and took off their shoes. Lizzie ran down to the water, her grandmother not far behind. "It's perishing," Flora exclaimed as a wave splashed over their feet. She pointed across the firth to the pleasingly shaped hill known as Arthur's Seat and the spires of Edinburgh. They walked along, filling their pockets with shells. As they ate their bread and cheese, they decided which ones were worthy of Hugh. The rest would be crushed with a rolling-pin, for the hens.

After lunch Lizzie ran into the dunes to squat behind a scrubby bush; the little pool vanished instantly. When she came back to the beach, a boy was leading a donkey along the wet sand. "Penny a ride," he cried. "A penny for a ride on Fife's best-tempered donkey."

She could have all the rides she wanted on Acorn, but she asked for a penny and joined the two girls already waiting. She was watching them play leapfrog when, like a small breeze stirring the kitchen curtains, something rippled across her brain. Was a picture coming? She hadn't had one since before they went to the fair. But no, it was nothing. Flora was strolling the tide line. Three children were paddling. A dog that looked like William was trotting behind an elderly man. A flock of seagulls, some white and grey, some fledgling brown, were pecking the sand. The donkey returned, a boy slid off, the smaller of the waiting girls climbed on. The other turned to her. "You're not from here," she said.

Lizzie explained they were taking a holiday after finishing the jam. She pointed to her grandmother, who was throwing a long strand of seaweed into the sea. The girl pointed to a spire visible above the dunes; she lived beside the church. They had made their jam last week and the girl on the donkey was her little sister.

The donkey trotted back. The younger sister slid off; the older one climbed on. Lizzie watched her grandmother bend to examine something. Maybe next time they could bring Acorn and offer rides. Then the donkey was back, his eyes brown as the river Elder and on his shoulders the cross of dark hairs which Mr. Robinson, the Sunday-school teacher, claimed was the donkey's reward for carrying Christ into Jerusalem on Palm Sunday. She clambered on and, from her new vantage point, searched the horizon. Somewhere in all this water was her father.

"Does he have a name?" she asked.

"She. We call her Gooseberry because she fancies them."

The boy began to run, Gooseberry trotted, and she held tight to the halter, delighted by the people, the waves, passing so quickly. When the ride was over, the boy helped her down. Gooseberry, released, opened her mouth and uttered a sound so angry, so sorrowful, that Lizzie jumped back.

"Och, she's tired of the rides," said the boy. "I'll take her home for tea."

All the way across the sand, the braying followed her. Her grandmother had wrapped up the shells and was shaking out the blanket. They retraced their steps through the dunes and were climbing up towards Largo Law when they heard the clip-clop of hooves and—what luck!—Johnny Stephens from the village was heading home with room in his cart. While the grown-ups chatted over her head, she calculated the money she and Hugh could make giving rides at the beach. They got down at Neil's house and walked the rest of the way. As they came through the farmyard gate, the hens ran to meet them, clucking furiously. "Hugh must have forgotten to feed them," her grandmother said.

Lizzie was leaving the granary when Alice came shooting down. She landed a few feet away and, looking over her shoulder, eyes glinting, began to walk towards the gate. When Lizzie didn't follow, she came back, pecked her shoe, and began to walk again. Still holding the pail of grain, Lizzie followed. Alice took to the air, circling, cawing. "Run," she was saying, "run faster." Lizzie set the pail on the wall and ran.

Hugh was lying on the grass between two apple trees. His face and neck were covered with bees, so many that no skin was visible between their brown and golden bodies. Flinging herself down, she used her skirt to wipe them away, not caring when she was stung.

"Hugh, Hugh, are you all right?"

His lips moved, but there was only a faint hissing sound. She wiped and wiped, her hands pricking from the stings. Still he said nothing. She turned and ran back to the kitchen. As soon as Flora understood what she was saying, she seized a sharp knife and a towel. "Bring some water," she called, and hurried to the door. Lizzie caught up with her at the edge of the trees. In the few minutes she'd been gone, Hugh's face had swelled so his eyes were almost hidden. Beside him, Alice hopped up and down, rattling.

"Don't look," said Flora. She put one hand under his neck; with the other, she drew the knife across his throat. Even as Lizzie cried out, she did it again. Blood sprang up against his pale skin. Alice cawed once, sharply.

"Push on his chest," said her grandmother. "Let go. Push again. Don't mind the blood."

She pushed as hard as she could. How could this be better? All this blood.

"Good girl. Let me."

As she moved aside, Hugh's eyelashes trembled; blood bubbled along the cut. Nearby the bees circled. "Find Rab," her grandmother said. "Tell him to fetch the doctor."

Once again she was running, calling for her grandfather in the house. Empty. In the barn. Empty. Past the granary and there he was, leaning against a cart, smoke rising from his pipe. As soon as she shouted, "Hugh needs the doctor," he was striding towards the village. Let Dr. Murray be home, she thought; he could be miles away, visiting another patient. Back in the orchard, Flora was still kneeling beside Hugh. If only he had kept his promise and waited for her to go to the hives. She knelt down on his other side. "Grandfather's gone to the village," she said. "Did you know this would happen?"

"How could I?" Her grandmother gave her a sharp look. "I doubt he knew. One or two stings wouldn't bother him but so many, all at once, made his throat close."

But I knew, Lizzie thought. She was glad when Flora sent her for more water, another towel. Then her grandfather came hurrying over the grass, followed by Dr. Murray. At the sight of her grandmother, hands and blouse smeared with blood, Rab burst out, "Flora, what in God's name happened?"

Before she could answer, the doctor, kneeling on Hugh's other side, said, "Good woman, you did just what I would have done."

Lizzie asked how Hugh would talk and the doctor explained that in a day or two the swelling would go down. He would bandage the cut and Hugh would be able to speak again. Together he and Rab carried Hugh back to the house and up the stairs to the spare room. Flora went ahead to spread a towel on the pillow. The doctor showed them how to raise his neck to make sure the cut stayed open. Promising to return first thing, he hurried away. He'd been visiting another patient when her grandfather found him.

"Read to him," her grandmother said. "If anything changes, fetch me."

She opened *The Princess and the Goblin* at a page with a picture. " 'The princess wiped her eyes, and her face grew so hot that they were soon quite dry. She sat down to her dinner, but ate next to nothing. Not to be believed does not at all agree with princesses: for a real princess cannot tell a lie.' " Deep in his swollen face, Hugh's eyelashes stirred, stilled, stirred. The princess had almost met the goblins when his eyelids slid open. As his lips moved and no sound came, she could see he was afraid. She ran to get her grandmother.

"Are you thirsty?" Flora asked. "Do you need anything?"

He made a writing gesture.

When she came back with her slate and some chalk, her grandmother was explaining why she had cut his throat. Hugh wrote *Thank you. Water.* When they were alone again, Lizzie told him how Alice had led her to the orchard but not about the feeling on the beach, or Gooseberry's braying, or her picture. That evening in her room she took out *Jane Eyre*. There was her drawing of Hugh and the bees, the date more than a year ago. She longed to show it to her grandmother, to tell her how, sitting beside Viola, she had seen Hugh lying in the orchard, but she remembered what Flora had said about Madame Solange. When the house was quiet, she tiptoed down the stairs and put the drawing in the stove.

II

＊

At night, after she said Our Father, she added a special petition to see no more pictures, and in the months following Hugh's recovery she saw only two: a wheel came off the cart; a tree in the north pasture was hit by lightning. In each case the picture came a few weeks before the accident. When she had bad dreams, her grandmother counselled her to forget them; now she tried to do the same with the pictures. They were more easily ignored because that autumn brought new worries. In the evenings, instead of reading, Rab and Flora sat at the table, adding and subtracting. If they didn't buy soap, they could afford medicine for the cows. If they didn't buy coal, they could buy seed corn. She tried to help by giving the hens and ducks smaller handfuls of corn. On Saturday mornings she packed the eggs in straw in the wagon Hugh had built. Around them she placed wedges of butter wrapped in cheesecloth, bottles of milk. She pulled the wagon into the village and visited their regular customers. Occasionally someone would stop her in the road and ask for half a dozen eggs or a pint of milk. She felt a pang of pleasure as she handed her grandmother the extra coins.

The Saturday after Hugh was stung, Mrs. Anderson, the joiner's wife—a dozen eggs and a pound of butter—asked how Flora knew to cut a hole in his neck. Lizzie said she didn't know, and that evening, over neeps and tatties, asked the same question.

"Before I met Rab," her grandmother said with a quick smile for her grandfather, "I worked for a family in St. Andrews. Mr. Rankin had a few hives at the bottom of the garden. His bees made the sweetest honey I've ever tasted. One day, their son Murdoch was chasing his brother and he knocked over a hive. Mrs. Rankin and I ran out with pails of water. That got rid of the bees. Then Murdoch stopped screaming and she sent me for a knife.

"Afterwards she told me that in ancient Greece a doctor had discovered when a person couldn't breathe, you could cut into their windpipe. Her father was a doctor and she had watched him do it once. So, when I saw Hugh lying there, I thought of Mrs. Rankin."

"I'm a fortunate lad," Hugh said. "Not many women would have cut my throat."

"That's why I married Flora." Her grandfather smiled across the table.

But in bed Lizzie kept thinking, What if Flora hadn't gone to work for the Rankins? What if Murdoch hadn't chased his brother that day? Should a person's life depend on a thin chain of coincidences? The next time she saw Neil standing in his cottage door, she asked if he had ever been stung.

"All the time," he said. "Sometimes I ask the bees to sting me, for my rheumatism." He held up his crooked fingers.

"No," she persisted, "stung like Hugh."

"Only once. I was trying to capture a swarm in an elm near the church, and had to jump into the horse trough. But I wasn't poorly like Hugh." He stepped inside and returned with a honeycomb, each waxy cell brimming. "A reminder that the bees have their sweet side."

THE NEXT ACCIDENT HAPPENED WITH NO WARNING ON A mild afternoon. She was in the meadow by the river, rounding up the cows, when she heard shouts. Mr. McEwen, the sternest of the church elders, was running along the other bank, his oldest son at his heels. Where the river grew shallow, rippling over the stones, they plunged into the water and bent down as if trying to catch a fish. They straightened, holding a dark bundle. As they carried her to the bank, staggering under the weight, water poured off the girl's clothes and her long, brown hair. They laid her on the grass. Mr. McEwen took off his cap and sat down a few yards away while his son ran towards Langmuir.

Walking behind the cows, Lizzie counted the dead bodies she had seen: Mrs. Frazer's son, who'd slipped through the ice on the lochan; Mr. Wright's father, who'd fallen over digging a grave for his dog; Syd the cowman, who hadn't woken up one morning; and many, many animals. Sometimes in church Mr. Waugh, the minister, asked them to pray for those dead in disasters: miners crushed at a local colliery, fishermen drowned near a town called Eyemouth.

In the barn she fetched her milking stool and, sitting beside Viola, told her grandmother what she'd seen.

"Poor thing," said her grandmother. "Did you recognise her?"

She shook her head. Almost all the older girls she knew, except for Christine Arnot, had long brown hair.

As they walked into the village after supper, to see if there was news, her grandmother pointed out the moon rising over the birch trees. Looking at the slender crescent, Lizzie wondered why she had had no picture of the drowned girl. Perhaps, she hoped, it meant the girl had revived? But as soon as she saw Morag's mother, and three other women, standing near the horse trough, she knew the worst was true. She would have liked to listen to their conversation, but her grandmother gave her a penny and sent her into the shop. By the time she emerged with her stick of toffee, they were talking about the Harvest Festival. Walking home, Flora told her what she had learned: a maid from the Blackhorse Inn in Cupar had gone missing; her name was Grace Henderson.

The next day at school, when she overheard the older girls talking about Grace, she elbowed her way into the conversation. Briefly, as she described what she'd seen, she was the centre of attention. Nora Anderson asked if Mr. McEwen had pressed on the girl's chest to get the water out. Phyllis Campbell said she'd heard Grace had had a little too much to do with a stable boy. From the way her lips twitched, Lizzie guessed this was an insult. That afternoon, when she and Hugh went to fetch the ducks, she repeated the remark. "Did she mean the stable boy hurt her?"

"Not how you're thinking," he said. "She meant the girl was going to have his child and he wouldn't marry her. She went into the river out of despair. Don't let on to your grandparents I tell you such things. Hamlet, supper time."

Four of the ducks—Hamlet, Ophelia, Gertrude, and Claudius— came running to Hugh's cry. The fifth, Polonius, continued to waddle along the bank, shoveling his beak into the mud.

She searched her grandfather's newspaper but read no mention of Grace. After a few days no one spoke of her; it was as if she had never existed. In the city, years later, Lizzie would see women begging, some with children, some with child, and think Grace might have found another way.

....

THAT WINTER TWO EWES DIED GIVING BIRTH. THEN ONE of the orphan lambs died. All the money went for seed corn, potatoes, turnips. The first planting of oats was washed away. Rab blamed himself for not knowing that a storm was coming. They burned wood in the stove; most nights they ate porridge for supper. There was no money for a new sketchbook. When the crops ripened, Rab hired four lads instead of the usual three, to help bring in the harvest. Flora went to the fields as soon as she had finished the milking, and Lizzie, once school ended, joined her. They followed the men, hooking the corn and the oats into stooks. The day after they brought in the last of the barley, Hugh kicked one of the barn cats and swore at Viola for not letting down her milk. When Lizzie asked what was wrong, he said Rab had paid the village lads more for three weeks than he paid Hugh for three months.

She often forgot that he was paid; her cheeks grew hot as she said he should ask for more money.

"I did. Rab said he didn't have it. He showed me the accounts to prove it. He had to pay the lads to get in the harvest. Christ, Lizzie, how can I argue with that?"

The next morning on her way to school she put the two shillings she'd been given for her birthday under his door. When she came home there was a piece of paper under her own door: *Thank you.* At school Miss Renfrew had taught them about the Great Chain of Being, God and his angels at the top, followed by Queen Victoria, followed by lords and ladies, then people like the minister and Mr. Douglas, who lived in the big house on the way to Cupar, going all the way down to poor people like the Scotts, who lived in a mouldering cottage on the road to the castle and couldn't read or write. She and her grandparents could read and write, they had the farm, but they were much closer to the Scotts than she had understood.

AT CHRISTMAS MISS RENFREW SURPRISED EVERYONE BY retiring. A new teacher, Miss Urquhart, came from Glasgow and moved into the schoolhouse. On her first day she made the pupils write a paragraph, introducing themselves:

> My name is Lizzie Craig. I am eleven years old and I live with my grandparents who own Belhaven Farm. They are always telling me not to be impatient and to work hard. I like drawing, history, and geography. I'd like to go to Asia Minor someday. When I'm in a thrawn mood, my grandmother tells me to think of the starving children in Glasgow but I have never been there. She and my grandfather work every day except the Sabbath. I wish I was a boy so I could help them more.

Miss Urquhart wore narrow skirts and a bright-blue hat with a pheasant's feather that Lizzie liked to watch in church. The girl who kept house for her reported that she read the newspaper and sometimes bought oranges. At school she started a library, took them on nature walks, made them draw maps of countries and famous battlefields, including Bannockburn, Robert the Bruce's great victory. When she heard that there was a circle of standing stones at Belhaven, she asked Lizzie to draw a picture and pinned it on the wall beside a drawing of Stonehenge. "What we call the Kingdom of Fife," she said, "was once the Pictish Kingdom of

Fib." One spring afternoon she marched the whole school down the main road, past the Scotts' cottage, to the ruined castle on the outskirts of Langmuir. "There has been a castle on this spot for eight hundred years," Miss Urquhart said. "Someday archeologists will dig here and discover statues and necklaces, like they're doing in the ancient city of Troy."

That evening, when she repeated the teacher's remarks, Hugh said, "Let's go and see what we can find." On Sunday after church he loaded two spades and a fork into the wagon. With Alice circling, they walked to the castle. Inside, Lizzie pointed out the tower in the west corner, which was the oldest part of the building, and the rectangular holes in the walls, which marked where the beams used to be. While Alice explored the battlements, she led Hugh into the huge fireplace. At the top of the tall, dark chimney, the sky was a brilliant blue.

He directed her to a nearby corner and started digging a few yards from the fireplace. As he cleared away stones and fallen branches, he remarked it was a pity they couldn't consult his brother, Stewart, who knew about castles.

"Do you miss him?" she asked, pushing down on her spade.

"I'm too busy to miss anyone, but if I did, he's the one I'd miss. I have this notion he and I will meet someday, wearing posh suits, and talk about bridges and buildings."

"You're not going to get a posh suit working at Belhaven." At once she wished she'd held her tongue.

"But you will," he said. "When you inherit the farm, you can bring in machines, plant new varieties of oats and barley."

"Why would I inherit the farm?" Her spade dinged against a rock.

"Who else will your grandfather leave it to?" He bent to his own spade. "Not his ne'er-do-well brother in Aberdeen. There's no one but you, Lizzie. That's why they adopted you, gave you their name. Look." He held up a fork, mossy with rust.

As she lifted another spadeful, her mind was busy with this new idea. The farm would be hers, hers and Hugh's. They would decide what to plant, which cows to breed, when to harvest the oats and the tatties. The other girls at school had sisters, pianos, nice neat cottages in the village; she had Hugh and Belhaven.

THEY WENT BACK TO DIG MOST SUNDAYS UNTIL THE ground froze, but they didn't find buried treasure, only something Hugh thought was a hairpin and a pot the size of a porridge bowl, decorated with black lines. Lizzie took the latter to school. "Oh, my," Miss Urquhart exclaimed when she unwrapped it. Setting it carefully on her desk, she leafed through one of her books until she found a drawing of a similar pot. "This kind of decoration was used by the Vikings," she said. "You should show it to someone at the university in St. Andrews."

Hugh seized on the suggestion. In late January he made his way to Cupar and caught the train to St. Andrews. Long after dark, Lizzie was reading aloud to her grandparents when the latch rattled. Hugh burst into the kitchen, flushed with cold and the excitement of his journey. Between spoonfuls of broth, he described the grand buildings of the university, the library with its rows and rows of bookcases. In the history department, he had exchanged their pot for a receipt. The man had said they would put it in the museum. The hairpin was only thirty or forty years old.

"Here, Lizzie," he said, "you'd better keep this."

On a piece of paper stamped with the university crest she read: *January 28th. 1886: Received from Hugh Irvine—1 pot, possibly Viking. Found at the Castle in the village of Langmuir by Cupar.* "Did they give you any money?" she said.

Hugh said he hadn't thought to ask. After handing over the pot, he had gone to a bookshop and bought a book, the pages full of diagrams of machines. Here was a seed drill: it had been invented nearly two hundred years ago and still only a farm near Ceres had one. Here was a new kind of harrow. Now, while she did her homework, he pored over the pages. Sometimes he got her to copy a drawing for him so that he could experiment with his own alterations. When he finished the book, he built a hoist in the granary to raise the sacks of grain to the upper floor. The miller paid him a pound for a similar hoist. He adjusted the grandfather clock so that it no longer gained ten minutes a week. He asked for an afternoon off to watch the trains pass in Cupar. When spring came, they went back to the castle, but on the way home he said he spent all week digging; he didn't want to spend his Sundays that way too. At Whitsun he announced at supper that after the harvest, he was going to find a job in Glasgow. "I want to work with machines," he said.

While her grandparents tried to change his mind, Lizzie glared at her plate. Belhaven without Hugh was unthinkable. The next morning, she slipped out of the house to find him in the barn, milking by lantern light.

"You can't leave," she said. "When the farm is mine, it will be yours too."

Hugh kept his face pressed against the cow's flank. "Lizzie, waiting for Rab to grow old is no way for me to live, or you either. Truth to tell, I'm fed up with farming. Everything depends on luck. I want to work with something reliable, like a steam engine: energy in, energy out."

"Please." She knelt beside the cow, clasping her hands. "I'll give you all the cows."

He shook his head. "You're so tall," he said, "sometimes I forget you're still a child."

Later she would think this was her first betrayal, and she had brought it on herself. If only she hadn't taken him to the castle.

They were all red-eyed as they bade him farewell on a misty September morning; Alice cawed and the cows were slow to let down their milk. "We miss him too," Lizzie told them. Rab said he'd hire someone else in the spring. Meanwhile he hired village lads to help get ready for winter, and Neil lent a hand. Hugh wrote he had found a room and a job at the Singer Sewing Machine factory, the new one they were building at Kilbowie. *It's as long as six football fields. We have our own railway to carry supplies.* He promised to return for the harvest.

Without Hugh, everything was harder. Now as she hurried home from school, she imagined herself not as the little princess but as Curdie, the miner's son, who defeats the goblins. That autumn she helped lift the tatties, pull the neaps, rescue a haystack that had blown away; she cut whins on the hillside; she scoured a ditch. Winter came like a fist. The man refused to go back in the weather house; the duck pond was frozen solid. Night after night they ate porridge. A late blizzard killed three lambs and a ewe. Her grandfather fell out with Mr. MacDonald over a cow and they moved from their pew behind the MacDonalds to one at the back of the kirk.

From their new pew Lizzie could no longer see Miss Urquhart's hat with its cheering feather. Instead, while Mr. Waugh preached about the parable of the hidden treasure, she stared at Miss Dawson's dowdy grey hat, which she had been wearing for as long as Lizzie could remember. Mr. Waugh was explaining that the good seed were the children of the kingdom but the tares were the children of the wicked one, when the hat disappeared. She was looking at a room, the walls lined with shelves of shoes and boots, big and small, some black, some chestnut brown. At a workbench a white-haired man with a fan-shaped moustache was studying the sole of a shoe. "So we understand," said Mr. Waugh, "that at the end of the world, the wicked shall be cast into the fire; there shall be wailing and gnashing of teeth."

ON MONDAY ALICE FAILED TO MEET HER AFTER SCHOOL. Flora said perhaps, at last, she had found a friend. But the next morning in the barn, as Lizzie hung up her milking stool, something moved in the straw: Alice, bloody, broken-winged. Cradling her carefully, Lizzie hurried to the house.

"Can you help me splint her wings?"

"Lizzie." Her grandmother stroked Alice's head. "We should put her out of her misery." It was what she always said about a sick animal.

"But she saved Hugh. I'll nurse her. I'll fetch her worms."

Alice's grey eyes followed their exchange. The next day Lizzie refused to go to school. She carefully dropped water into Alice's throat; she cut plump worms into squirming pieces; she read to Alice from her namesake; the Mad Hatter told riddles and the Dormouse told a story. But in the morning, Alice's eyes were closed. Lizzie buried her in the orchard, close to William, marking the grave with two branches tied in a cross.

III

At school, Miss Urquhart taught the older pupils about the pathetic fallacy. As rational beings, she said, we know the weather doesn't care whether we behave well or badly, although poets often suggest the contrary. But day after day, as the rain fell, or the fog hung over the fields, or the sleet cracked against the windows, it was hard not to believe that Belhaven, and its inhabitants, were being punished. No wonder Hugh had wanted to go to Glasgow. One morning she and Morag arrived at school to find the room filled with smoke: a nest had fallen down the chimney. As she opened a window, Miss Urquhart reminded them of the date: the Ides of March. "Remember, children, we read about that in *Julius Caesar.*" Throughout the day they shivered with the windows open or coughed with them closed. When the last bell rang, she and Morag ran to Morag's house; then Lizzie kept running to get warm.

In the kitchen her grandmother was at the table, peeling apples. "Look at the state of you," she said. "Hang up your coat and sit down. The hens will wait."

Trying to think what she had done, or failed to do, she took her usual chair. Flora reached for another apple. As the peel unfurled, the tick of the grandfather clock seemed to grow louder and louder. "You know," she said at last, "your parents bided with your other grandparents in Kirkcaldy. What you don't know"—her blue eyes fastened on Lizzie—"is that you have an older sister. Her name is Kate MacLeod, your father's name. When Helen was poorly, she asked me to take you, but she wouldn't let me take Kate."

She was on her feet, her chair falling to the floor, hugging her grandmother so hard that Flora laughed. "Calm yourself, Lizzie. What a commotion."

When she was seated again, Flora explained that she and Granny Agnes had decided not to tell the girls about each other, but Agnes had died the week before Christmas, and today a letter had come from Grandpa John: he was giving up his cobbler's shop and going to live with his brother. As soon as the weather cleared, Rab would fetch Kate. "Can you finish the apples while I skim the milk?"

Alone, too excited to peel apples, Lizzie paced between the sink and the pantry. Since Hugh left, there had been three places at the table; now there would again be four. She thought of the sisters she knew. The three Findlayson girls, all curly-haired and broad-shouldered but the middle one a soprano in the church choir, the other two croaking like frogs; the Millers, Lillian so studious, her hand always up to answer Miss Urquhart's questions, Annie never opening a book unless she was scolded; Sarah and Jane Dobbs, both pale and freckled and good dancers. Would she and Kate be like, or unlike, or some mixture of the two?

HOW LONG THOSE DAYS OF WAITING SEEMED AS SHE woke every morning to the man coming out of the weather house, rain lashing on the windows. On Saturday no rain but fog so thick the ducks vanished into the field. At last on Sunday, an hour before the usual time, she heard footsteps on the stairs. In the kitchen her grandfather was eating his porridge while her grandmother cut slices of bread and cheese. "Can I come?" she begged.

"It's too far," he said. "You need to stay and help with the cows."

As the cart disappeared down the track, Flora went to fetch the lantern and she headed to the barn. From the doorway, she could make out the dark shapes of the cows and hear their slow breathing, a sound like the sea. She would teach Kate to milk, she thought, and to gather the eggs. Perhaps she too would be good at drawing. They would walk to school and everybody would want to meet her sister with a different surname. Together they would inherit the farm. Then her grandmother was back, hanging the lantern on the hook. As they settled to milking, she described her plans.

"Lizzie," her grandmother said, "you mustn't expect too much. Imagine if you were sent to live with strangers."

"But we're the opposite of strangers."

After church, Flora gave her various tasks—cleaning Kate's room, sewing on a button—but the hours crept by. When she gathered the eggs, the hens pecked at her and the ducks, when she went to bring them in for the night, headed into the field, quacking loudly: too soon, too soon. In the barn the cows fidgeted from hoof to hoof and she almost tripped over one of the cats. Dusk had fallen before they heard the creaking of the cart. In the lantern light Acorn plodded along. Sitting beside her grandfather, as far away from him as possible, was a figure wrapped in a blanket.

"Welcome to Belhaven Farm, Kate." Her grandmother held out her hand. "I'm your grandmother Flora."

"I'm your sister, Lizzie." She too offered her hand.

Her sister, hidden by the blanket, neither moved nor spoke. All that could be seen of her was four fingers, red with cold, clasping the blanket, and two shiny, brown boots.

"There's no help for it, lass," said Rab. "We're here, like it or not."

At last the girl, still ignoring them, jumped down. To her surprise, Lizzie saw she was several inches taller than her older sister.

"Come inside," said Flora. "You must be frozen." She led the way to the house; Kate followed slowly. Before she could go after them, her grandfather asked her to hold Acorn. "Lizzie, my dear," he said, "I hope I never have another day as long and sad as this one." He hoisted Kate's box out of the cart and carried it towards the lighted doorway.

"I wish you could tell me everything you've seen today," she said, stroking Acorn's nose. Then her grandfather was back. She ran to the farmhouse. In the kitchen, Kate was standing by the door, holding the blanket close, while her grandmother urged her to come and warm herself by the stove. "We'll have supper as soon as Rab feeds Acorn."

"I don't want supper." The voice was sharp as a slap.

"How about some hot milk?"

"Do I have a bed?"

Did she think they were going to make her sleep on the floor? Not looking up from the stew she was stirring, her grandmother said, "Lizzie will show you."

She led the way back into the hall, up the stairs. "This is our grandparents' room, this is mine. And this is yours." She opened the door, raising the lantern so that the light fell on the bed, smooth save for the hump of the hot-water bottle she had filled three hours ago. She was explaining about the WC when Kate took the lantern, stepped past her, and closed the door.

Lizzie reached for the door, about to pull it open. Then, remembering her sister's "Do I have a bed?" she ran downstairs, threw her arms around her grandmother, and allowed herself to be enveloped by the fragrance of green soap and tea.

"Lizzie, Lizzie, don't upset yourself. She's weary after her long day."

"Weary!" she was exclaiming when her grandfather stepped into the room. He crossed the kitchen, disappeared into the pantry, and reappeared with the bottle of whisky he got out on New Year's Eve and Burns Night and the last nights of sheep shearing and harvesting.

Her grandmother carried a tray upstairs. "Your supper's in the hall," they heard her say. Then she was back, closing the door behind her. "Not a murmur."

Her grandfather raised his glass. Even when he was up all night with a sick ewe or a cow in labour, the next day he'd be following the plough across a field. Now, seeing his hair grey as ashes, the lines scoring his forehead, the plum-coloured shadows around his eyes, his hawklike nose, she understood that the long hours in the cart had made his bones ache and his head hurt, and Kate, for whom he had done all this, had offered no word of thanks. Between mouthfuls of stew, he described how he'd got stuck behind a flock of sheep, then had to find an inn to water and feed Acorn. When he reached Kirkcaldy, the streets were filled with people in their Sabbath clothes. He had tied Acorn up in the square and got directions to the shop.

"John stepped out to talk to me. He said Kate had been in an awful state. She claimed she'd rather go into service than come here, but that was nonsense—she would hate people telling her what to do all day long. I offered to go home, she could write to us when she was ready, but he said he couldn't go through this again. Her box was packed; a cousin was taking over the shop at the end of the month. I wish you'd been there, Flora." He looked at her grandmother. "I'm no good at this sort of palaver."

When he came into the house, Kate was standing in the kitchen. "She was so like her mother," he said, "it gave me a turn. I said I was her grandfather Rab and she glared at me until John asked her to make tea. I told them about the farm, about you. She served the tea and sat in a corner with a book. When I asked what she was reading, she said, 'A book.' John told her to mind her manners.

"He and I carried out her box. When we came back, she was still in the corner. I said she might be glad of a cushion, if John could spare one. 'In the summer, you'll come and visit me,' he said. 'Until then, rain or shine, I'll write every Sunday. And every Sunday you must put on the shoes I made you and go to the kirk and when you get home, write me a letter.' Poor man, I was worried he was going to weep. The three of us walked to the cart. He patted her cheek and headed back to the empty house. She climbed up and didn't speak another word."

"Poor John," Flora agreed. "And poor Kate. She needs to recover from her journey."

In bed, Lizzie thought about the picture she had had in church. Perhaps someday she could tell Kate she had seen Grandpa John with his fan-shaped moustache and his shelves of shoes. She was almost asleep when faintly, through the wall, came the sound of crying.

THE NEXT MORNING WHEN MORAG ASKED WHERE HER sister was, she repeated her grandmother's phrase about recovering.

They compared the maps of Scotland they'd drawn for homework, marking the places where someone they knew lived, and the major cities. Lizzie had marked Hugh in Glasgow; Kate in Kirkcaldy; St. Andrews, where the Viking pot was in a museum; Balmoral, where the queen spent the summers; Stirling, where Robert the Bruce had won the battle of Bannockburn. She did not mark Aberdeen, where James, the uncle they never spoke of, lived. Morag had marked the same towns, and included Scrabster, the town near John o' Groats where her father had grown up watching the northern lights.

At school Miss Urquhart said of course Kate needed to rest; they'd see her tomorrow. Sarah had already moved to another desk to make room for her, and lesson after lesson, the empty seat reminded Lizzie of her absence. When the bell rang, she told Morag she had to hurry home, but in the kitchen, there was only her grandmother, mixing mash.

"I haven't seen her all day," Flora said, bending over the pail. "She's as thrawn as her mother."

"But she'll starve!"

"You don't starve in a day or two. When we forbade Helen from marrying Teddy, she didn't leave her room for three days. Now help me take this to the horses."

They did the normal things, but everything felt different as they listened for the sound of a latch, a foot on the stair. Rab said if this nonsense continued, he'd fetch her down; Flora told him not to be hasty. That night Lizzie fell asleep to the wind wuthering around the chimneys. Hours later the silence woke her, and in the silence she heard, again, the faint, determined crying.

The next afternoon her grandmother reported Kate had eaten some bread and cheese, but at supper the place Lizzie laid for her remained empty. When she woke to the now familiar sobbing, she carried *The Water Babies* to Kate's room and opened the door. "Please, please, please, stop crying," she whispered. From the doorway she could make out Kate's dark hair on the pillow. "I brought you a book."

"I hate it here. It smells of animals."

That must be true, Lizzie thought. When she was doing the deliveries, each house had its own smell: mince or babies or cloths boiling or stale cheese. "Did your old house have a smell?"

"Leather." Kate began to sob again. "Grandpa's pipe. Shoe polish."

She set the book on the chest of drawers and stole away.

That afternoon when she came home Kate was at the sink, scraping carrots. If she passed her on the road, Lizzie thought, she would never have guessed this person was her sister. Kate's eyebrows were straighter, her cheeks paler, her lips thinner, her hair nicely wavy. Her blouse and skirt fitted like Miss Urquhart's and her boots shone. She did not speak at supper but she sat at the table, she ate.

SHE STILL MISSED HUGH EVERY DAY, AND NOW, WALKING down the track to Langmuir with Kate silent beside her, she missed the sister whom she'd imagined would be her best friend. At school Miss Urquhart asked what Kate had studied at her last school—everything—and what her favourite subject was—French. "You'll find we do things differently," Miss Urquhart said. "Lizzie will help you with the timetable."

"But I'm nearly sixteen. She's only thirteen."

Briskly Miss Urquhart explained that everyone did the same subjects at the same time, except for French and Latin, which only the older pupils did. "You'll sit with Lizzie today. On Monday you can stay after school so I can figure out where you belong."

"I belong with the older pupils," Kate said.

Lizzie was glad when lessons began and she could think about geography and history. Beside her, Kate sighed and wrote in answers, sometimes before Miss Urquhart finished speaking. At lunch, Lizzie went to sit with Morag and Sarah and tried not to notice Kate, alone at their desk. When the bell rang, she walked home with Morag, leaving Kate to follow. Morag kept glancing over her shoulder, but Lizzie insisted Kate wanted to be on her own. After they reached Morag's house, she started running and didn't look back. She was changing her pinafore in the kitchen when Kate appeared, pink cheeked, her shiny boots dulled with mud. "Where are you going?" Kate demanded. "Where is everyone?"

"Working," Lizzie said, and pushed past her out of the door.

In the henhouse she slid her hand under the hens' feathery bodies. Twenty-three eggs, one without a shell. She set the warm, quivering mass on top to throw on the midden; the hens must not discover they enjoyed eating their own eggs. Let Kate see what it was like to be ignored. In the barn, Flora was already milking Queenie. Lizzie retrieved her stool and settled down with Isabel.

"Kate was rude to Miss Urquhart. When is she going to help with things?"

"She's homesick. On Saturday you can show her how to do the deliveries."

"I already show her things at school. Why should I have to help her at home too?"

"She's your nearest relation. We're glad you'll have each other when we're gone. Rab lies awake worrying about you and the farm."

She had not known anything could keep her grandfather awake. Now, as the milk frothed in the pail, she began to make a list of village boys, not the ones still at school but the older ones who worked at the mill, the smithy, the wheelwright's, the joiner's, the cooper's. There must be someone other than Hugh who could drive a straight furrow, who knew the care of sheep and cattle, whom she could learn to like. Flora finished Queenie and went to start supper. Lizzie moved on to Fanny. Her second pail was almost full when a picture came. Acorn was standing in a corner of the field, her head hung low, her legs oddly stiff. Beside her the blackthorn hedge was covered with white flowers, which meant it was high summer. And the mare's lips were white as if, despite the thorns, she had been eating the blossoms. Perhaps she had colic, Lizzie was thinking, when Fanny whisked her tail, and Acorn was gone.

ONCE, WHEN SHE HAD FORGOTTEN TO BRING IN THE ducks, her grandfather hadn't spoken to her for three days, and sometimes at school the girls teased her about the ink blots on her fingers or the manure on her boots, but she had never, hour after hour, been ignored by another person. She vowed to follow Kate's example, to pretend her sister didn't exist, but she couldn't stop herself from watching this new person: what was she doing? what was she thinking? On Saturday, when her grandmother reminded her to take Kate with her on the deliveries, she said she would be quicker alone. But Kate was right there, saying she needed to learn her way around Langmuir. She helped load the wagon, doing exactly what Lizzie ordered, and even offered to pull it, but Lizzie said no; she knew where the potholes were.

"Do you think your grandmother would let me bake some scones?" Kate said as they passed the farmyard gates.

"I don't see why not." It made sense, she thought, that they each had their own grandmother. Forgetting her vow, she asked what it was like living in Kirkcaldy.

"It was grand. After school, I used to help Grandpa with the ladies' shoes, and there was always something going on: a concert, a lecture, a football game, a ceilidh. Where do you post letters?"

"Letters?" She steered the wagon around a puddle.

"You've heard of letters, haven't you?" Kate said, forgetting to be nice.

Lizzie concentrated on pulling the wagon. Why should she answer when Kate was so rude? She stared at the ground while they passed Neil's house. But she kept thinking about Grandpa John, with his fan-shaped moustache, waiting for the postman. As they reached the potato field, she said Mr. Ross, at the shop, took care of letters. Kate thanked her and asked how many deliveries they made.

"Fifteen. I always go to Mrs. Mitchell first. Her son died in the Crimean War. When she's upset, she thinks there are soldiers in the village."

They passed Morag's house, the coal merchant's, and the road that led to the mill. "Stand back," she warned as she knocked on the door. Sometimes Mrs. Mitchell appeared in her nightdress, already talking furiously. Today, however, she wore a neat blue skirt and a dark blouse, as if expecting company.

"You must be nearly the age your mother was when I last saw her," she said to Kate. "She was always one for the lads, first the blacksmith's son, then mine, then your father. You look like you take after her."

"She loved my father," Kate said.

"How would you know?" Mrs. Mitchell's voice was kind and curious.

"How would *you* know?" Kate said, stepping back into the road.

As she handed over the eggs and butter, Lizzie stammered an apology, but Mrs. Mitchell was holding out sixpence. "Lizzie," she said, "you're a grand girl."

Why today of all days would Mrs. Mitchell praise her? She seized the handle of the wagon and led the way down Mill Street to Miss Dawson's. "Do you think it's true?" she said. "About our mother and her son?"

"Not in a month of Sundays. You told me she's away with the fairies."

"But neither of us knew her."

"I did, for two years. We went for walks on the beach. She made me a woolen ball."

Gazing at Kate, her thin lips and neat eyebrows, Lizzie wondered if this could possibly be true. In her own early memories—her first picture, William shaking a dead rat, falling in the lochan, a bee sting—she was much older than two. But perhaps remembering was something you could learn. If she tried very hard, might she recall her mother drawing a picture, undoing a knot?

In the shop, surrounded by sacks of sugar, flour, oats, potatoes, salt, they waited behind Mrs. MacDonald, small, rumpled, smelling of camphor, and Mrs. Anderson, tall, angular, listing to one side. At last Mr. Ross turned to them, and Kate produced an envelope from her pinafore.

"Mr. Callum Menzies," Mr. Ross read, "18 Mill Street, Kirkcaldy. Och, it doesn't have far to go. It should be there by Monday."

Back in the road, Lizzie said, "Who's Callum? I thought you were writing to your grandfather."

"The boy I'm engaged to. We're going to get married as soon as we can." Now that she was talking about him, Kate couldn't stop. He was two years older and apprenticed to a joiner. They had met when he made a set of shelves for her grandfather's shop; afterwards he sent her a valentine. "I worry your grandparents will forbid us. Grandpa said they didn't think Teddy was good enough for their daughter. That's why he and Helen eloped."

No one Lizzie knew had ever eloped, but at once this explained why her grandmother never spoke of Helen's wedding. "Where did they elope to?" she asked.

"Gretna Green. Please don't tell your grandparents about the letter."

"What will you give me?" Seeing Kate's face, she laughed. "I won't, but tomorrow, at church, Mrs. Anderson will probably mention seeing us at the shop. Why don't you write to Callum on Sundays, when you write to your grandfather?"

"If they try to stop me writing, I'll run away."

"Where to?" she scoffed, but Kate was already running, towards the farm.

That evening, in her room, Lizzie studied her own face in the mirror and beside it the drawing of her mother. Kate had Helen's nose and eyebrows but Lizzie had her full mouth, her untidy hair and her capable hands. Looking back and forth between the drawing and her reflection, she felt a sudden longing for this person she did not remember who could make thrushes sing and had boldly run away to Gretna Green.

SHE WOKE TO A HAND ON HER SHOULDER. KATE HAD forgotten to bring in the ducks, her only task in the farmyard. At once Lizzie was out of bed. Years ago, when she had forgotten them, the drake, Arthur, had disappeared, leaving only a few white feathers. Downstairs she lit a lantern, chose a pail, and led the way to the farmyard. After dark, the granary was the kingdom of the busy, bright-eyed rats; even before she opened the door, she could hear them rustling among the sacks of grain. Her grandmother always said they were afraid of her, that was why they ran away, but in her dreams they darted towards her, sank their teeth into her leg. Now, as she dropped a handful of corn into the pail, their eyes gleamed from the corners.

She opened the gate of the field and closed it behind them. "Hamlet," she called, rattling the corn in the pail.

"Polonius," called Kate. "Ophelia."

The pond was empty; the surrounding grass was empty. As she led the way along the hawthorn hedge, the lantern flickered on several dark mounds: sleeping cows. She walked faster, Kate at her heels, peering into the darkness, calling, rattling the corn. Perhaps they had taken shelter among the standing stones, but again there was no sign. The foxes had had hours to do their work. She and Kate had almost circled the field when they came upon them, all five, heads neatly tucked under their wings.

As they walked to school the next morning, Kate said, "I'd have been wretched if they'd been eaten."

Lizzie recognised the peace offering. In exchange, she asked which girls Kate liked.

"Agnes seems nice. She liked my boots, and Marian lent me her penknife to sharpen my pencil. Sarah, the Sarah who shares your desk, is nice too. I like her freckles. The older one looks like someone's about to hit her. How old do you think Miss Urquhart is?"

She had never thought about it. "Forty?" she suggested. "Fifty?"

"No," Kate said. "She's not that old. Maybe twenty-nine, thirty. Have you noticed her shoes? She must have bought them in Glasgow."

A LETTER CAME AND KATE READ IT ALOUD AT SUPPER. Her grandfather was well; he missed her scones. Another letter came, in a different hand; she pounced and carried it to her room. That afternoon when they were milking—on fine days they sat beside the cows in the field—her grandmother remarked that her sister had a lot of correspondents. Lizzie's hands kept moving while her mind darted between difficult choices: how to keep her word to Kate, how not to lie. Happily, Flora was still talking. When Helen met Teddy, she said, they had forbidden her to write to him, but she had found a way. And Kate will too, Lizzie thought. She, and the other girls she knew, might grumble, but they did what they were told; her sister was made of different metal.

On Saturday, when they were packing the wagon, Flora appeared in the door of the dairy to ask Kate to help with the baking. As she walked into Langmuir, a journey she had made thousands of times, Lizzie felt alone as she never had before; in the village every customer asked what she had done with her sister. She hurried home, dreading to find Kate once again shut in her room. But the kitchen smelled of scones and Kate was at the sink, washing bowls. Next Saturday, Flora announced, if the rain held off, Kate's friend Callum would bicycle over for the day.

At Sunday school they read the parable of the talents. When she asked why the third servant was punished for burying his single talent to keep it safe, Mr. Robinson said it was a sin to waste the gifts God gave you. "Each of you is good at something," he urged, scanning the pews of girls and boys. That afternoon, as they searched the cows' field for wild garlic, Kate asked what she was good at. "You could be pretty," she added, "even though you're so tall."

No one had ever suggested she might be pretty. Bending to uproot a shoot of garlic, she stored the idea away to examine later. "I'm good at drawing," she said, "swimming, history, milking, taming Alice, helping Grandfather. What are you good at?"

"Baking, making shoes, singing, looking nice, getting people to do what I want."

Why did she choose that moment to speak? Was it because Kate had been nice, or because of that unexpected feeling of being alone, or because Isabel, grazing nearby, had raised her head to examine Lizzie with her kind brown eyes? Cautiously, she asked if Kate ever saw things that hadn't happened yet. When Kate asked what she meant, she described her picture of Hugh.

"You can see the future," Kate said. "Can you teach me to do that?"

"No, the pictures just come to me. I thought they might come to you too."

Kate was watching her as if, for the first time, Lizzie had something she wanted. "I wish they did," she said. "What's going to happen to you next?"

"I don't know. I never see myself."

Then Kate asked if the pictures were accompanied by a special feeling. "Like the witches in *Macbeth*? 'By the pricking of my thumbs, something wicked this way comes.'"

She was about to say no—the strange rippling she had felt on the beach at Lower Largo had not heralded a picture—but she recalled how, before she saw Acorn, her heart had begun to race. Next time a picture came, she would try to notice if it happened again. She told Kate about seeing the mare's white lips, her stiff legs.

"Poor Acorn. And do you know when the things you see will happen?"

She said she didn't. She had seen Hugh being stung more than a year before it happened, but now, as she grew older, the pictures came only a few weeks early; often some detail—like the black-thorn in bloom beside Acorn—suggested the date.

"Have you ever had a picture of me?"

"How could I? I didn't even know I had a sister until the Ides of March." She spotted a shoot of garlic and bent to pick it.

"You didn't know?" Kate's neat eyebrows rose.

As she repeated what her grandmother had said about keeping the sisters secret from each other, Kate was already shaking her head. "Maybe Flora decided that," she said, "but Granny Agnes often talked about you." They had reached the circle of standing stones. "Even if she hadn't," Kate continued, "I can remember you crying, being a nuisance."

Again she wanted to argue—no one remembered before they were three or four—but something about Kate's inward gaze suggested she was telling the truth. She set the garlic shoots on one of the fallen stones and bent to wipe her muddy hands on the grass.

At supper Kate asked if there was an illness that made a horse's legs go stiff.

"You're speaking of lockjaw, lass," said her grandfather. "There's no help when a horse catches it. The muscles get so tight they can't open their mouths."

Lizzie asked how a horse caught it and he said usually they got a cut on a leg and some dirt got in. His father's mare had caught lock-jaw when he was a boy. It had taken the best part of a day to dig the grave. "I ran into Mr. Elliot at the mill this morning," he said. "He was saying there's been another mining accident in Lanarkshire. The roof of a shaft collapsed."

While Kate and her grandmother exclaimed, Lizzie was still thinking about Acorn's stiff legs. Since her failure with Hugh, she had never tried to change what a picture showed her. But there were several weeks before the blackthorn bloomed. Whenever she had a free moment, she would go to the field and remove any sharp branches on which Acorn might cut herself.

THE NIGHT BEFORE CALLUM ARRIVED, KATE WASHED her hair, ironed her pinafore, and polished all their shoes. Soon Lizzie would understand her preparations, but that evening she thought only of how she detested pushing the iron back and forth. The next morning she was steering the wagon through the gates when she saw a boy standing beside a bicycle.

"Good morning," he said. "Are you Lizzie Craig?"

"I am. Are you Callum Menzies?"

He agreed he was. As he spoke, she noticed that his dark blue eyes were rounder than other people's. He showed her the copy he had made of the map at the library, marking the crossroads and the names of villages, ending in Langmuir and Belhaven Farm. "Kate wrote that the farm was east of the village," he said, "but it's south. I had to get directions at the shop. What's in your cart?"

She explained about the deliveries and asked if she could try his bicycle when she returned. "If there's time," he said. "Is my hair sticking up?" When she said yes, he spat on his hand and ran his palm over his head. She nodded approvingly even as the hair sprang up again. Her grandmother had said Dr. Murray might not be the bonniest man in Fife but he was the most openhearted. As

Callum wheeled his bicycle into the steading, she thought perhaps he had that same quality. The deliveries were her favourite task, but today she couldn't wait to be back at the farm. In her haste, she forgot about the pothole by Neil's house. She was picking up the fallen eggs—miraculously only two had cracked—when she heard a cuckoo calling: a sweet, faraway sound. Usually her grandfather, out in the fields all day, was the one to hear the first cuckoo of spring. Surely it was a good omen.

Back at the farm, her grandmother asked her to finish churning the butter and then, seeing her face, said, "Oh, go and find your sister." She ran to check the barn and the hayloft before heading to the field. Callum and Kate were kneeling beside the pond, throwing handfuls of grass to the ducks. She ran over to kneel on the other side of Callum.

"Tell Callum who's who," Kate said. "I get Ophelia and Claudius muddled."

"Are you the one that names them?" Callum threw his handful of grass into the water.

"That's Ophelia." She pointed. "Grandfather and I chose the names. Would you like to visit the horses? They're called Acorn, Ivanhoe, and Rob Roy."

"I'm going to show him the lochan," Kate said.

Lizzie was standing, ready to lead the way, but behind Callum's back, her sister made a shooing gesture. Quickly, before they could see her burning cheeks, she turned and ran back to the dairy. As she ladled cream into the churn, she remembered helping Kate find the ducks and, with each swing of the handle, she recalled something else that fanned her anger: she had shown her where to post a letter, loaned her books, praised her boots. She was vowing never to help her again when the curds began to rumble.

Over Scotch broth her grandfather mentioned that a couple of slates had slipped on the barn roof. Soon Callum was straddling the ridgepole with a stack of slates and a bag of nails while Rab, from the ground, called instructions and Kate paced back and forth, torn, Lizzie guessed, between pleasure at her grandfather's approval and dismay at the loss of her precious hours with Callum. By the time the last slate was nailed, the sky was growing pink. Flora asked if his parents would fret if he didn't come home, and he said no; several times he'd bicycled too far to get back and slept under a hedge. "There's a nice hedge near the duck pond," he added.

Her grandmother smiled and said no need for that; he could have the room over the dairy.

At supper, Callum asked about the livestock, the crops. Did they have to buy seed? Who helped with the harvest? Rab went from answering politely to answering expansively. They didn't have their own bull but borrowed Mr. Wright's. The sheep took care of themselves except at lambing and shearing; the fleeces went to a mill in Cupar. "You seem gey interested, lad," he said. "Kate said you're a joiner."

"An apprentice," Callum said. "How do you decide what to plant?"

After supper they played Happy Families, which Kate won gleefully, and gin rummy, which Flora won. That night Lizzie woke to the click of her sister's door, stealthy footsteps. She imagined Kate and Callum, in the room above the dairy, holding hands, talking. Then she imagined Grandfather finding them. I must warn her, she thought. But remembering that shooing gesture, she forced herself to lie down. Let them get in trouble. The steps stopped and, after a long moment, reversed.

IV

*

Once Callum had pedaled away, Kate became nice again, thanking her for taking care of the ducks, asking if she would make a drawing of her for Callum. At first, she said no, she didn't have time, she didn't have paper but Kate persisted; she would pack the wagon, buy her paper. When at last she gave in, she enjoyed the way that drawing put her in charge. "Sit still," she commanded. "Raise your chin." As she drew Kate's dark eyebrows and thick eyelashes, she thought about their mother, carefully drawing herself and Teddy, perhaps making each of them a little more handsome. Now she was tempted to make Kate's lips thinner, her eyes narrower but her pencil, almost despite her, depicted her sister's bright glance, her mouth about to smile. When she finished, Kate clapped her hands.

The next day as she hurried through the orchard to fetch Acorn, she heard the sound of neighing. Ivanhoe was leaning against the gate of the field, calling. At the sight of Lizzie, he fell silent and stepped aside to allow her entry. Rob Roy, grazing nearby, did not raise his head. Nor did Acorn, who often came to the sound of her name. But today she remained standing in the far corner of the field, where the blackthorn hedge grew thick with starry flowers.

As she skipped over the grass towards her, Lizzie thought how, in the autumn, she would gather the tiny dark fruits of the blackthorn and Flora would make sloe gin, the colour of an emperor's robe. Perhaps that was why she had almost reached the mare before she realised she was seeing what, weeks ago, the picture had shown her: Acorn's legs oddly stiff and far apart, her head low, her nose white.

She turned and ran back past Ivanhoe, past the apple trees. In the farmyard her grandfather came to meet her. Before she had finished speaking, he was striding towards the orchard. At the gate he shoved Ivanhoe aside and continued across the field.

"What ails you, lass?" he said.

A tremor passed over Acorn. Foam bubbled on her lips. Lizzie waited for him to lead the mare to the barn, where he could make her better, but he told her to wait while he fetched Flora. Alone, she backed away. Beneath Acorn's dull brown coat, the muscles were taut and twitching. Uselessly, she began to recite: Henry VIII, Edward VI, Mary I, Elizabeth, James I and VI. She had reached Queen Anne when her grandmother came hurrying over the grass, carrying a pail and some rags.

"Oh, Acorn." Gently she wiped the foam from Acorn's nose. "We'll fetch some straw for her to lie on."

"What about a hot mash?" Lizzie said. "Or one of your potions?" Other animals died—sheep, cows, hens—but she had known Acorn all her life.

Her grandmother shook her head. "One horse in a thousand recovers from lockjaw."

"She could be the one. Can't we bring her to the barn?"

"We made that mistake once with a cow and had to drag the body out to the field to bury it."

All day Lizzie went back and forth between her chores and

Acorn. She had spent hours removing fallen branches from the field, but she must have missed one. Soon Acorn was lying on her side, legs sticking straight out, lips pulled back over long yellow teeth, but Lizzie was no longer afraid. She sat beside her, stroking her neck. "When you get well," she said, "we'll go to the seaside." She poured water over Acorn's nose, offered handfuls of grass. At supper, when they told Kate what was happening, she turned to Lizzie. "Isn't this—?"

Quickly Lizzie asked if she had found the thread she needed.

By the time the dishes were washed, darkness was pushing at the windows. Her grandparents protested as she put on her coat and boots but she begged until they let her go. She was at the gate of the field when behind her Kate called, "Wait. I brought a blanket."

Acorn was lying where Lizzie had left her; Ivanhoe stood a few yards away, keeping vigil. In the lantern light, the whites of her eyes shone; her breathing rattled. "You're going to be all right," she said. She stroked Acorn's neck, feeling the heat beneath her hand.

Kate spread the blanket nearby and sat down. "Do horses go to heaven?" she asked.

"Maybe." When she had asked her Sunday-school teacher that question, Mr. Robinson had said everyone God deems worthy will be in heaven. So, Bertha, the hen who used to follow her, Alice, William, the Red Queen.

"Granny Agnes used to say our parents were together in heaven," Kate said, "but it seems daft to think they're making meals and fishing in the sky. And what happens when people remarry?"

Lizzie repeated what Hugh used to say: heaven was a way to make poor people behave. If they believed in the rewards of the afterlife, they wouldn't complain about this one.

"I think"—Kate spoke slowly—"our parents are dead as dodos.

They've disappeared into the earth or the sea. They don't care if we're good girls or bad. Look at poor Acorn. She didn't bite or kick anyone, yet here she is, suffering."

She lay back on the blanket, and, after stroking Acorn, Lizzie did too. The darkness sorted itself into various shades, the blackest being the trees edging the field, the next-blackest directly overhead. Small, lacy clouds drifted between the dark centre of the sky and the dark trees.

"This is the picture you saw," Kate said.

She admitted that it was. "I tried to remove the sharp branches, but I couldn't be with her every minute, and Grandfather wouldn't have listened. Kate, you nearly said something at supper."

"But why are your pictures a secret? If you'd told him beforehand, he would listen now. Maybe he could have saved Acorn."

That she had failed Acorn twice over was a charge she could not bear to consider. But Kate was still talking, asking if she had noticed the bruise on Sarah Elliot's cheek? "I think her brothers hurt her," she said.

Every Sunday Sarah sat between her brothers, two pews in front of the Craigs. Oxlike, they towered over her, but that they would hurt her, Lizzie said, made no sense. "Besides, their father would stop them."

"Maybe," Kate said, "her father hurts her too."

Later she would understand what her sister was suggesting. At the time she thought only that Mr. Elliot was a church elder. If Sarah did something wrong, he would send her to her room, or give her extra chores, not inflict a purple bruise. Before she could say any of this, Acorn gave a deep groan.

....

WITH ACORN'S DEATH, THEY FELL EVEN LOWER ON THE Great Chain of Being. After hours doing accounts at the kitchen table, her grandparents reluctantly sold a field to Mr. Wright in order to buy a new mare, Nutmeg, and three cows. Walking to and from school, she and Kate discussed how to help. No new pinafores this year. She tracked down every last hen's egg, milked every cow dry, weeded the peas and beans and carrots. At the sheep shearing, she tied up her skirts and helped to dip the sheep so they only had to hire two lads from the village. When Callum visited, it was understood that he helped Rab. In July she and Kate picked the fruit and made the jam. She counted the days until Hugh's return. Surely he would tell her how to rescue the farm.

Her grandfather let her come with him to the station. As they waited on the platform, he smoked his pipe and they both watched a pheasant strut along one of the rails, long tail bobbing. She was telling him what Miss Urquhart had said—that pheasants came over with the Normans—when the bird took wing and the train appeared. She stared at the engine as it ground to a halt, puffing clouds of steam; only two hours ago this black beast had been in Glasgow. A dozen doors opened. Through one of them, a person she knew must be Hugh climbed down, wearing a strange, dun-coloured jacket. His hair no longer flopped over his forehead and his cheeks, after a year indoors, were pale. Then he was lifting her off her feet, swinging her round, Hugh again.

When they were settled in the cart, Nutmeg clopping along, he remarked that he was looking forward to meeting her sister. She said Kate was eager to meet him too. In truth she was worried Kate might take against him; her likes and dislikes were still a mystery, changing from one day to the next. But as soon as they stepped into the kitchen, and Kate set down a plate and came over saying, "I'm

Lizzie's long-lost sister," she knew all would be well. They talked about Glasgow, which Kate had visited with Granny Agnes. He likes her, Lizzie thought, but not as much as he likes me.

When she was younger, she had loved harvest time, everyone working together, the picnics in the fields. Now, aware that an hour of rain could ruin months of work, she dreaded the man coming out of the weather house. As she followed her grandmother, hooking the grain into stooks, she glanced anxiously at the sky. They had finished the oats and were starting on the barley by the time Callum arrived. He and Hugh entered into a friendly rivalry: who could scythe a row faster. At lunch they declared a draw and shook hands.

That evening Kate pleaded an errand at the shop. While she and Callum headed to Langmuir, Lizzie and Hugh walked to the lochan. The afternoon clouds had cleared and the sun was still above the trees, the swallows swooping in the evening air. As soon as they passed the farm gates, she told Hugh about Acorn, about selling the field.

"Poor Acorn," he said, "but Lizzie, you know Rab is stubborn as stone. He's grand with the animals, but he won't try the new strains of oats or potatoes. He won't hear of keeping pigs. That was one reason I couldn't stay."

She had overheard the girls at school, the lads who helped with the harvest, make similar comments. "I thought I could find work in the village," she said.

He nodded. "Maybe you could earn a few shillings minding someone's bairns."

She asked if there wasn't something better paid and he said he didn't know. They made their way past the bank of willow herb and through the birch trees to the lochan. Close to shore the still water held a perfect image of each tree. "You should paint this," Hugh said. "How often is Callum here?"

"Most weeks." She bent to choose a stone and threw it as he had taught her; it skipped five times, the reflection breaking and uniting. "He comes on Friday and helps Grandfather on Saturday. Sometimes they even do repairs after church."

"Well, as long as he doesn't dawdle, that's your answer." Hugh skipped his own stone. "Good for Kate, saving the farm."

His words reached her like the widening ripples. Ever since Callum nailed the slates back on the barn roof, she had watched her grandparents courting him. Flora had stopped asking where he and Kate were going; Rab sometimes thanked him.

"It's gey fortunate," Hugh went on. "Kate's doing what she wants, and you'll be able to do the same. I didn't like to think of you marrying some lad because he could follow a plough."

"But the farm is mine. You said so." She heard her voice splinter.

"Lizzie, that was when I didn't know you had an older sister. Kate and Callum will inherit the farm. Now you can be the younger sister who does what she likes. Come to Glasgow, and have adventures."

He was looking at her as he had sometimes when she made a mistake in long division, or failed to thin the carrots. She stepped closer, clenching a rock in either hand. How had she not understood that Kate's arrival changed everything? That she was now the younger sister? She hurled first one rock, then the other. "Belhaven is mine," she said. "My home."

"It is," Hugh said, "but people find new homes. Don't say anything to Kate. She might not like the idea that she's doing what everyone wants."

She watched the circles of ripples, each fainter than the last. All along she had been certain she would save the farm. She would find a gold necklace buried in the field or, more plausibly, meet someone like Hugh, only devoted to the farm. Now her daydreams scattered in the evening air, tiny as gnats, flimsy as dandelion seeds.

AS THEY SAT BESIDE THE STOVE AFTER SUPPER, READING *The Water Babies* aloud, she could feel her grandparents' worries, Kate's worries, prowling the room. Despite the good harvest, they were still burning logs in the stove, eating porridge twice a day. At the harvest ceilidh, Callum had danced every dance with Kate but still he said nothing. The week after the ceilidh, Lizzie went to the shop and asked Mr. Ross if he knew anyone who needed a hand.

"What kind of hand?" His eyebrows rose above his spectacles.

She listed the things she could do: clean a house, do the washing, milk a cow, mind a child, give drawing lessons, tend a garden.

"My," he said, "you have a lot of accomplishments, but aren't you still at the school?"

"I can work after school. I could help you here."

He smiled and said he and his wife managed fine but he would ask around.

Walking home, she imagined her grandparents thanking her as she paid for the seed potatoes or a sack of coal. They would remember that Belhaven was hers. On Friday, when she and Kate arrived home from school, a folded piece of paper with her name on it lay on the table. Ignoring her grandmother and Kate's curious glances, she opened the note and read it, first to herself, then aloud.

Dear Lizzie,

Mrs. Dougherty tells me she needs help with her mother.
She lives at 7 King Street.

Good luck.

Mr. Ross

Her grandmother, potato in one hand, knife in the other, was frowning. "Lizzie, have you forgotten you're still at school?"

"Plenty of girls leave at my age. I can study later."

Kate, also frowning, started to say if anyone worked, it should be her, she was older, but Lizzie pulled on her pinafore and hurried away to the henhouse. As she reached for the eggs, she thought her grandfather would understand; he knew how sorely they needed money. At supper, he was in good humour—he had got a bargain on the turnips and stopped for a beer at the Royal Hotel—until he grasped what she was telling him. Then his hawklike gaze flashed. "No granddaughter of mine is leaving school at fourteen to mind some sick wifie," he said. "You'll go by tomorrow and thank Mr. Ross for his trouble. If you want to help, clean out the henhouse. I've asked you twice."

"But I could buy coal."

"Lizzie Craig, haven't we taught you your elders know best? Money will come in the spring with the crops, the animals."

"But—" she was saying again when, under the table, Kate pinched her thigh.

That night Flora came to her room. "We know you mean well," she said. "Rab's going to fell some firs in the north pasture. Timber is fetching a good price."

She felt a wave of relief: they would not have to sell another field.

But alone in the darkness, her feelings lined up like the English and the Scots at Bannockburn. On one side the long-held belief that Belhaven would be hers. On the other the bitter facts: Kate was older; she had Callum; her grandfather would never trust a girl to cut down a tree. She was staring at the shadowy outline of the window, remembering how she had taught Kate everything about the farm, when her heart began to race. Instead of the window she was looking at a field of barley, the grain golden, a couple of rows already cut. Her grandfather was swinging his scythe, Hugh was in the next row, with two lads from the village. Behind them a lad she didn't recognise was clumsily hooking the grain. He straightened to wipe his forehead and stood staring down at his hands, as if surprised they were still there.

SHE TRIED, AND FAILED, AND TRIED AGAIN TO HOLD A grudge against Kate. How could she blame her for being older? When Kate came to her room at night to whisper her fears about Callum, she whispered back, of course he likes you. He's here nearly every week. But Kate would list the times he'd failed to compliment her, had repaired a wall rather than taken a walk. At Halloween, she asked Lizzie to go with her to the churchyard at midnight. "We can summon the spirits," she said. "They'll show us our future husbands."

As soon as she heard the word "future," Lizzie knew their grandmother would forbid them. She said as much, and Kate said they wouldn't tell her. They would go to bed as usual and, only once their grandparents were safely asleep, steal out of the house. "Please, Lizzie," she said. "I've got everything ready—a candle, a mirror—but I can't go alone."

Lying in bed, feeling the rough material of her pinafore beneath her, she thought how easily Kate spoke of deceiving Flora. Not long after her grandfather cut himself with the scythe, she had broken a plate and hidden the pieces behind the flour bin. When her grandmother found them, she had looked deep into her eyes and said, "Anyone can break a plate, but a lie will always find you out. Promise me, Lizzie, you'll always tell the truth." She had promised and, save for the pictures and an occasional fib, kept her word. But Kate's feelings for Callum seemed to sweep away all other considerations.

She was already sitting on the edge of her bed when she heard the tap at the door. They tiptoed down the stairs and let themselves out of the house. The sky was overcast, with a few random stars. As they walked along the track, the darkness was full of shadows. "Why do we have to go to the churchyard?" she asked.

"That's where the spirits can come most easily," Kate said. "All Hallows' Eve is the one night of the year when they can return and talk to the living."

"But what if a witch or a warlock comes, like in 'Tam o' Shanter'?"

"We'll take sanctuary in the church."

Neil's house was dark; Morag's house was dark; every house they passed, except the minister's, was dark. Perhaps he was up late, working on his sermon. At the gate of the churchyard, they stopped to listen. She heard only the faint scratching of the yew trees. "Come on," Kate whispered. She opened the gate and led the way past the upright gravestones to one that lay flat. She set the candle in a jar on the stone and lit it.

As the flame steadied, Lizzie was afraid. So long as they were part of the darkness, no one could find them. Now anyone could, and all around were dead people—her great-grandparents, Miss Renfrew who had died last spring, Syd the cowman—dressed in their best clothes, lying beneath the grass. "What do we do next?" she whispered.

Kate got out the mirror and knelt before the candle. She made Lizzie kneel beside her. "Whatever happens," she admonished, "don't turn around." She raised the mirror, holding it to reflect not her face but the darkness behind her. "Mirror, and you beings who walk tonight, please show me my beloved husband."

Scarcely daring to breathe, Lizzie pressed her hands against the gravestone. At any moment someone might appear, not a person but a spirit, cold breath misting the mirror.

"You came," Kate whispered, letting out a long sigh.

"What did you see?"

"A lad with untidy hair and round blue eyes."

"Callum!"

Her sister's lips curved in a smile; she held out the mirror.

Lizzie wanted to refuse. It was one thing when you knew who you were waiting for, another when he was still unimaginable. But she took the mirror, angled it to catch the darkness and repeated Kate's words, leaving out "beloved." Come, she thought fiercely. Come if you're going to come. Show yourself. Did she hear the grass bend underfoot? Catch the rub of fabric?

The next thing she knew Kate was taking the mirror out of her hand, saying it was fine, it didn't matter. They hurried home, half running, not speaking. At the house it was Kate who hung up their coats and led the way upstairs. In the morning as they walked to school, she apologised. "I shouldn't have asked you to do that, not when you already have your pictures."

From the field where they'd lifted the potatoes last week came the cry of the curlews pecking the newly turned earth with their long, curved beaks. Watching them, Lizzie thought there were the things she understood—animals and crops and the weather and her grandparents—but running beneath them, beyond her understanding, was a dark river where a girl could drown; where brothers could hurt a sister; where Kate would risk anything for Callum.

FROST FLOWERED ON THE WINDOWPANES; THEY HAD TO break the ice in the well. At school Miss Urquhart made them touch their toes between lessons to keep warm. In early December, Kate went to visit Grandpa John. She returned, her cheeks marked by tears. He had mistaken her for Granny Agnes. "I told him he has to stay well until I get married and he said I must wear a pair of his shoes when I walk down the aisle." But soon after Burns Night, a letter from his brother brought the news John had died in his sleep.

In the wintery weather, Callum came less often. When he did, Rab showed him how to handle the sheep and lambs. They rebuilt the sheep-folds. Despite herself, Lizzie could not help liking him. He smiled often and teased Kate about her dainty ways. On a mild March day he made good on his promise to teach Lizzie to ride his bicycle. As she pedaled along the track, the breeze in her hair, she remembered riding Gooseberry.

At last, after lunch on Easter Sunday, Callum spoke his piece. "If Kate will have me," he said, "I'll give up my apprenticeship and work here." He's proposing to all of us, Lizzie thought. Kate's face gave her answer. Her grandfather nodded. "I'll be glad of the help, lad. You can have the room over the dairy." But Callum had other plans. Neil had a cottage which had been standing empty since

Syd died. If Callum fixed it up, he could have it for a small rent. That afternoon the five of them walked down the track and along the overgrown path.

Neil was waiting beside a lilac bush already tinged with purple buds. "No one's been in here since Syd," he warned as he pushed open the garden gate and unlocked the door. The air rushed out, bringing with it the smell of mice and mould. Inside, whitewash flaked off the walls, cobwebs laced the windows, the floor was thick with dust and dirt; the few pieces of furniture—a settle, a table, two chairs, a bed—were spotted with bird droppings.

"Only a pig could live here," Kate exclaimed, and fled to wait beside the lilac.

While her grandparents and Neil stood in the doorway, Lizzie followed Callum around the three rooms. He wet a finger and drew it down a windowpane, a clear streak in the dirt. "With a bit of work," he said, "this will suit us fine."

Walking back to the farm, he and Kate lagged behind. She caught their words on the wind. "Pigsty . . . hovel . . . a week . . . if you . . ."

"Let them sort it out," her grandmother said, and took her arm.

On Thursday evening Callum returned, a bag of tools strapped to his bicycle. For two days, only Flora was allowed across the threshold. Then, on the way back from church, Callum said, "May I invite you to Lilac Cottage?" Apologising for the long grass, he'd scythe it next week, he again led the way down the path. As the garden gate swung open, Lizzie could see the bright windows. Inside the floor was spotless, the walls freshly whitewashed, the stove blacked, the table covered with a blue cloth. Kate walked from room to room, brows knit. Lizzie watched her, bewildered and furious. What would become of them if her sister rejected Callum?

She was trying to make up for Kate's scowl, saying how nice every-thing was, when her sister burst into laughter. She was delighted with the cottage, delighted with herself for hiding her pleasure. "I'll measure for curtains," she said.

Callum told the joiner and his parents; a date was chosen in June. While Kate hemmed the curtains and made her wedding dress, he borrowed the cart and returned with two armchairs his parents had given him and a bed he had made. On the headboard the initials K and C were surrounded by a wreath of roses.

The night before the wedding, Kate came to sit on Lizzie's bed and asked again if she had had a picture of her. She shook her head. They didn't come often nowadays and were mostly quite ordi-nary: Mr. Wright's bull getting out of the field; Morag wearing a new hat.

"You'll tell me if you do," Kate said. "Hugh didn't understand when you told him about the bees, but I'll listen. I don't want to die before I'm twenty."

She closed her eyes and pressed her hands to her temples. "I see you in a white dress, coming down the aisle with a handsome lad. I see you eating cake and dancing an eightsome reel."

But Kate would not be distracted. "Promise you'll tell me," she insisted until Lizzie did.

V

Once again there were only three places at the table, and her grandparents, from one day to the next, grew older. Rab used his arms to push himself out of his chair; Flora stooped even when empty-handed. Most days, Lizzie visited Lilac Cottage, but she was still in the world of childhood, going to school, coming home to chores and homework, while Kate, in that bed with the carved headboard, had entered adulthood. One windy afternoon, when they were walking to the village, discussing Flora's birthday, she caught sight of her sister's belly, swelling beneath her skirt. "Are you in the family way?" she exclaimed.

Kate's eyes shone. "I wondered when you'd notice. He'll be a winter baby, January at the latest."

"But it's too soon." Morag had told her a baby took less time to grow than a calf, only nine months, which meant . . . She did not finish the thought.

As if she had only been waiting for Lizzie's permission, Kate grew rapidly. Soon she could no longer see her feet; she guided Lizzie's hand to feel the baby kicking against the confines of his first home. "It's a boy," she insisted. She talked often about what they would do when their son arrived, but Lizzie could not help being afraid. Last year Frances McEwen, who had sat behind her at school for five years, had died having a baby, and several other graves in the churchyard were of women taken in childbirth. Then there were the small stones with a single name: James, Angus, Mary, Mary.

Four days before Christmas, on a night of freezing rain, she woke to a volley of knocks on the farmhouse door. Downstairs her grandmother was already buttoning her skirt. "Should I come?" she asked, and could not help being relieved when Flora said no, this was women's work. Back in bed, her feet numb from the stone floor, she tried again and again to summon a picture. Show me, show me Kate's baby. But the rain kept beating on the window; her heart kept beating steadily. Instead she began to pray—"Dear God, please let Kate be safe. Please let her son be safe."—until the words lulled her to sleep. The next morning, she was laying the table, when Callum rushed in, his jacket unbuttoned.

"We have a daughter," he cried.

She dropped the spoons she was holding. "Is Kate all right?"

"Flora says she will be." He flung himself down in a chair and laid his head on his arms. Although it was not yet light, her grandfather poured two drams. On the first Sunday in January, the baby was christened May Flora Menzies.

THAT YEAR LIZZIE TURNED SIXTEEN. IN CHURCH THEY prayed for the children who had lost their lives on a Sunday-school outing in Ireland when a train ran down a hill. Kate whispered news of a woman named Jessie King who was hanged in Edinburgh for murdering two babies left in her care. What sort of person, they asked each other, would kill a baby? May was rosy cheeked and cried often. Hugh wrote that he was bringing a friend from the bowling club to help with the harvest. When the cart rolled into the steading, he jumped down to hug Lizzie. Only as he stepped back did she notice the lad standing awkwardly behind him, his hair the colour Flora's used to be.

"Lizzie Craig." Hugh stood between them, arms outstretched. "Louis Hunter."

Louis's eyes, blue flecked with darker blue, sought hers. "How do you do, Lizzie." Her name sounded differently in his mouth. The hand he offered was pale and, when she clasped it, smooth. Her own hands were always grazed, callused. Louis had grown up in Paisley, a town by Glasgow, and was apprenticed to a tailor. "I've never been to a farm before," he said. "Maybe some of the tweed I sew comes from your sheep."

"Maybe." She hadn't thought of their sheep ending up in Glasgow.

She worried how Louis would fare in the fields, but when she came up the first morning, he was hooking the corn into stooks steadily, if slowly. As usual, she worked beside Flora, but with Louis to watch, the rows seemed shorter. On the fourth day rain came in the late afternoon. Rab shook his fist at the sky and declared they'd be back first thing tomorrow. As everyone gathered their discarded clothes, their hook or scythe, she managed to end up near Louis. "If the rain stops," she said, "would you like to visit our sheep?"

"That'd be grand," he said.

By the time she finished milking, the clouds had passed. Hugh had an errand in the village and Flora said she could manage supper. She found Louis sitting in the doorway of the dairy. As she led the way out of the farmyard, she studied him in sidelong glances. From this angle she could see he had a small bump on his nose and his ears were a little large. "Tailoring must be very different from harvesting," she said. She longed to hear more about his life in Glasgow.

"In lots of ways," he agreed, "but today I was thinking cutting a row of corn isn't so different from sewing a seam. You have to keep going in a straight line. Are you still at the school?"

She was glad to be able to say she had finished in June. "You must have left years ago."

"Five years. I was sorry to quit. We were reading about North America. What will you do after the harvest?"

"Help my grandparents, help Kate. Do you ever go to dances in Glasgow? We have a grand dance after the Harvest Festival. You and Hugh should come back."

He said he wished they could and asked what was her favourite dance. She said Strip the Willow, she liked how fast and furious it was, or maybe the Duke of Perth. Leaning over the wall of the field, she explained how the sheep were still white from being shorn in June. Beatrice and Benedick, the lambs she had nursed that spring, trotted over, bleating hopefully. Louis praised the thickness of Benedick's wool, and she told him how the lanolin softened the skin. As they walked back to the farm, he asked if her grandfather owned the fields they were passing.

"Most of them. That field in the distance"—she pointed—"belongs to Mr. Wright, and our neighbour Neil has a long lease on the land by his house."

When she glanced over, he was biting his lower lip. "Everything I own fits in a box," he said, "except for Father's fiddle. It must be grand to walk around and know this is all yours."

"It's like having brown hair," she said. "I never think about it."

"Very pretty hair, if I may say. So what do you do in the winter for company?"

She said they read, played cribbage; she worked on her drawings. No one but Hugh had ever spoken as if her life were one thing and could, perhaps, be another. Back in the farmyard, Louis asked about the birds he heard every morning billing and cooing on the henhouse roof.

"You mean the turtle doves," she said. "In winter, they go to Africa."

"'The voice of the turtle is heard abroad in the land.'" He smiled. "We learned that at Sunday school but I never knew what it meant."

As she carried her milking stool out to the cows, she repeated the mysterious, lovely words.

WITH HUGH AND LOUIS AROUND EVERY DAY WAS DIFFERENT. Sometimes after supper, Louis played his fiddle and he and Hugh sang. On other evenings, they went to the orchard and hung the badminton net Hugh had brought between the trees. Louis showed her how to hold the racquet. "Good shot," he called. One evening Callum and Kate joined them, bringing May in her basket; she cooed like one of the doves. After they finished playing, the five of them were sitting, drinking lemonade when Hugh remarked that a reaper binder would have finished the barley before lunch. "We could have spent the rest of the day at the seaside." He was lounging beneath an apple tree. Callum and Kate were leaning against another tree, May beside them. Louis was sitting cross-legged on the grass, and she was sitting nearby, not far from the spot where Hugh had lain covered with bees.

"Mr. MacDonald has one," said Callum, "but it needs half a dozen men to work it."

"It's worth it," Hugh said. "Machines are the future. At the Singer factory we'll soon be making thirteen thousand sewing machines a week. Imagine"—he gestured beyond the trees—"enough for everyone in Fife."

"I can't speak about the reaper binder," Louis said, "but with a sewing machine who uses it is the key. Mr. Rintoull, the tailor I work for, his seams are straight as a ruler. Mine sometimes wander."

Kate said her grandfather had doubled his business when he got a machine to fasten the soles of shoes to the uppers. "That engineer you're so keen on"—she looked at Hugh—"he invented it."

"Brunel," Hugh said. "He did everything."

Louis said he had read a story in which a man builds a machine that is meant to resemble a man, but everyone is afraid of it.

"I read that," she said. Miss Urquhart had lent her *Frankenstein* last spring. "Then the machine asks the man to make him a woman."

"Do they fall in love?" Kate said.

She was saying no, the machine ends up going to the Arctic, but May was crying and Kate was on her feet. Then Louis was standing over her, holding out his hand, which after ten days in the fields was as sunburned and calloused as her own. By the time she had brushed the grass off her skirt, the others were at the edge of the orchard. He stepped forward and, before she knew what was happening, pressed his lips to her cheek. As he stepped back, she recognised the lad she had seen, months ago, harvesting the barley.

ON THEIR LAST EVENING, HUGH CAME TO THE FIELD TO help with the milking for old time's sake. A thrush was singing in a nearby hawthorn tree. As their pails began to fill, he confessed there was a girl he liked. "Another Elizabeth, but she goes by Beth." She was his landlady's oldest daughter, a teacher at the primary school.

"Does she like machines?"

"She likes her sewing machine," he said, "and she knows the kings and queens of England better than you."

He's hers already, Lizzie thought. She had lost him once; now she was losing him again.

"What about you?" he said. "Is there a lad you fancy?"

"A different one every week." She told him about Douglas, whose father owned the mill. "He's always covered in chaff and can lift a hundredweight of flour."

"Does he fancy you?"

She had liked Douglas and his attentions until Morag told her he was walking out with the minister's daughter. "We have a chat," she said, "while I'm waiting for Grandfather, but it's a game he plays with lots of girls."

"Clever Lizzie. What do you think of Louis? I can vouch for him being a grand fiddler and a good bowler. He told me he likes you. You'd never have to sew on a button again."

Her hands faltered as she recalled her picture of him, their visit to the sheep, the kiss in the orchard, how he had complimented her hair, her drawing. While the thrush sang, Hugh went on, "I told him all the bad things I knew about you. Think about it, Lizzie. Now Rab and Flora have the son they need, we could be neighbours in Glasgow."

That night at supper she noticed how Louis praised Flora's mutton pie and asked Rab's opinion of the Scottish Labour Party. Afterwards he played his fiddle and he and Hugh sang, "O ye'll tak' the high road, and I'll tak' the low road." Watching Hugh, she knew from his faraway expression that he was already back in Glasgow.

Suddenly she sensed she in turn was being watched. Louis winked, a tiny gesture, gone in an instant, and began to play "My luve is like a red, red rose."

The next morning, as she was milking Queenie, a voice said, "Excuse me." Louis was standing by the gate, cap in hand. "May I write to you, Lizzie?" Even as he spoke, Hugh was shouting, "Time to go," and he was hurrying away.

"Yes," she called after him. "Yes, please."

She was carrying the milk to the dairy, still thinking about his question, worrying he had missed her answer, when she heard shouts of "No!" "There!" "For heaven's sake!" As she turned the corner, she saw dark smoke rising from the hayloft. Not stopping to set down the pails, she hurried towards it. The flames were leaping from place to place. Her grandfather and two of the lads he'd hired for the harvest were raking the burning hay onto the ground.

"Well done, lass." Before she could stop him, Rab had seized the pails; the air filled with the smell of scorched milk. She ran back to refill them at the water trough. By the time she returned, the fire was mostly out, blackened hay smoldering. "Do you not have the brains you were born with?" her grandfather asked the lads. At supper he said ten more minutes and they'd have lost the barn. "I didn't know it was the milk you brought, Lizzie, but it served its purpose."

EVERY DAY SHE HOPED, AND GAVE UP HOPE. IF HE DIDN'T write within a week, she thought—no, a fortnight—she would write to Hugh and ask him to pass on a message. She recalled his exclamations over her drawings, his fluttering kiss, the books they shared, his pleasure in Benedick's wool. Kate had said she was almost pretty, but there must be no shortage of pretty girls in Glasgow. Eight days passed before she came in from helping net a haystack to see an envelope with her name, *Lizzie Craig*, lying on the table: the first letter she had ever received.

Rintoull's Tailor.
57 Balveny Street,
Glasgow

26th August 1889

Dear Lizzie,

I haven't had an hour to write until today. My boss, Mr. Rintoull, joked that Tom and I—he's the other apprentice—had forgotten everything he'd taught us. When I was cutting out the sleeves for a jacket this morning, I thought about your sheep. I told Mr. Rintoull about the farm and he said we ought to visit a tweed mill. He's always saying never skimp on fabric. A good suit can last twenty years.

My brother says I'm daft to be an apprentice when I could be earning a good wage working in the shipyards but I couldn't stand hammering metal all day. When I finish, I'll make a decent living. People always need clothes.

One of the things I liked best about your farm (besides you) was how peaceful it was, only hens and cows and turtle doves. The shop is on a busy street and we live upstairs. There are always carts making deliveries, people shouting, factory bells. I wonder what you'd make of the hubbub, Lizzie. Write and let me know what you're doing. Don't forget me at the harvest ceilidh.

Yours, Louis

She stared at the words, in amazement. Louis had written them sixty miles away, in Glasgow, and she was reading them here. When she went downstairs, her grandmother was kneading the bread. "So you have a suitor," she said.

"He wrote to me about the tailors."

"Lizzie, you won't hear what I'm going to say, but I'll say it anyway. Be careful. One thing leads to another. You're not just choosing a person, you're choosing a road in life—and you can find you've made a choice you never expected to make. When I married Rab, I didn't know I was marrying Belhaven Farm."

"Why didn't you have more children?" Last week Kate had confided she was again in the family way.

Her grandmother's hands folded and flattened the dough. "Some women are lucky," she said, "some aren't. The midwife told me to drink cinnamon tea and I did, month after month, but it made no difference. Not having a son was the worst thing that ever happened to Rab. There's no justice in these matters. My sister Shona has five boys."

And you could only know if you were lucky, Lizzie thought, once you were married. Or—she remembered May's early arrival—a little before. She had got her monthlies a few weeks after Kate came to Belhaven. Flora had explained every girl got them, but at the time it was as if her sister had brought the blood.

VI

That autumn, for the first time in eleven years, she did not go to school. For all her talk with Morag and Sarah about longing to be done, she missed the other girls, writing the answers to problems as fast as she could, conjugating Latin verbs. The days, filled only with chores, were longer. She took care of the cows, the hens, the deliveries. Her grandmother left the milking and the dairy entirely to her. Louis wrote that a building had collapsed in Glasgow, killing twenty-nine weavers. *I'm lucky to be in a solid house.* She wrote back trying to make her life interesting. *I went to Cupar with Grandfather. We got a good price for the heifers. The two older Frazer brothers are marrying the two older Findlayson sisters. People are laying bets on whether the younger brother will marry the third sister.* At Christmas, Callum trapped a goose in the meadow; at New Year, she went firstfooting with Dr. Murray's family. On Valentine's Day a card arrived, a red rose on the front, and inside: *Be mine. From your not so secret admirer.*

As she sat on her bed, studying the tiny blot beside the "mine," her heart jolted and raced. She was looking at a street of tall, grey houses, much taller than the ones in Cupar, the pavements filled with people dressed in city clothes, carts and wagons and what must be a tram rumbling along. There was Hugh, in his nice jacket, walking briskly along the pavement and up three broad steps to a grand wooden door. She was trying to read the name above the door, when the picture disappeared. What was the building, she wondered, and why hadn't she seen Louis?

ANNIE ARRIVED THE WEEK AFTER VALENTINE'S DAY. SHE was smaller than May, red and puling; nearly three months passed before Kate baked her famous scones. Lizzie went to Lilac Cottage whenever she could to clean and cook, to fetch water from the well, to play with May. Since Kate got married, she was calmer and kinder—she thanked Lizzie often for her help—but as Lizzie peeled the potatoes at one kitchen table, then the other, wrung the clothes through one mangle, then the other, she thought, This isn't what I want.

Through his letters, she began to piece together Louis's life. The year he turned nine, his father, a cooper, had sailed to Canada, promising to send for the family once he was settled. Before he left, he had given Louis his fiddle. "You'll play me a tune in Montreal," he had said. Louis had practised every evening, but week after week the postman had walked past their door. Then his mother had died of consumption; an aunt had come to take care of him and his three older brothers. They all worked in the shipyards. He had left school at twelve to be a messenger boy in a department shop. Last year, before she died, his aunt had arranged his apprenticeship at the tailor's. Sometimes, in the evenings, he played games with the Rintoull children, or Tom, the other apprentice, read a story, using different voices. *It'll be grand to see you*, he wrote, *when we come for the harvest.*

Once again she counted the days, imagining the conversations they would have by the lochan, how he would play his fiddle. Or perhaps Hugh would play and she and Louis would dance. She would show him her drawings and tell him how she had been sure she would save the farm until Kate arrived, bringing Callum. Louis and she were more alike than he understood.

She was at Lilac Cottage, passing a sheet through the mangle, when Kate reported that their grandfather wanted to hire more village lads, so there'd be no need for Hugh and Louis's help. "He's worried you like Louis too much," she said. She was sitting by the fire, nursing Annie.

"They can't not come," Lizzie exclaimed. The sheet fell from her hands. "Besides, there's no money for more lads." Everything she had imagined was suddenly in jeopardy.

"That's what Callum said." Kate shifted Annie to her other breast. "He persuaded Grandfather we need them, but he and Flora will be watching you."

"They can't watch us every minute." As she fed the next sheet into the mangle, she resolved to stop mentioning him: no more Louis said, Louis told me. Meanwhile Kate was saying there was something else she had to tell her: she was in the family way again.

"But Annie's barely five months."

Kate shrugged. "I've told Callum we need a rest, but in the night he forgets."

And not only in the night, Lizzie thought. A few weeks after the wedding, she had arrived at Lilac Cottage to find the door ajar. Standing in the kitchen, she had heard sounds she couldn't name. Through the bedroom door, she glimpsed Callum, his bare shoulders moving above her sister, his groans mingling with her gasps. She had backed out of the cottage and run all the way to the lochan. On the shore she had flung herself down, pressing her hands against the pebbles. What she had heard sounded like pain but she had to believe it was pleasure. Now she watched Kate nursing and saw how her sister's lips were chapped, her blouse stained, her hair lank. "He loves you," she said.

"He wants a son," Kate corrected.

EVERYTHING FILLED HER WITH IMPATIENCE. WHY WERE they making jam again? Why was she weeding the turnips and the carrots? Kate warned her not to get her hopes up. "He lives in Glasgow," she reminded her. Lizzie said that was part of what she liked about him; his life was not bounded by fields and weather.

At the sight of him jumping down from the cart, she heard herself utter a little "Oh." He was the person she remembered, but not. The little bump in his nose was still there but a moustache, the hair a shade darker than that on top of his head, now framed his red lips. "Lizzie!" He held out a pale, clean hand.

Kate had told her not to warn him about their grandparents' disapproval. Now she trusted him to read the gladness in her gaze as she shook his hand and turned to greet Hugh, who also looked mysteriously different: taller, smarter, wearing a jacket that fit and neat boots. At supper, he said he had left the Singer Sewing Machine factory and was working at a firm of engineers. "Is the name of the firm above the door?" she asked.

"It is," he said sounding surprised. "Why do you ask?"

Before he could press her, Rab reminded them of the time—

they needed to be in the field by six—and everyone was on their feet. As Hugh and Louis headed to the room above the dairy, she busied herself with filling the stove.

THE NEXT MORNING, AS SHE SLICED BREAD FOR LUNCH, Flora announced she wouldn't be harvesting this year. "I'm too old to stoop all day." Even as Lizzie agreed she deserved a rest, she was thinking her grandmother's absence would make things easier. By the time she arrived at the field, bringing a second breakfast, lunch, and as many bottles of water as fit in the wagon, they had cut half a dozen rows. Louis waved and blew her a kiss. Thankfully Rab was bent over his scythe. They had breakfast—Louis's arm brushed hers as he reached for a hard-boiled egg—worked, had lunch—Louis whisked a fly out of her hair—worked. Her grandfather let the lads from the village go at five but he, Callum, Hugh, and Louis stayed on for another hour.

Year after year she had prayed for the rain to stay away; now only rain would let her talk to Louis. At last, on the fourth morning, the man emerged from the weather house. She was gathering the eggs when she heard the pitter-pattering on the henhouse roof. As she stepped outside, Hugh emerged from the dairy. She hurried across the yard. "I need you to help me talk to Louis," she said.

"He's having his porridge." He nodded over his shoulder.

Quickly she explained that her grandparents wanted to keep her and Louis apart. "They're worried I'll follow your example and run away to Glasgow."

"So that's the way of it," Hugh said. "Why don't you go to Lilac Cottage? I'll make an excuse to go to the village and bring Louis by. The two of you can have an hour together."

In the kitchen she ate her porridge silently while her grandfather glowered at the newspaper and her grandmother swept the floor. I must try to behave like Kate, she thought, but only when she was at the sink, her back safely to the room, did she manage to say that Callum had mentioned they needed milk at Lilac Cottage. Maybe she should take it over? "Take a loaf too," said Flora, bending to sweep dust into the dustpan.

At Lilac Cottage, Kate smiled when she heard why Lizzie was there. "Auntie Lizzie needs to rest," she told May, opening the door of the children's room.

Inside the small room, she sat on the bed and looked at the books on the table: a Bible and a dreary book she remembered called *Willy Russell and His Little Friends*. She opened it to the first page: *Ever since he learned his numbers Willy Russell had wanted to be a good boy*. She had wanted to be a good girl, she still did, but there were other things she wanted more. Outside the window, the clouds were already lightening. What if her grandfather stopped Hugh and Louis from coming? She was turning back to *Willy* when she heard the door of the cottage open, voices, and then he was in the room, hair beaded with rain, cheeks glowing. Before she knew what he was doing, his arms were around her. "Lizzie, Lizzie, Lizzie."

At last she pulled away to explain. "If my grandparents find out about this, you'll be on the next train. They don't want us to see each other."

"But I came to see you." A little line appeared between his eyebrows. "We can't keep writing letters forever."

"What else can we do?"

Sitting beside her on the bed, he asked, Did she ever think about living in Glasgow? All the time, she said. Maybe, he suggested, she could find work, not too far from the tailor's. He had three more years of being an apprentice, but they could see each other most Saturdays. "Wouldn't that be grand?" he said.

"How would I get a job?" she said. "Where would I live?" Even to ask such questions was thrilling.

"If you got a position as a housemaid," he said, "you'd have your board and lodging. Maybe Hugh can help you find a nice Protestant family."

They were still talking about how to find a position when someone knocked at the door. Indignant, she went to answer—Kate had promised them an hour—and discovered it was past ten. Hugh was there, to walk Louis back to the farm. "Wait twenty minutes," he told Lizzie, and they were gone.

May demanded a ride and she knelt to let the little girl climb on her back. "Tell me everything," Kate said.

As she crawled around the room, she described how Louis wanted her to come to Glasgow, work as a housemaid. After circling the table twice, she gently lifted May down. "I hate the thought of not seeing you every day."

"I hate that too, but I know it isn't fair. I have Callum and the girls. You're working all the time and have nothing."

How was it, she wondered, that they were both already talking as if she were going to leave? That afternoon she worked harder than ever, hooking the barley.

SHE WAS IN THE ORCHARD, LEADING NUTMEG UP TO THE field, when Hugh called her name. He caught up with her beneath a tree heavy with apples. "Is it true," he said, "you're coming to Glasgow?"

"Yes." She tried to sound certain. "I'm hoping you'll help me find a position."

"Lizzie." His voice was solemn. "Louis seems like a grand lad, but I only know him from the bowling, and here. He's got a long road ahead of him. All kinds of things could happen."

"You were the one who said I'd never have to sew on a button again."

"I did." He was standing a few feet away. "But Flora and Rab are older. They need your help."

"No, they don't." Her grandparents were older, frailer, but they still worked all the time and they still treated her as if she were twelve, always ready to do their bidding. "I didn't want to believe it," she said, "but what you told me beside the lochan is true. They have Callum and Kate, they don't need me. If they did, if Belhaven would be mine, I would stay. But you forget what it's like, night after night, reading in the kitchen, day after day tending the cows and the hens."

She slapped Nutmeg's neck and started to walk again; Hugh fell in beside her. "You'll be doing housework in Glasgow too," he said. "Someone will be telling you what to do."

"But I'll get paid. There'll be shops and people, concerts, a library." At the field he opened the gate and she led Nutmeg inside. "Maybe Glasgow won't suit me," she said, "but I need to see for myself, like you did."

From his frown she knew he was trying, and failing, to think of objections. All of this is your fault, she thought; you should never have abandoned us. But he had brought her Louis. At last, reluctantly, he said he would ask Beth how to find a position. Before he could change his mind, she kissed his cheek.

VII

*

At the harvest ceilidh she danced every dance. Lads who for years had barely nodded to her asked for an eightsome reel or a Strip the Willow. Like bees round a honeypot, Flora remarked as they walked home; she and Rab had danced only a couple of times. Beside her, Lizzie studied the waning moon, shining through a thin veil of cloud, and said nothing. She knew her new popularity was all because of Louis; his attentions had changed her. When one of her dancing partners, Colin, who worked at the smithy, came by the farm the following Saturday, she got him to fix the harrow. Watching his hands, black with grease, tighten the bolts, she tried to imagine living beside the smithy, taking an interest in whose horse he had shoed that day, how many ploughs he had welded. She told him Morag thought he was a fine dancer, and he did not call again.

At Kate's urging, she did not mention Glasgow to her grandparents. "When you have a position," Kate reasoned, "they won't be able to say no." Meanwhile she did her usual tasks as if she would never do anything else. In the evenings, she and her grandfather took turns reading aloud from *Mansfield Park*; everyone condescended to Fanny, the poor, unmarried niece, and told her what to do. She was beginning to give up hope when, nearly a month later, a letter came from Hugh. Beth had found her a position in a nice Protestant household.

She touched the paper, wanting to make sure the words were real. At last, just when it had begun to seem impossible, she was going to Glasgow. From the wall her parents watched approvingly. When she broke the news, tactless in her excitement, her grandfather banged the table so hard the plates jumped. "No granddaughter of mine is going to be a skivvy," he said. "Your place is here, helping Flora."

"If you want something else to do," said her grandmother, "why not see if Miss Urquhart needs a hand at the school."

"You went to St. Andrews to be a housemaid."

"Because my parents couldn't afford to feed me, which is not"— Flora gestured at their plates —"your situation."

In the days that followed, she thought often of those weeks after Kate's arrival when she had felt not merely invisible but shunned. Once or twice her grandmother gave her a quick glance, but her grandfather looked past her. They'll come around, Kate kept saying. Over and over, Lizzie imagined telling them she had changed her mind: how her grandfather would nod and get out the cribbage board; her grandmother would embrace her. Then she thought of Louis, of the winter ahead. Lying in bed one night, after another silent supper, she heard raised voices and tiptoed to the hall.

"Rab, if you drive Lizzie away like you drove Helen, I don't know how I'll forgive you. It isn't a sin to want to see other places."

"Honour thy father and mother," said her grandfather. "That's what we say every Sunday. And now our granddaughter is behaving like those words mean nothing. Maybe if she were going to

Glasgow to study, I could countenance that, but she's going to clean other people's privies, and run after that tailor."

"That tailor mended my skirt so you wouldn't know it was torn. And he worked hard in the fields."

There was the sound of footsteps, her grandfather pacing. "He did, and that's part of what I have against him. He cuts his coat according to the fashion. You can't trust a lad who's always trying to please everyone."

"Rab, she'll go whether we like it or not. But if we forbid her, she won't come back."

He said something that sounded like "Good riddance."

In the morning, she carried her porridge out to the barn to avoid the silence. Only Kate's assurances that they would eventually relent enabled her to stand firm. Then on Sunday Mr. Waugh preached on the text "For if you forgive men their trespasses, your heavenly Father will also forgive you." Our souls are closer to heaven, he claimed, when we forgive each other. As they walked home, her grandfather stooped to pick a flower from the hedgerow. "I'll miss my bonnie lass," he said, holding out the purple vetch. She put the flower to press between the pages of *Gulliver's Travels*.

On her last evening she was in the dairy, skimming the milk, when she felt the familiar jolt. There was Kate, weeding the garden at Lilac Cottage. Nearby May was making a daisy chain, and Annie was crawling. The new baby was slumped against the gatepost, his mouth opening and closing in big gulps, like a fish craving water. Spit dribbled down his chin. He's poorly, she thought. But before she could determine what ailed him, she was back spooning cream into the churn.

As soon as the butter was made, she hurried to Lilac Cottage. Kate was bending over the oven, checking on her oatcakes. "What are you doing here?" she said. Straightening, she took in Lizzie's tangled hair and flushed cheeks. "Is something wrong?"

"I had a picture of you while I was churning the butter. You're right, the baby is a boy, but he's different from May and Annie. He just stared and—"

She was still talking when Kate interrupted. "I won't hear another word about your daft pictures. Now kiss the girls goodbye and get home to your packing."

She started to remind Kate of her promise, but again her sister cut her off. Later she would understand—the new baby was coming as surely as her train tomorrow; he could not be stopped, or changed—but, walking home, her eyes stung with fury.

IN THE CONFUSION OF THE GUARD TAKING HER BOX, HER grandfather shouting "Haste ye back," the doors slamming, there was no time to wave. Then the platform was gone and the fields were rushing by. She had never before travelled faster than she, or a horse, could run, and at first she held tight to the armrest for fear the train would balk or swerve. As it kept hurtling forward, as the two men opposite kept discussing the price of coal, she relaxed her grip and pressed her face to the grimy window, staring at the unfamiliar fields and villages. They passed Kinross, Stirling with its castle, other towns, until there were no more fields, only houses and more houses.

At the station, she followed the men onto the platform and came to a breathless halt. More people than she had ever seen in one place were hurrying in different directions. A woman with a red feather in her hat walked purposefully through the crowd, followed by two men carrying a trunk. Clouds of steam rose from the engine up to a ceiling made of glass. She was looking around for the station entrance when she saw Hugh making his way towards her; by his side was a girl wearing a blue jacket Lizzie envied and carrying a book. While he fetched her box, Beth explained that they'd be taking one tram, then another to the Phelpses' house. She had a quick, warm manner which made her appear to be in motion even when standing still.

Outside the station Lizzie was again struck dumb. No grass, no trees, no animals, so many buildings and everywhere the noise of carts, carriages, trams, people, bells. But not everyone was well-dressed; some people wore rags worse than the poorest villagers. Before she could ask Hugh about them, he was pointing out the streetlights. At dusk men called leeries lit them one by one. The tram, like the train, ran on rails and was pulled by two horses. At first, she tried to memorise their journey, but after they changed trams, she lost count of the number of streets they turned down before they got off. Hugh hefted her box onto his shoulder and led the way to a street of tall houses. She was about to seize the gleaming knocker on the Phelps's front door when he said, "This way." He led her down the stairs to the servants' door, put her box on the doorstep and held out a piece of paper. "Here are the directions to my boardinghouse. Good luck, Lizzie."

She knocked twice at the much more modest door. Before she could lower her hand, it opened and a woman wearing a capacious apron was studying her with bright brown eyes. "You must be the new girl," she said. "I thought you were the fish. I'm Cook." Her voice, Lizzie thought, sounded like Louis's.

In the kitchen she introduced Bert, a sturdy, red-cheeked boy. He gave an awkward wave as he lofted Lizzie's box onto his shoulder and disappeared up the stairs.

"You'll be hungry after your journey," Cook said. Not waiting for an answer, she set a cup of tea and a thick slice of treacle cake on a table twice as long as the one at home and motioned Lizzie to sit down.

She was eating her second slice of cake when Edith, the head housemaid, appeared. She had fair, wispy hair and, as she later demonstrated to Lizzie and Cook, delicate ankles. "My best feature, if anyone looks down." In the same conversation she told them she had grown up in Glasgow, near the cemetery called the Necropolis. After her mother died, she had kept house for her father. But two years ago, he had remarried. The day after the wedding, his wife had come into Edith's room at seven a.m. and told her to find herself a place. This sounded terrible to Lizzie, but Edith seemed resigned.

On that first day, as she showed Lizzie round, Edith told her she had a gentleman. Ralph worked at his father's public house. "But I haven't reeled him in yet," she added. At the news of Louis, she nodded approval: tailoring was a good trade. They weren't allowed callers, but Mrs. Phelps was generous about time off. Ralph used a jar on the stairs for notes. Louis could do the same, only a different stair.

Lizzie stared in wonder as Edith led her from one grand room to the next—the drawing room, the dining room, the morning parlor and study on the ground floor, then up to the bedrooms, up another floor to the nursery and the schoolroom. At the top of the house, reachable only by the back stair, were their attic rooms. "This is you," Edith said. "Mind your head." Alone, she took in the angled ceiling, the narrow bed, the chair tucked into a corner, the chest of drawers with a jug and basin. From the window she could see the garden, more houses, rooftops, and chimney pots. Bert had put her box at the foot of the bed. She hung up her two dresses and set the drawing of her parents and the weather house on the chest of drawers. *Let me know when I can see you,* Louis had written.

Downstairs she was taken to meet Mrs. Phelps. Seated at the piano, her long, smooth neck and upswept hair made her appear tall, but when she stood, Lizzie was half a head taller. "Welcome to Glasgow," she said. "We hope you'll be happy in our household."

That first night she missed her grandparents and Belhaven so fiercely she almost packed her box and stole away, but in the days that followed there was so much to do, so many things to get wrong, that she had no time for missing. Most of her skills—milking, making butter, minding the hens, rearing a calf, cleaning the barn— were useless here. Instead, she had to learn how to polish a table until her reflection rose out of the wood, how to clean and trim the lamps the Phelpses used along with gas lighting, how to dust the wainscoting and beat a rug and replace the furniture in exactly the same place, how to plump the pillows so they looked as if no one sat on them, how to clean the privies. Time was measured not by the sun, or the animals, but by the clock. Every morning Edith had a list: which rooms to clean, what guests were due. Mrs. Phelps's sister came several times a week to lunch or afternoon tea, bringing her daughter. On Friday or Saturday, the Phelpses went out to dinner or a concert, or there were guests. After practicing for a week on Edith and Cook, Lizzie was allowed to serve the vegetables.

Her favourite part of the day involved the Phelpses' daughters, Marie and Celia, aged seven and five. While Edith served breakfast to Mr. and Mrs. Phelps, she helped them wash and dress, sat with them while they ate breakfast in the nursery, and delivered them to the schoolroom. Sometimes she drew pictures for them of Nutmeg or the ducks or the neighbour's dog. From Edith's comments, she understood that the choice not to replace the nursery maid, who had left last month, was unusual; Mrs. Phelps liked to spend time with her daughters. Last year they had attended a nearby school, but after Marie caught pneumonia, a governess had been hired. Miss Cameron walked to and from her mother's house in all weather, arriving on rainy days the hem of her skirt dark with water. She would unlace her boots and place them by the fire to dry. "Nobody sees me but the girls," she said, wriggling her toes in their damp stockings. "And you," she added, with a smile for Lizzie.

One morning, when Lizzie delivered the girls, Miss Cameron said, "Marie tells me you grew up on a farm."

Had she done something wrong? So many rules emerged only when she broke them. Miss Cameron was a servant, but not like her and Edith. Lizzie had overheard her speak quite firmly to Mrs. Phelps about new books for the schoolroom. "I asked," Miss Cameron went on, "if we could borrow you for a couple of hours. I thought you might draw a map of your farm, tell us about the animals and crops."

Marie wrote *Belhaven Farm* in wavering capitals at the top of a large sheet of paper. Miss Cameron fetched an atlas and together they found St. Andrews and Cupar and the place where Langmuir would be marked if it were larger. Lizzie told them about going to the beach at Lower Largo to gather shells for the hens. "So the hens change seashells into eggshells," Miss Cameron said. "I didn't know that." Lizzie did not mention the occasional shell-less eggs. Carefully she drew the house and the farmyard, the orchard, the horses' field and the cows' field with the duck pond. Then she drew the fields farther away, with corn, oats, barley, turnips, and pota-toes, and the rough land where the sheep grazed. She explained how they sold eggs and butter in the village, took the grain to the mill. She was taken aback when Miss Cameron announced it was eleven, time for their daily walk. "Will you help us tomorrow?"

"Please," said Marie, clapping her hands.

The next morning, she made new drawings, described how a butter churn worked, how they sheared the sheep and sent the fleeces to Cupar to be spun into wool which was woven into cloth. "In Glasgow," Miss Cameron explained, "we don't grow food. Instead we make things: ships and sewing machines and books and carriages. Farms, like Lizzie's, send us food."

When she came downstairs, Edith was waiting in the hall, arms folded, face folded. "Miss Cameron," she said, "is paid to mind the girls."

"But Miss Cameron—"

"—wasn't here last year, and won't be next. Your duty is to help me."

By way of atonement, she offered to wash the windows, a task Edith had mentioned several times. In her coat, armed with water, vinegar, newspapers, and rags, she set to work on Mr. Phelps's study. Peering through the panes of glass at the tall bookcases, the wide desk, she wondered what sort of house she and Louis would have. Nothing this grand, but perhaps they could have gas lighting, an indoor tap. The wind nipped at her face, and she moved on to the drawing room. As she rubbed the glass, she looked at the painting which hung to the left of the mantelpiece. It showed a young woman sitting in a chair, a letter forgotten in her lap. What Lizzie liked best was the way her golden hair sprang back from her broad forehead, and how her blue eyes, set a little farther apart than most people's, were looking intently at something no one else could see.

The next day she delivered the girls to the schoolroom and slipped away while Miss Cameron was taking off her boots. An hour later, she was polishing the dining-room table when a voice said, "We missed you today." Miss Cameron, only her head and shoulders visible, was leaning around the door. "Do you not like helping with the girls?"

"I like it fine." She kept moving her hand in circles. "Edith needs me."

Miss Cameron started to say something about Mrs. Phelps, broke off, and stepped fully into the room. "I didn't mean to make trouble," she said. "If you ever want to come by the schoolroom, you're welcome."

LOUIS WAS WAITING ON THE LIBRARY STEPS. AT THE sight of her, his face widened in a smile. "'The voice of the turtle is heard abroad in the land,'" he said. "This is the best thing that ever happened to me."

They stood, holding hands, and she could tell he too was amazed: here they were, in the city, no one telling them what to do. They walked over to the tailor's and he proudly pointed out the window with the words in gold: MR. RINTOULL, TAILOR BESPOKE. He did not invite her inside but pointed out the various windows: the living room above the shop, the family bedrooms, the attic room he shared with Tom. Then they walked to the park that lay between the shop and the Phelpses'. He showed her the Stewart Memorial Fountain, the water arcing from the mouths of strange beasts, and the bowling club with its neat privet hedge.

When she told him about the kerfuffle with Miss Cameron, he at once understood: keeping on Edith's good side was what mattered. As they circled the flower beds, still bright with roses, he told her they'd worked late every night that week, making suits for three brothers. She heard the excitement in his voice. Despite his small wages, his long hours, he was learning a trade. And I am too, she thought: how to live in the city, how to make you yearn for me. Later, when he walked her home, he drew her into the shadow between two gaslights. They did not move, scarcely breathed, until a clock chimed nearby. In her room, she caught sight of her face in the mirror. A few days ago, she had met Edith returning from an evening with Ralph and seen the same expression: flushed, excited, ready for anything.

KATE HAD A HEALTHY BOY, HER GRANDMOTHER WROTE. *Callum is beside himself.* She felt a swoop of relief. Her picture was wrong; surely Kate would forgive her. When she told Edith about her nephew, Edith said she could meet him at New Year, which was how she learned that every Hogmanay the family went to visit Mr. Phelps's brother in Perthshire and the staff had five days off. She could stay in the house if she wanted, Edith would be here, and Cook, or she could go home. Louis protested—their first New Year together—and then relented; of course she must meet her new nephew.

Outside the station her grandfather was waiting with the cart. "Welcome home, lass," he said. His hair, during her absence, had turned from pewter to white; she glimpsed the darkness of a missing canine. While Nutmeg clipped along, he told her Callum had persuaded him to try a new kind of turnip called the Achilles. "I fancy the name," he said. "Dr. Murray told me he's delivered two sets of twins this month."

In the kitchen her grandmother said, "You're pale as paper. They must be working you hard." But she was the one who was pale, and, more surprising, smaller; for the first time Lizzie had to look down to meet her eyes. She put on her pinafore and set to the New Year's cleaning. Everything seemed dirtier, or perhaps she was judging by Edith's standards: there was dust on the settle, mud and crumbs between the flagstones, dead flies in the pantry. She changed her grandparents' sheets, washed the windows, blacked the stove. She dusted the Toby jug on the mantelpiece and polished the grandfather clock. Her grandmother, when she returned from taking a pot of soup to Neil, thanked her. "What with the farm and the cooking," she said, "the house gets short shrift." It was as close as she came to complaining that, in Lizzie's absence, all the work fell to her.

At last she was free to go to Lilac Cottage. She hurried down the track, sliding on the frozen puddles. In the kitchen Kate led her to the cradle where Michael was asleep, dark hair rising like a crest, tiny fists. "What a handsome boy," she said. She had been ready to apologise for her picture but, seeing Kate's smile, she knew there was no need. While the kettle came to the boil, she played "Pat-a-cake, pat-a-cake" with Annie and let May ride her around the kitchen. At last the girls quieted, and she turned to her sister. Kate's face was still thin, but her hair was neatly gathered and her liveliness had returned. In the spring, she said, they were going to hire a lad, but the big thing she and Callum were talking about was exchanging houses. "We're tight as peas in a pod," she said, "meanwhile Rab and Flora are rattling around and Callum's walking back and forth to the farm half a dozen times a day."

Only Kate, Lizzie thought, taking in the cosy kitchen with the two bedrooms right there, could come up with something so obvious, and so outrageous. She was asking what their grandparents thought of the idea when the door opened. She jumped up to embrace Callum; he smelled of the frosty air. "Has Kate been telling you our scheme?" he said.

"She has. I can see you need more room."

"We need more room, and we need more help." Annie toddled over and he bounced her gently while he described the arguments with Rab about the turnips, the winter wheat.

Like her grandparents, Callum had changed. His eyes were still rounder than most people's, his hair unruly, but his easy smile was gone. A vertical line punctuated his eyebrows, and the bones in his temples were visible. Day after day of following orders, of being paid tuppence ha'penny, had drained his reserves of good will. "I'll talk to Grandmother," she promised. "Kate says you're taking on a lad come spring. If you're the one that hires him, he'll listen to you."

A small cry came from the cradle. Heedless of his muddy boots, Callum crossed the room to pick up his son. He has your eyes, she was about to say, but she was wrong. Michael's eyes were grey and, something she had never seen before, the pupils were circled by lighter dots.

"He's such a good boy," Kate said. "We'll firstfoot you when they're safely asleep."

As she walked into the village, she kept thinking about Michael, the way he had lain so quietly in his father's arms. May and Annie at that age had been restless and demanding. But perhaps he was drowsy. In the doorway of the shop, Miss Urquhart greeted her. "Hello, Lizzie, how's Glasgow treating you? Have you visited the Hunterian Museum?"

She said she was hoping to in the new year. How were things at school? As Miss Urquhart answered, she took in her wool coat, her shiny boots. Kate was right, she thought; the teacher was not many years older than them.

That evening she laid the table with cheese and meat, freshly baked oatcakes and shortbread, the chocolates she had bought. As the grandfather clock struck midnight, she imagined Louis playing his fiddle for the Rintoulls. *Please*, she thought, sending her wishes to that room above the shop she had never seen. The rest of the sentence was banished by fists on the door. Kate and Callum tumbled over the threshold, holding a lump of coal and a shining shilling.

The five of them sang "Auld Lang Syne" and toasted the New Year. Her grandmother urged them to try the shortbread. In the lamplight, Lizzie thought, her grandfather, with his white hair and missing tooth, resembled a warrior king, her grandmother his queenly consort; Kate was the sister who had sat with her while Acorn was dying and Callum, once again, the amiable boy on the bicycle.

VIII

*

Back in Glasgow a note from Louis was waiting in the jar on the stairs; could she meet at a tearoom to celebrate his Christmas bonus? "Oh, fancy," Edith said when she told her. She pinned up Lizzie's hair so that only a few strands escaped and loaned her a necklace of red beads. But taking in the room full of smartly dressed people from the doorway, Lizzie hesitated. Then Louis, his hair neatly combed, his jacket freshly brushed, waved to her from a table near the window and she made her way towards him. Once the tea was served in delicate floral cups, she handed over the basket of eggs she had brought. "You can tell Mrs. Rintoull they were laid yesterday."

At the sight of the eggs, carefully nestled in straw, Louis burst out laughing. "How on earth did you manage on the train?" he said. "She'll be delighted. Think, Lizzie, three years today I'll be a proper tailor. We can come here every week."

"You said three years when we talked at Lilac Cottage."

"Yes, three years from New Year." His moustache moved in a smile.

"Why does it take so long? Kate taught me to make a blouse in three days."

"Lizzie, you're so impatient. Women's clothes don't have to fit in the same way. Look"—he pointed to his own jacket—"the way the sleeve follows my arm." As he described learning about patterns, his face assumed what she thought of as his tailoring expression: earnest and slightly smug.

"But don't you want to live in your own house?" she pressed.

He gave an emphatic shake of the head. "Not without money. After my father left, we had no food, no coal. You don't know what that's like." One afternoon, as they circled the park, trying to keep warm, he had told her about the months following his father's departure. How he had kept insisting that his father's letters had gone astray; that they would be going to Canada soon. Then one day, on the way home from school, his brothers had waylaid him and shaken him until his teeth rattled. "He's not coming back," they had said. "He's never coming back."

Before she could say she did know what it was like to worry about money, all those nights eating porridge at Belhaven, he was saying he had heard the queen might visit Glasgow on her way to Balmoral that summer. "You could make drawings of her and sell them as souvenirs. Sixpence each."

"Why not a shilling?" she said.

That evening as she stood at the window, brushing her hair, she felt the familiar jolt. Instead of the lighted windows in the house at the end of the garden, she was looking at a field of grain, the new plants a few inches tall. Barley, she thought, nicely sowed, maybe in the field next to the potatoes. Then her grandfather appeared, but why was he shaking his stick, shouting as if the rows of plants had disobeyed him? A footstep sounded on the stairs; the field was gone. So the pictures still came in Glasgow, she thought, as she set aside her brush. But what she longed to see was not a field but her own future with Louis.

WHEN THE DAYS GREW MILDER, LOUIS BORROWED A KEY to the bowling clubhouse. While he fiddled with the lock, she admired the smooth grass, not a daisy or dandelion in sight. "It looks as if you cut it with your scissors," she said. Every Friday, he had told her, he or Tom took their scissors to the knife sharpener.

"Madame." He opened the door with a little bow. "It's a bit spartan, but we can have a chat and stay dry without spending money."

How strange that here in the city was a cottage from a fairy tale, everything made of wood and smelling of dry grass and polish. Two of the walls were lined with shelves holding bowling balls, each slot labeled. On the third hung photographs of club members; beneath stood a bench. Louis pointed out himself in the most recent photograph, and here was Hugh; he was a much better bowler but had given it up when he took his new job. She asked if Mr. Rintoull played, and he said yes, but not Tom. He showed her his bowling ball, black and shining, his name on the slot: *Louis Hunter*. "Can I try it?" she said.

The bowl was smooth and pleasing in its heft. He fetched another. On the edge of the green, he demonstrated, leaning forward and swinging his arm low. The bowl rolled almost to the end. She swung a couple of times without letting go. Then, keeping her eyes on his bowl, she sent hers on its way. It idled to a halt a few inches away. "You should be on the team," he said. They walked over the grass. She nudged her bowl until it almost touched his. He nudged his until it did. Back in the clubhouse they sat on the bench and he produced a bottle of lemonade; he had brought it by yesterday. She described how last week one of the supper guests, a minister from a big church, had told a joke that made Mr. Phelps say ladies were present. When Louis pressed her to repeat it, she couldn't recall the offending phrase. "You're such a well-brought-up girl," he said, putting his arms around her.

Dear Lizzie,

Something dreadful has happened. Back in March, Grandfather wouldn't hear of planting barley in the middle field. Callum gave up trying to persuade him and sowed the barley secretly. As soon as the seeds came up, Grandfather saw what he'd done. The two of them shouted back and forth while Grandmother and I tried to make peace. For days they didn't speak to each other. Then Grandmother came and begged Callum to apologise. "I believe you're right," she said, "but you're breaking an old man's very stubborn heart."

I was scared he was going to refuse. His anger's been building for years. Finally, he said he'd eat humble pie this time but no more. He worked from dawn to dusk, and what did he have to show for it? If he had stayed a joiner, he'd be making a good living. Grandmother put her hand on the Bible and promised: after the harvest, we'll move into the farmhouse and Callum will be in charge.

We've hired George Thompson to help with the planting. Lizzie, please come as soon as you can. There are things I can't put in a letter.

Love, Kate

....

SINCE THE DAY SHE ARRIVED, SHE HAD MET HUGH ONLY twice—her precious free hours were for Louis—but on Thursday, when Edith announced the Phelpses were going to the theatre, she followed the directions he had given her and took one tram, then another to his boardinghouse. Beth answered the door, wearing an apron. "Lizzie," she exclaimed, "are you all right?"

She said she was fine, she just needed Hugh's advice. Beth showed her into a room off the hall and went to fetch him. Alone, she looked around with interest; this was only her second Glasgow house. Two green armchairs and a couch ringed the fireplace, and in one corner a large dimpled egg—perhaps it belonged to an ostrich?—stood on a small table. She was studying the picture above the mantelpiece—it was titled *The Poultry Market*—when Hugh came in, asking what was the matter. She handed him Kate's letter and perched in the nearest armchair, watching his eyes move down the page.

"Good for Callum," he said. "I didn't think he had it in him."

"He's changed." She tried to explain what she had seen on her last visit. "Having a son has made him more ruthless."

"Do you know if Rab has made a will?" Hugh said.

"I don't, but you said Callum and Kate will inherit the farm. Who else would he leave it to?" Even as she spoke, she remembered her grandfather's temper, how he had ignored her when she said she was going to Glasgow.

"Doesn't Rab have a brother, up near Aberdeen? I'm no barrister, but if he died without a will, I worry the brother could inherit the farm and put you all out on the midden."

She promised to ask her grandmother when she went home. "Hugh, I know you and Beth have plans, but will you come for the harvest? If you're there, Grandfather and Callum won't quarrel."

She could tell from the way he stared at the hearth rug that he wanted to refuse. The thin, pale scar across his throat was still visible, and as she left her chair to stand beside him she kept her eyes fixed on it, trying to remind him of that afternoon in the orchard.

"All right," he said at last. "I'll talk to Beth."

THE NEXT TIME THEY MET AT THE CLUBHOUSE, LOUIS said they wouldn't be able to use it much longer; the bowling started soon. Shyly he produced two lengths of material and hung them on the nails already driven into the window frames. On the bench, he edged closer. When he pulled away, it was to retrieve a blanket. "Lizzie," he whispered, "you're the girl for me. Soon we'll have our own home, not a blanket on the floor."

She let his hands slip under her blouse. Her hands unbuttoned his shirt. In the dim light she saw that his chest was patterned with little freckles and golden hairs. She heard herself making sounds she had never made before.

Afterwards, walking home, she thought, Why did no one tell me I could feel this way? She remembered the list she had made of village lads, how she had thought nothing mattered besides ploughing a straight furrow. Now she studied the women she passed, wondering if they too knew this feeling that all the adults in her life, except Kate, had kept so carefully hidden. Louis had straightened her skirts, she had straightened his collar, but beneath their neatly buttoned clothes there was something marvelous, unimaginable. Back at the Phelpses', she stole away to the drawing room.

The golden-haired woman in the painting was still looking into the distance. She's thinking about her lover, Lizzie thought.

Had Edith lain down with Ralph? There was no way to enquire, but as they polished the silverware she asked did he like working at the pub? Edith said he'd never known anything else. In the autumn his father was at last moving to Bute, leaving him in charge. "Why not bring your tailor by next Saturday?" she suggested. Louis turned out to already know the Tam o' Shanter; one rainy evening last spring he had taken refuge there. As they walked down Grey Street, he pointed out the sign—Tam riding his good grey mare, the witches and warlocks in close pursuit—and she told him how her grandfather recited the poem every Burns Night. Inside, the pub was paneled with dark wood, furnished with tables large and small; around two sides of the room ran a red velvet banquette. Edith waved to them from a corner table. In her conversation, Ralph had loomed large. But as he rose to greet them, Lizzie saw he was several inches shorter than her, his chest solid as a shield. His upturned moustache made him look as if he were always smiling.

"We all quake in our boots," he said, "when Edie comes around."

He brought tankards of beer for Louis and himself, glasses of ginger beer for Edith and her. She watched the tiny bubbles rising in the cloudy liquid. When she drank, she could feel them prickling inside her mouth. Ralph remarked they always had their best nights after football matches. "Business will be even better when Edie's here," he said, squeezing her shoulder.

"You can tell when a place has a woman's touch," Louis agreed. "Have you set a date?"

"December 28th."

While Louis said congratulations, Lizzie looked at Edith with sudden understanding. So that explained the new lightness in her step, her equanimity when Cook complained about dinner guests: she had reeled him in.

"You should follow our example," Ralph said.

"As soon as I finish my apprenticeship"—Louis raised his tankard—"I plan to make Lizzie an honest woman."

As he and Ralph fell to discussing the feud between Celtic and Rangers, her mind snagged on the phrase. She knew what they did in the clubhouse belonged to married people, that for the unmarried, it was a sin so grave her grandmother had never thought to forbid it; but when she lay down with Louis, she felt as if they were already married. Now, as he enthused about Rangers' new goalkeeper, she wondered if he felt the same.

WHEN SHE CAME BACK IN AUGUST, CALLUM WAS WAITING at the station, the cart full of sweet-smelling hay. All the way back to the farm, he talked about Mr. Wright's reaper binder. It did the work of six men but broke down every few hours. Only at the gate of the farmyard did he thank her for inviting Hugh and Louis. "They'll make us mind our manners," he said. While he went to unload the hay, she stood looking at the farmhouse with its white harled walls, its bright windows, the rowan tree beside the door already heavy with berries. Her home for eighteen years, and now seven more days. In the kitchen Flora was tapping a loaf out of a pan. As they embraced, Lizzie smelled the familiar commingling of green soap and tea.

On the train she had thought surely her grandmother would sense the momentous discovery she had made in the clubhouse, but Flora smiled and spoke as if nothing had changed. When the tea was brewed, they carried their chairs outside to sit beneath the rowan tree and enjoy the sunshine. She asked if there was much to do to get ready for the move.

"I've packed what I can," her grandmother said. "Everything else we'll do on the day."

"Will you miss the house?"

A breeze shivered the rowan and a single orange berry landed in Flora's lap. "Truth to tell," she said, "it's been too much for me for years. What I will miss is the wind wuthering in the beech trees. It kept me company the night your mother was born. I used to hope it would do the same for her when I was tending the cows and hens, but she'd be crying when I came back. Sometimes I think that's why she eloped; because I had to leave her alone so often."

Like rocks in a field, memories were surfacing. Her grandmother had never mentioned the elopement, yet now she spoke as if it were common knowledge. Lizzie seized the opportunity to keep her promise to Hugh and ask if Rab had made a will. She had feared Flora would take offence, but she nodded and said Lizzie was right to ask; he had made a new one soon after Kate got married. As she spoke, a rooster in the farmyard crowed.

"I'm worried about Michael," she went on. "Kate keeps saying he's an easy baby because he never cries. But babies cry because they want something. It's a bad sign: not wanting. Callum says Michael will grow up to farm the whole of Fife. I dread the day he realises this isn't the son he needs. Why not take the loaves to Lilac Cottage and see for yourself?"

Lizzie carried her bag up to her room. When she opened the door, a breeze was lofting the curtains over the bed. The first time in the clubhouse Louis had asked, "Is this all right?" After that, four more times, he did not stop to ask; their hands reached for each other. Looking at the smooth counterpane, she thought, this was why people got married: so they could share the night as well as the day.

Sitting beside Callum in the cart, she had admired the crops. Now, walking to the cottage, she appreciated the hedgerows blooming with red campion, bluebells, buttercups, forget-me-nots, lady's slippers, so different from the pavements of Glasgow. What was it, she wondered, that Kate couldn't write? In the garden, May and Annie ran to greet her. She set down the loaves and kissed them. Kate was picking peas, Michael propped against one of the poles that held the washing line. "Tell me everything," she said.

While she reached for the pods, Lizzie described a dessert Cook had made and the boat trip she and Louis had taken down the Clyde. They had seen swans and children paddling, a man in a boat fishing, and two women swimming. As she spoke, Michael slowly slumped to one side.

THE ROOKS HAD FLOWN HOME FOR THE NIGHT BY THE time Hugh and Louis reached Belhaven. Over a late supper, Hugh said they hadn't seen each other at the station in Glasgow and each boarded the train convinced the other had missed it. Only on the platform at Cupar did they discover their mistake. "And here we are," Hugh said. "What field are we doing tomorrow?"

"The oats," said her grandfather. "They're the colour of Flora's hair."

While her grandmother protested—her hair hadn't been that colour in years—Callum pushed back his chair. "We'll start with the oats," he said. "I'll be back at six."

With his departure, they discovered how late it was. Hugh went to his old room above the dairy; Louis was allowed back in the parlor. There was no moment for a private word, scarcely for a glance, but she felt the connection between them, stretching like the thread he unspooled every day.

In the morning she was by the duck pond, milking a brown-and-white Galloway whose name she didn't know, when the porridge rose in her throat. She leaned her forehead against the cow's dusty flank and breathed deeply. She had eaten quickly, but at once she was sure this was the sickness Kate had described that heralded a baby. As she started milking again, she thought she must be lucky; after only five times, she was in the family way.

In the field, Hugh, Callum, four village lads, and her grandfather were each scything a row; Louis and George followed, gathering the oats into stooks. She spread a cloth in the corner by the gate and set out meat and cheese, a bowl of hard-boiled eggs, slices of bread, a screw of salt, a jug of water. "Breakfast," she called.

Louis was the last to arrive. Cheeks red, hair dark with sweat, he flung himself down, laughing. "Just as well I'm a tailor. George does two rows for every one of mine, and his are neater."

"But you should see me sew on a button," George said.

"Give me your shirts," Louis said, "and I'll fix the buttons so they stay on for a year."

She would tell him, she thought, when they were safely back in Glasgow.

ON SATURDAY, WHILE RAB WENT TO PLAY DOMINOES with Neil, and Kate and Flora supervised the move, she minded the children. In the garden she propped Michael against a laburnum tree and tried to get him to take part in the dolls' tea party. As she poured imaginary tea, ate imaginary cake, she wondered would

Louis mind whether they had a boy or a girl. Once or twice she heard his voice among those of the men moving the furniture: "Up on the right," "Slowly."

In each house they left the settle and the table and chairs, but by late afternoon everything else had changed places: the plates on the settle, the armchairs and rugs and beds, the lantern on the hook by the door. She remembered Kate, when she first arrived, complaining about the smell of the farmhouse. Already at Lilac Cottage the smell of Kate's baking was fading and objects Lizzie had known all her life took on a different aspect. On the mantelpiece Flora's Toby jug seemed to smile. On the wall a plate depicting Robert Burns frowned. In the smaller room the grandfather clock ticked more loudly.

The three of them sat down to a cold supper. As her grandfather reached for a slice of pie, he said, "Flora, I owe you an apology. I didn't want to leave the house where I was born, but you were right. We'll be snug here when winter comes."

Lizzie imagined the others sitting around the table in the farmhouse, talking, laughing, never noticing her absence. She was thinking she'd join them as soon as the dishes were done when she heard music. Louis was walking down the track, playing his fiddle, Hugh beside him. In the kitchen they sang "Comin' Thro' the Rye." Her grandfather poured everyone a dram. Lizzie coughed and Hugh patted her back. "This isn't lemonade," he said, which made everyone laugh.

EACH MORNING WHEN SHE PUT A PIECE OF BREAD IN her pocket and walked to the farm to do the milking, everything she saw—the standing stones, a foxglove, a robin perched on the gate, lambs jumping in the fields—was transformed by the thought she might not see it again. She and Louis would come back for a week or two, but this was no place for a tailor. Only the cows noticed when she jumped up from her stool to be sick. In the henhouse, she had to hold her breath. Even loading the wagon made her queasy.

As she made the deliveries, everyone asked about the harvest except for Mrs. Mitchell. She looked Lizzie up and down, from her hair to her boots. "You're in the family way," she said.

Startled, Lizzie stepped back. "You're thinking of my sister. I put in a duck's egg for your baking."

"No," Mrs. Mitchell said. "Your eyes have changed."

How unfair, she thought, as she headed to Miss Dawson's, that the first person to guess about the baby was this daft old woman. Perhaps that was why, when they took the children to play by the lochan that afternoon, she told Kate. She had imagined her sister's delight, but she cried out as if she had been stabbed, "Oh, Lizzie, what will you do?"

She explained the plans she'd gone over and over while she milked the cows. "I'll work until Christmas. Then we'll get married and rent a room near the tailor's. I can mind someone else's children. We'll be like you and Callum, our baby a bit early."

"But we had a roof over our heads. Louis is still an apprentice. Has he spoken of marriage?"

"Yes," she said stoutly. "He wants to make me an honest woman."

While Kate continued to point out obstacles, she watched the heron standing, grey and motionless, beneath a nearby willow. From the angle of its head, she could tell it was waiting to strike.

When her sister fell silent, she said, "Why is Michael so quiet? What was it you couldn't put in a letter?" She gestured towards him, listing against a birch tree.

Kate clasped her hands. "I'm scared your picture is coming true, that he's going to be like the McClaren boy." For years Marcus McClaren had come to church every Sunday, empty-eyed, open-mouthed, but last spring his mother had forgotten to tie him up and he had wandered down to the river. "I worry it's because I had him too soon. My body wasn't strong enough to make a healthy baby."

"No!" May shrieked. There was a loud splash. Kate jumped up to rescue her. Alone with Michael, Lizzie tried to make him sit up. "There's a good boy," she kept saying, but as soon as she let go, he slumped to the ground like one of the puppets she had seen lying backstage at the Punch and Judy show on Argyle Street.

IX

In the kitchen Edith was at the table, polishing the spoons, wearing the smart uniform she wore when important guests were due. "Look at your rosy cheeks," she said. "You've filled out."

Quickly Lizzie explained she had been working in the fields all day. "My grandfather is almost as hard a taskmaster as you. How many guests tonight?"

"Eight. Can you be ready in fifteen minutes?"

Upstairs in her attic room she studied herself in the mirror. From one angle her cheeks did seem fuller, from another not; her eyes, she was sure, were unchanged. She would ask Louis when she saw him on Saturday. If only her stomach didn't turn while she was serving dinner. Right now, the thought of food made her hungry. Ravenous.

AT THE PARK GATES, LOUIS CAME TO MEET HER, FROWNING. Something must have happened at the tailor's, she thought, but no, he was only worried it might rain. She reassured him. In her attic room, the woman had come out of the weather house. They chose a bench beside a flower bed, glowing with scarlet and bronze dahlias. "That red would suit you," he said, holding out a bag of humbugs.

Unthinkingly she took one. "I've some news," she said. But her words were muffled by the large sweet. Moving it to the other cheek, she repeated what she had said to Kate.

It was as if a giant jar had descended, trapping the two of them. She could still feel the wooden bench, still hear the bees in the dahlias, the conversations of passersby, but everything was far away. Only the smells of Louis's hair oil and her own lavender soap were real. He did not move, did not blink. A few yards away a mistle thrush stabbed its beak into the grass.

"Are you sure?" There was no gladness in his voice.

She could not tell him about the new veins in her breasts, how every morning her stomach roiled, how the monthly blood hadn't come. "I talked to Kate," she said.

"But there were only a few times. I thought we were being careful."

"You shouldn't have taken me to the clubhouse if you wanted to be careful." Trying to push away his words, she hit his arm, glancingly.

The silence inside the jar thickened. "I'm very, very sorry," he said at last, "but you know I can't get married until I finish my apprenticeship."

"You're over sixteen. You can get married, if you want to." She plucked the humbug from her mouth and hurled it among the dahlias.

"I've more than two years to go. I can't take care of a family until I finish." As he described, yet again, how Mr. Rintoull would help him when he was qualified, she saw his smooth, pale hands tighten into fists. "I'd lose everything if I left."

"You don't have to leave." She explained her plan. They would rent a room. She would make money minding babies. He would go to the tailor's every day.

"Minding babies pays pennies. Will your grandparents help us?"

"No!" How could he even ask such a question? Lowering her voice, she asked whether Mr. Rintoull might advance a loan against his future prospects. From the way his eyes retreated, she saw he found her suggestion equally shocking.

"Lizzie, you know what my life was like before Mr. Rintoull took me on: porridge twice a day, wearing my brothers' castoffs. How could I want that for you?"

So why had he come to the barn on his last morning, written her letters, urged her to move to Glasgow, taken her to the clubhouse? "What am I going to do?" She turned not just her face but her whole body towards him. "Edith said I'd filled out."

"Not yet," he said, "but you'll have to go home."

She thought of her grandmother praising how she'd arranged the china at Lilac Cottage, her grandfather saying she managed the cows like no one else, their good opinions blown away like chaff. "I can't. They thought I was making a life in the city. Now I'm having a child with no father in sight."

"I'm in sight." He put his hand on hers. "We did no more than Callum and Kate. No one wants an early baby, but they'll take you in. I'll visit. We'll get married as soon as we can." He talked on, trying to convince her, but all she heard was that his life would continue running along the rails, while hers hurtled towards ruin. He was still talking when she started walking towards the park gates.

"Lizzie."

She stopped to look at him: the mouth she had kissed, the clothes she had unbuttoned, the body she had touched. If they had been alone, she would have pummeled him to the ground, hit him over and over, demanded he take back every word. She kept walking. He walked alongside, saying again and again that he was sorry, please wait. Passersby glanced at them and turned away. At the gates of the park, he fell back and she walked on alone. She passed a butcher's, a church she had never seen before. The shops and houses grew smaller, blackened by soot. Two boys ran up to her, barefoot, begging. When the rain began to slant down, she asked a newspaper seller for directions.

Back at the house everything was quiet. Edith was at the Tam o' Shanter; Bert had gone home; Cook was at her mother's; the family was visiting Mrs. Phelps's sister. She climbed the four flights to her room, to change out of her wet clothes. "What am I going to do?" she asked her parents in their wooden frame. As usual, they said nothing. She remembered Grace, the drowned girl in the river, the water streaming off her hair. But she was not ready to walk down to the river Clyde.

In the empty kitchen she made herself a cup of tea and sat down to write to Kate. First, she wrote a letter to be read to Callum and her grandparents: the journey, Louis, the Phelpses. Then she turned to the one that mattered.

Dear Kate,

you were right. Louis is very sorry but he says he can't afford to get married until he finishes. I'll work here for as long as I can. Then I don't know what I'll do. I overheard Cook talking about a home somewhere in Glasgow for girls who are caught. Maybe I can go there. I hope you won't hate me for being so stupid. I didn't think a few times was enough.

Please forgive your bad sister, Lizzie.

THAT WEEK SHE WORKED LIKE A WOMAN POSSESSED. THE girls at school had talked about babies lost because of a fall, or hauling a sack of coal. Please, she thought, as she beat the rugs, heaved the coal scuttle, dragged an armchair to the other side of the window. "What's got into you?" Edith said when she found her trying to straighten the rug beneath the dining-room table. "You're making the rest of us feel guilty." But her exertions made no difference; the blood did not come. Later she would learn there were people who could persuade a baby to leave, and be glad she had not known about them during those desperate weeks.

On Monday there was a note in the jar on the stairs, another on Wednesday. She put them between the pages of her Bible. As long as she didn't read them, anything was possible. On Friday, a letter came from Kate and a third note from Louis.

Dear Lizzie,

I'm very sorry but Callum and I think Louis is right. To quit his apprenticeship would be madness. He'd lose everything he's worked for. Stop this nonsense about some place in Glasgow. This is your home. If Rab and Flora won't have you, we will. Plenty of babies in the village arrive early. You should hear the midwife's stories.

Don't be too angry with Louis. He's a good lad and you

should see your face when you look at him. You'll have a husband and your baby will have a father, only a wee bit late.

Love, your equally bad sister, Kate

When she opened Louis's notes, nothing had changed; he was worried; he wanted to see her. The last one, a single line, said he'd be at the library after lunch on Saturday.

WHEN THE BOWLING SEASON ENDED, THEY RETURNED to the clubhouse. The first time he took her there, she asked, again, what she was meant to do, but beneath his kisses her questions dwindled. The worst had happened, was happening. She thought only about what his hands were doing, what her hands were doing, the freckles on his chest. During a stretch of beautiful autumn days, she enjoyed a trip to the shops with Edith, a concert. and a visit to the docks with Louis. She went to the museum Miss Urquhart had recommended and stood in front of a painting so blue she wished she could step inside it. Cook remarked on her refusing a second helping of black-currant pudding, and she joked about wanting to fit into her dress for Edith's wedding.

When Mrs. Phelps stopped her in the hall, her first thought was she knew. She and Edith had often speculated about what lay behind their mistress's calm brown eyes and smooth forehead. In the face of household crises, badly behaved guests, Marie and Celia's tantrums, her sister's surprise visits, she never lost her tranquil air. Perhaps she doesn't notice, Edith suggested. Only at the piano, which she played every morning, did she show passion. Now she was asking Lizzie to take the girls for their morning walk; Miss Cameron had sprained her ankle.

They walked to the park where she met Louis, but to a different gate. As they passed their old school, Marie said they were going back in the spring; they were looking forward to seeing their teachers. Inside the park the girls let go of her hands and ran down the avenue of elms towards the fountain Louis had shown her last year. Today the water was still, no jets arcing into the air. When she leaned over the rim of the pool, several golden fish rose to the surface.

While the girls gathered grass for the fish, she sat on one of the benches circling the fountain. In the sun, out of the wind, it was almost warm. Last night Edith had confided Ralph was pressing her. "Some days are safer than others," she'd said, "but I worry about being caught." When Lizzie said she didn't know there were safer days, Edith had laughed. "Didn't you learn anything on your farm? Close to your monthly is best—right before and right after. The middle of the month—your month, not the calendar's—is the riskiest." If only, she had spoken to Edith sooner. She closed her eyes, letting the warmth spill over her.

"Don't," shouted Celia.

Opening her eyes, she was momentarily dazzled. A figure, arms outstretched, was swaying on the rim of the fountain. A picture? No, Marie. She jumped up, ran over, and lifted her down. "Miss Cameron will be very cross if you fall in. Promise not to do that again."

"Promise. Can we visit the birdhouse?"

In a corner of the park where she'd never been, a large cage was divided into half a dozen smaller ones housing a parrot, several budgerigars, a shiny black mynah bird, and a drab female peacock. "Morning, morning," said the mynah bird. As they walked home, she told the girls about Alice. They both wanted a pet jackdaw when they grew up. At the house, she delivered them to the nursery and went to fetch elevenses.

"Can you sit for a minute?" Miss Cameron said when she brought the tea. She gestured at the other armchair. "I hope the girls behaved themselves."

"More or less. Marie said they'll be going back to school in the spring."

"So it has been decreed."

As Miss Cameron took off her spectacles and carefully wiped each lens, Lizzie saw that, like Miss Urquhart, she was younger than she looked. "What will you do?" she said.

"Currently," Miss Cameron said, "I haven't an inkling." Spectacles restored, she described how last April her mother had lost her way coming home from the bakery. Since then, she couldn't go out alone; often she made tea at midnight, or mistook Miss Cameron for her sister.

When she asked who was minding her now, Miss Cameron's face constricted. "I lock her in every morning," she confessed. "The neighbours know where the key is and take turns visiting. Sometimes when I'm walking home, I imagine finding her dead, but she's always there, smiling."

For a wild moment, Lizzie thought, she could offer to take care of Miss Cameron's mother in exchange for a place to live. She could pretend to be a widow. Then she imagined being alone all day with a madwoman and a baby. "Isn't there anyone else who can help?" she asked.

"No," said Miss Cameron, quietly setting down her cup.

....

THE WEATHER TURNED COLD; HER FITS OF SICKNESS dwindled; she moved through her days in a trance of cleaning, polishing, fetching, and carrying, trying not to eat too much. Night after night she pleaded for a picture to guide her, but none came. The happiness she had felt on that first morning, milking the cows, was utterly gone. By early December she was grateful for the fullness of her housemaid's apron. One frosty morning, as they cleaned the lamps, she broke the news to Edith that she would have to leave at Christmas; her grandparents were growing frail and needed her help. The next day Mrs. Phelps called her to the drawing room. "We've enjoyed having you in our household," she said, "but of course your first duty is to your family." Suddenly the days were even busier as she trained her replacement, the cack-handed Hilda, and Edith trained hers, the dauntingly upright Miss Shaw. "She acts like she has a poker up her back," Edith said, but Cook, who complained they were both abandoning her, said she'd unbend when she got the hang of things.

The day after the Phelpses left for their annual New Year's holiday, Edith's father gave her away in the icy church. The minister mumbled and the only words Lizzie heard were Ralph's ringing "I do." Then he and Edith were walking down the aisle, Edith smiling as if her slippers didn't touch the floor. Everyone repaired to the Tam o' Shanter. After the meal, they cleared the tables, the fiddlers struck up, and Edith and Ralph sailed onto the floor. Louis held out his hand. Her last night in the city; they must dance every dance.

The next morning at the station, they took shelter from the bitter wind aboard the waiting train. In an empty compartment, noses red, eyes watering, they held each other. "I'll be thinking of you," he said, "every hour, every day." He jumped off as the train began to move. Alone, searching for her handkerchief, she came across the envelope Cook had given her. Inside were her wages and four extra five-pound notes. *Please accept this contribution to your upcoming expenses*, Mrs. Phelps had written. She had also included a reference. *To whom it may concern: Elizabeth Craig* . . . Lizzie's cheeks burned. Here was the answer to her and Edith's speculations. Despite her unshakeable calm, Mrs. Phelps noticed them.

At the station, Callum was waiting to carry her box to the cart. As Nutmeg clip-clopped along the icy road, he said the geese were back in the meadow by the river; he had trapped one for Christmas dinner. They had planted a new stand of firs in the north pasture. She did her best to listen, but all she could think about was the terror of facing her grandparents. At Lilac Cottage she hurried to the door, desperate to meet their anger. There was Flora in her grey shawl, smiling; Rab pushing himself out of his chair.

"Hello, hello," said Callum. "I'll bring in Lizzie's box."

Her grandmother's smile vanished. Her grandfather—he hadn't caught the significance of the box—asked about Christmas in the city. Lizzie forced herself to describe dinner at the Phelpses, Edith's wedding. Meanwhile, her grandmother ate in furious silence. As soon as the table was cleared, the dishes washed, Lizzie went to her room. Ice lined the bottom of the windowpanes, but she did not dare to light the fire. She was folding her nightdress into a drawer when her grandmother came in, without knocking, and sat down on the bed.

"Being so tall you don't show much," she said. "When is it due?"

She had counted dates over and over: her last monthly, her last visit to the clubhouse. "March, I think. Late March."

"Is Louis the father?"

If this was the worst her grandmother said, she would be lucky. "I didn't understand he couldn't marry me until he finishes his apprenticeship."

"But he did. He never should have started courting you with so much time to go."

She wanted to say he was swept away, but any argument would only fuel her grandmother's anger. "I'm sorry," she said. "I thought we'd get married, rent a room, and make do until he finishes, but Mr. Rintoull won't hear of his apprentices living out. I didn't know how to tell you in a letter."

"You knew fine. You didn't want to read our reply. When I was at the Rankins', my friend Mary got caught by an apprentice brick-layer. She went home, telling everyone they'd be married as soon as he finished. Two months later he was engaged to the bricklayer's daughter. She ended up marrying a widower, twenty years older, with three bairns."

"Louis isn't . . ." she began, but no defence was possible. Help-less, she knelt at her grandmother's feet. "I'm truly sorry. I hate that you're ashamed of me. I hate that the baby won't be wanted. Please let me stay. I'll help you. I'll help at the farm. I don't know where I'll go if you turn me out." She kept her gaze fixed on her grand-mother's skirt, carefully mended by Louis, and her shoes, dusty and scuffed.

At last she felt her grandmother's hand, warm against her hair. "Lizzie, you've committed a sin, not one that can be undone, but we'll manage. Truth to tell, I can use the help. My eyesight's not what it was, and Rab needs company. We'll speak no more of this until the new year. Now go and help Kate with the deliveries. With your coat on, no one will guess."

....

BY THE TIME LOUIS'S FIRST LETTER ARRIVED, HER DAYS
had a routine: a quick bowl of porridge in the dark kitchen, then
walking to the farm to help with the cows, the hens, the ducks.
Once the milk was skimmed, the butter churned, the eggs washed,
she helped Kate clean, bake, wash, mind the children. Some days
she stayed for lunch. Others, she headed back to the cottage. On
Saturdays she took the wagon into the village. Yes, Glasgow was
grand, but it was good to be home. She had worked hard at the
Phelpses'; now she never had a moment. When Louis's letter came,
she left it lying unread on the table until after supper.

My very dear Lizzie,

   I am writing this at the cutting table, using a piece of
blotting paper to make sure I don't spill any ink. I hope your
journey was easy and that you and your box arrived safely.
Happy New Year and may 1892 be peaceful, prosperous and
healthy. My body will be spending New Year's Eve with the
Rintoulls but my heart will be with you. I am glad I can picture
Lilac Cottage.

   Next week Mr. Rintoull is taking us to see Buffalo Bill's
Wild West Show. There are wild animals and cowboys and they
re-enact battles. I'll write and tell you about it.

   Please give everyone my regards.

   Love, Louis

He didn't realise, she thought, that no one at Belhaven spoke
his name.

....

ON THE MORNING OF BURNS NIGHT, EVEN BEFORE SHE opened her eyes, she recognised the silence of snow. She pulled on her thickest stockings, her warmest petticoat. The snow already reached almost to the top of her boots and was still falling. No wind, no birds, only herself making the first footprints. I might be the only person in all of Fife, she was thinking, when the baby gave a hearty kick. In Glasgow she had constantly prayed for her to go away. Now she waited impatiently for her arrival. Only when she was here could Lizzie's life begin again. She milked the cows and gave them hay, fed the hens and ducks. While Michael sat watching, she, May, and Annie made a snowman, using branches for arms, a carrot for the nose.

In the kitchen, as she dried the girls' hair, Kate said, "You're too big to go to the village. We need to come up with a story."

She had tried, and failed, to think how to explain the baby. Could they have found her, like Moses in the bullrushes?

"I was thinking," Kate continued, "maybe Callum has a sister."

"I thought he has two brothers."

Kate said he did and now he would have a sister too. Poor Shirley was recently widowed; soon she would die in childbirth. "I'll ask you and Flora to take care of the baby because I have my hands full."

"But what will happen when we get married?"

Kate had the answer to that too. They would adopt the baby; such arrangements were common.

By the time she walked back to Lilac Cottage, her footsteps from the morning were gone. Snow filled her boots. When she came into the cottage her grandfather rose to meet her. Before she under-stood what was happening, he stepped forward and slapped her, first one cheek, then the other.

"I didn't believe Flora when she told me," he said, "but it's plain as day. That a granddaughter of mine should grow up to be a whore. I'm ashamed of the day you were born."

Those were the last words he spoke to her until the baby came.

X

From the hour of her birth, soon after dawn on a Thursday, Barbara nursed greedily, yelled lustily, seized whatever lay within her grasp. She weighed more than a hen, less than a lamb, and was usually awake at midnight. Her head was too large, her arms and legs frighteningly thin. Lizzie had watched Kate's affection for her daughters, there from the moment they arrived; but when Barbara woke for the fourth time in a night, when she cried for hours, refusing all comfort, she longed to put her down and walk away. She was glad Flora wanted to rock her, Rab to sing to her. In Barbara's presence, he had forgotten his anger. "You sinned," he said to Lizzie, "but God has given you a bonnie daughter."

Kate had written to Louis when Barbara arrived and he wrote back he was glad that mother and baby were well. A fortnight later, he wrote again.

Dear Lizzie,

I hope you feel stronger and the baby doesn't cry much. Here it's a dreich day. I was meant to be going to the haberdashers for buttons but Mrs. Rintoull said it was a fool's errand in this weather. Mr. Rintoull has given me an extra day off for the May holiday so I can stay for three days.

Last Saturday I went by the Tam o' Shanter for a pint. I had my fiddle with me and Ralph asked me to play a tune. He and Edith were mostly behind the bar but they took a turn on the floor. We had a lively evening and Ralph wants to have regular ceilidhs.

In the paper it says the shipyards have built a boat that can carry a thousand people to North America in a week.

Love, Louis

Leaving her grandmother to watch Barbara, she walked to the farm. For once the house was quiet—the children were asleep— and Kate was sitting by the fire, hemming May's pinafore. As Lizzie confided her fears of Louis meeting another girl, she sewed steadily. "When would he have the time to court someone else?" she said. "You're always telling me what long hours he works."

Lizzie watched her needle flashing. "What if Callum had looked at another girl?"

"He did." Kate lowered her voice. "My friend Nell wrote that she'd seen him walking with the older Abbott girl. That's why I finally went to the hayloft. Rose Abbott lived in his street and she had hair like a mermaid. I always knew Callum was the one for me, but he could have found a dozen girls who suited him fine. Lizzie, there's no use in fretting. Write Louis a cheerful letter. We'll make him welcome when he visits. Now, put the kettle on."

Walking back to Lilac Cottage in the gloaming, Lizzie wondered if Callum would have lain down with one of those girls. She remembered seeing him and Kate that summer afternoon. Only after she visited the clubhouse with Louis did she understand their gasps and groans. Now she could not imagine having those feelings for anyone else. Her heart was a locked door to which only he had the key. But Louis's heart . . . Before she could finish the thought, a fox, tail low, ran across the track.

AS HER STRENGTH RETURNED, SHE TOOK ON HER OLD duties, the cows, the hens, the garden, glad to leave the baby with Flora. She wrote to Edith, saying how much Louis enjoyed playing at the Tam o' Shanter. *I wish I could hear him. I hope there aren't too many pretty girls around.*

A week later Edith replied. *Touch wood, we'll have a baby in the new year. It'd be grand if you came back. Ralph says you can have a room here in exchange for helping out.* She read the last sentence over and over. If she wanted, she still had a home in Glasgow.

Two jackdaws on a wall meant his visit would go well. So did the first primroses, the ducks laying an extra egg. A cow not letting down her milk, the barn cats fighting, meant it would go badly. As Kate had used to do, she washed and ironed her good dress, polished her grandparents' shoes and her own. The day before his visit, she was kneeling by the fire, drying her hair, when Kate appeared with a plate of scones. While their grandmother filled the kettle, Kate whispered she would put a blanket in the hayloft. "But don't get caught again."

"What are you girls plotting?" Her grandmother looked over from the sink.

"How Lizzie should do her hair," Kate said. "I think she should leave the little curls at the front loose."

That evening as she and her grandfather played cribbage, he

talked about how the lads in Langmuir had got up a football team; they were playing Cupar next week. When he paused, she said, "I need a favour."

"What is it, lass? Now you've let me win and got me in a good mood."

"Please don't scold Louis."

His eyes sparked. Hours after he slapped her, her cheeks had still borne the imprint of his hand. "He wronged you, Lizzie. He stayed here, summer after summer, eating at our table. Now he won't marry you."

"We'll be married as soon as he finishes. I'm to blame too."

"You are," he said sternly. "We raised you to obey the commandments. But a good lad doesn't take advantage." He studied the cribbage board as if counting the rows of holes. "I'll hold my peace," he said at last, "but if he doesn't marry you as soon as he's able, I'll be on the next train to Glasgow."

"And I'll be with you," she said.

SHE WAS LIFTING THE SHORTBREAD OUT OF THE OVEN when she heard the first notes of "My Luve is like a red, red rose." Leaving both doors open, she ran to meet him, not caring if her grandparents saw their embrace. He kissed her, and kissed her again. His eyes still had those flecks of darker blue; his moustache was a little fuller. "Lizzie," he said, saying her name as only he did.

In the kitchen, her grandmother remarked he had brought the sun. Her grandfather gave the slightest nod. She led him to the cradle, where Barbara, for once, was sleeping peacefully. Over and over, she had imagined this moment: Louis meeting his daughter.

"Barbara." He made their daughter's name sound different too.

Hesitantly he reached to touch her hand. "Her skin is like silk," he marveled. And then, "She has your hair."

She wanted to reciprocate, to say she has your chin, your hands, your ears, but so far she had searched Barbara's small features in vain for traces of Louis. While the four of them had a cup of tea, he told them about Hugh's wedding; he had married Beth at Easter. Louis had helped her make her dress and played his fiddle.

"A pity you weren't thinking about your own wedding," her grandfather said.

The blood rose in Louis's face. He pushed back his chair, saying he'd better get along to the farm. As she got up to follow him, a small sound came from the cradle.

"Lizzie," said her grandmother.

"It won't hurt her to wait twenty minutes." She followed Louis through the door.

"Shouldn't you—?" he began.

But she kissed him until he kissed her back. When they started walking again, she asked about the suit he'd mentioned in his last letter. Had they got it done in time? They had, but only by staying up until midnight. "Your hair is shining in the sun," he said. "Have you done any new drawings?"

"A few of Barbara."

At the gate of the farmyard, she left him and, as if still a schoolgirl, ran back to the cottage. Even from the lilac bush, she could hear Barbara's cries. Inside, Flora was rocking the cradle. "Lizzie," she said, "what kept you?"

"I'm sorry. Louis's only here for three days. You could have given her the rag, like Kate showed us." Holding Barbara close, she filled a saucepan and heated the milk until it was as warm as her hand. Gently she put a few drops of milk on Barbara's lips, then dipped the milky rag into her open mouth. Soon the saucepan was half empty.

EVERY FEW MINUTES SHE WENT TO THE WINDOW, HOPING to turn back the burly clouds, but by the time Louis knocked, rain was falling. Beneath his black umbrella, his face had a somber cast. Perhaps they should stay here, he said, but she insisted they take a walk. "I have the umbrella I bought with Edith," she said gaily. The prospect of sitting around the table, talking with her grandparents, made her want to jump out of her skin.

"Don't get too wet," Flora said. "You're welcome to supper, Louis."

As she led the way towards the village, heading for the bigger roads where walking was easier, she asked about the bowling club, about playing at the Tam o' Shanter. At last, they were almost at the river, he broke in. "Lizzie, tell me how you are. Tell me the things you don't write about."

"I'm fine," she said, and caught herself. No, she was not fine. Her grandparents treated her as they had before she went to Glasgow, at their beck and call; the cottage was cramped, especially in bad weather; Barbara always needed attention, and she still hadn't dared go into the village. "I worry people will notice I'm different."

"Only because you're prettier." He squeezed her arm.

"I was thinking of coming back to Glasgow. Maybe getting a job in a factory." Startled by her own words, she stepped in a puddle.

"Where would you stay?" He held his umbrella higher.

"Ralph says I can have a room at the Tam o' Shanter, in exchange for helping out."

"That's handsome." His voice brightened. "But what about Barbara?"

"We can get a girl from the village to help. I can send money." She and Kate had talked about a girl, but the idea of sending money had just come to her.

Louis said working in a factory was hard. You did the same thing over and over, with fifteen minutes for lunch.

"So, I could work in a shop." She imagined herself like the girl who had sold her the umbrella, saying "Much obliged to you."

At the old bridge, they took shelter under an arch beside the river. The dull-green water flowed smoothly, pocked by rain. "Last month," Louis said, "we made a jacket out of a tweed this colour. Lizzie, we're getting soaked. Let's go back."

"We have to stay close together." If she could ignore the dampness seeping into her shoes, down her collar, why couldn't he? But he hated getting wet. He pulled her to him, briefly, then set off towards the road. He was describing the greengrocer's that had opened next to the tailor's as they passed the path to Lilac Cottage. She allowed herself to keep walking. At the farm gate, she warned him not to mention Glasgow to Kate and Callum; she must talk to her grandparents first.

In the kitchen the girls were sharing a scone; Michael was patting a ball. Kate asked about Barbara and, when Lizzie said she'd nursed her before leaving, urged her to stay to supper. "Flora will guess what's happened," she said. With the four of them, it was a merry table. Callum asked about the building of the underground; Kate said she'd heard the university was going to admit women. The girls, basking in adult company, begged to stay up late. Kate asked Louis to give them a song and got out last year's sloe gin. By the time he walked her home, the rain had stopped. She made him say goodnight where the path met the track. When he slid his hand inside her coat, she whispered, "Tomorrow."

As soon as he disappeared into the darkness, she started running, and as soon as she started running, she heard, above her footfalls, the sound of wailing. Before she could take off her coat, her grandmother was thrusting Barbara, red-faced, outraged, into her arms. "She doesn't want the rag," she said. "She wants you."

That night Barbara nursed at eleven, twelve, two, three thirty, and six. Lizzie remembered the story of Jessie King, the woman in Edinburgh who had murdered the babies in her care. She would never hurt her daughter, but she glimpsed why a person might.

AT BREAKFAST THE COMPLAINTS CAME THICK AND FAST. "She cried for two solid hours," her grandmother said. "She was turning herself inside out."

"You can't pretend you don't have a daughter," her grandfather said.

She built a wall to protect herself from their words and threw her own words over it, saying whatever was needed to buy two more days with Louis. After breakfast, while her grandfather walked over to Neil's to pick up a honeycomb, she washed the dishes, wiped the table, made the soup, swept and washed the floor. She was putting coal on the fire when at last her grandmother spoke. "I don't remember wanting someone this much," she said, "but perhaps I did. If the weather holds, maybe the three of you can have a picnic this afternoon."

It took her a moment to understand "the three of you." She nursed Barbara for as long as possible, trying to store up food, good temper. They played peek-a-boo and Barbara offered one of her rare, enchanting smiles. After lunch Flora agreed to mind her for an hour while she took Louis to the castle.

He was waiting at the farmyard gate. Kate and the children, he reported, were in the garden; Callum and George were repairing a wall. She led the way past the hens to the hayloft. They climbed high into the hay. Louis unfolded the blanket Kate had left. Then he was embracing her, his hands under her blouse. She told him they had to be careful. Between kisses, he promised. When he began to groan, she gave him a little push.

Afterwards she watched him sleep. She was studying his moustache, trying to recall how he had looked before he grew it, when her heart jolted and raced. There were the wooden walls of the clubhouse, the bowls and the photographs. Louis was sitting on the bench. He took off his jacket, the brown one he always wore, and rolled up his shirtsleeves. Beside him sat a woman—no, a girl about Lizzie's age, but full-figured. Around her long, pale neck she wore a string of beads which matched her dark-green dress. Louis reached for her hand. "No," Lizzie was whispering when the picture vanished.

She shook him awake. "I was afraid you'd forget me," she said. It was the closest she could come to an accusation.

He blinked sleepily. "I hate you being so far away," he said. "Sometimes I almost have to forget you to manage. Why did you name her Barbara?"

"It's Flora's middle name. We should go. Remember to say you liked the castle. Then we'll take Barbara for a picnic."

"Goodness, what a lot of coming and going." But he was smiling as he buttoned his trousers. He folded the blanket, lining up the edges; they checked each other's backs for hay. At the cottage Barbara was still asleep. While Lizzie organised shortbread and lemonade, Louis examined the garments Flora had set out for him to mend; he would take care of them after the picnic. The food in one basket, Barbara in another, they headed to the lochan. Beneath the birch trees, with their tender green leaves, they set down the baskets and stepped to the water's edge. The lochan was rippling in the slight breeze. Last night, Louis said, he had had a dream about his father. "He was standing on the steps of a building, making a speech to a crowd, but I couldn't hear what he said."

"Did he make speeches?"

He turned to her, frowning. "How would I know? Sometimes I think of getting on a ship to Canada. I know he meant to send for us."

"When you finish your apprenticeship, we can go together." She was pointing out the minnows, how they swam close together, first one way then another, when a voice called "Good afternoon." Miss Urquhart, in her brown suit, was walking through the trees.

Lizzie felt her face grow hot as she introduced Louis Hunter, a friend of the family.

"And this must be Callum's niece?" Miss Urquhart bent down beside the basket where Barbara, newly woken, was staring at the sky, reaching with both hands. "Oh, look, she's smiling." Gently she touched Barbara's cheek. "Bye, baby Bunting," she sang in a clear soprano, "Father's gone a hunting. Well, enjoy your afternoon." Still humming to herself, she carried on around the lochan.

A few minutes later they were sitting on Lizzie's shawl, eating shortbread, when the teacher reappeared, almost running. She had found a rabbit trapped in a snare. Lizzie jumped up. She chose a fist-sized rock from the shore and followed Miss Urquhart, Louis trailing behind. When the rabbit came into view, its hind leg almost severed by the trap, he and the teacher halted. She stepped forward and brought down the rock.

XI

*

A week ago, she had cared how the lambs were doing, whether the potatoes and oats were flourishing, if Michael's tooth had come in, that the village shop had a new kind of soap. Now she kept thinking about the picture of the clubhouse, of how Louis had welcomed the idea of her return to Glasgow. As they sowed the carrots, Kate asked what he had made of his daughter. "He said she had my hair," she said. She planted two sticks at opposite sides of the vegetable bed and unfurled a string between them.

"She does," Kate said. "Callum scarcely noticed May till she was walking." She made a trough as Lizzie had taught her, deep enough to foil the birds, not so deep the seeds wouldn't sprout. "Should we do two rows of carrots?"

"If you have the seeds." As she moved the sticks to mark the next row, she described the picture of the girl in the dark-green dress.

"Maybe you were imagining things?" Kate handed her the seeds. "Or maybe he took a girl there before he met you. The weather's been so unsettled since you came back. No girl would go to a shed in winter. Did I tell you we'd asked George's sister Amy to help five mornings a week?"

As she sprinkled seeds in the small, dark trough, she thought it had been cold since the New Year but her pictures were always of the future. There was still time to stop Louis taking the girl in the dark-green dress to the clubhouse, but how much she couldn't tell. Given his shirtsleeves, the day was warm, June or July. She could not be in Glasgow then, but if he knew she would be there in the autumn, surely that would deter him. It was a good omen that Kate, without her prompting, had asked a girl from the village to help.

Dear Edith,

I hope all's well with you and Ralph. We're busy here—six calves so far—and Kate's son Michael is starting to walk, at last.

If you have a room free, I'd like to take it, maybe starting in November. I'll need to find a position when I arrive but Louis says people are hiring.

Love, Lizzie

Once the letter was written, she had to post it immediately. She left Barbara with Flora and walked to the village. In the potato field the plants were already nodding with white flowers. She would be here to help with the oats and the barley, but would she be here to help lift the tatties? Her own future, as usual, was hidden. She passed Dr. Murray's house, where Morag, since her marriage to Colin, no longer lived. She had missed the wedding because of Barbara. Since she left Glasgow, it was as if she had two lives: one at Belhaven, where everyone knew about Barbara, and one in the village, where no one did.

Instead of going straight to the shop, she turned in to the church-yard. There was the flat stone where she and Kate had tried to summon their future husbands. The letter weighed less than a handful of corn, yet to send it would change everything. She imagined tearing it up, hiding the pieces in the grass, and trusting Louis to make her an honest woman. But the long months of his apprenticeship stretched before her; she remembered her picture, her grandfather saying Louis was too eager to please. I'm just knocking on the door, she told herself. I don't have to open it.

THE BLACKTHORN BLOSSOM BLOOMED; SHE AND KATE thinned the carrots; the sheep were sheared, the calves weaned. Thoughts of Glasgow hummed in her head so loudly, she was surprised no one heard them. She tried, once again, to be the best possible granddaughter, sister, aunt, saving up virtue to pay for future misdeeds. She helped her grandmother, she helped Kate, she played cribbage with her grandfather, she tended both gardens and milked the cows and once again did the deliveries. When she came home, she would find Flora playing "Pat-a-cake, pat-a-cake," with Barbara, or Rab reading to her. She began to offer her spoonfuls of mashed potato, or stewed apple. Usually Barbara pushed the spoon away, spat out the contents. Flora said she was too young, but she already had three teeth; sometimes she swallowed a morsel.

In August Louis came again. He mended everyone's clothes and helped with the harvest. Barbara smiled at him and he held her on his knee and sang "Molly Malone." They slipped away to the hayloft a couple of times. On his last day he was so tired that as soon as he lay down, his eyes closed. Within a minute, he was snoring gently. She watched his moustache moving slightly, the little flakes of white on his nose where the skin was peeling. She would be twenty by the time they married, and here he was sleeping away one of their few hours together. When she shook his shoulder, he startled. "Forgive me, Lizzie. I'm not used to being outdoors all day." He laughed. She tried to laugh too, but her throat closed. How could she keep her hold on him if they did not do this thing they did only with each other?

When he stopped at the cottage to say goodbye, she walked with him along the path and retrieved the bag of clothes she had hidden in the hedge the day before. "Will you leave it at the Tam o' Shanter?" she said, and he clapped his hands.

SHE HAD ANOTHER PICTURE OF THE CLUBHOUSE; THIS time the girl in the green dress, still wearing her beads, was reaching for Louis's hand. When Barbara had eaten porridge six days in a row, she wrote to Edith asking her to invite her for a weekend. Once she was safely in Glasgow, she thought, she would write to her grandparents, explaining that she needed to stay for a few months. She could not bear to imagine their anger.

Edith wrote back a week later: *Would it suit you to come for the weekend of November 3rd? Come on the Saturday, early, so you can help me choose new china. We're having a ceilidh at the pub that evening and Louis will be playing.*

"You've been working hard for months," said her grandmother.

"But can you manage without me for three days?"

"Of course we can, can't we, Barbara?" On her grandmother's knee, Barbara gurgled obligingly. "You'll show me about her food and Amy will lend a hand."

"Go and enjoy yourself, lass," said her grandfather from his armchair.

She feigned reluctance for a little longer and after lunch wrote to Edith, and Louis, and walked into Langmuir. They had lifted the potatoes last week, five days of backbreaking, muddy work. Now, in the newly harrowed field, the curlews were back. How can you go? their melancholy cries asked. She remembered Barbara reaching for Rab's pipe, smiling as Flora tickled her toes. This time she did not stop at the churchyard.

"More letters, Lizzie," Mr. Ross said when she came into the shop. He himself had had a letter yesterday from his son in Canada; in Edmonton they already had a foot of snow.

DURING THOSE WEEKS OF WAITING THE ONLY TIME SHE felt like herself was when she was doing the tasks she had always done: collecting the eggs, milking the cows, churning the butter. Over and over she decided not to go and then recalled the girl at the clubhouse. Later, she thought she must have already known how hard it would be, once she was there, to leave Glasgow again. The Friday before her train, she lingered at the farm, playing with the girls, until Kate reminded her of the time. "Can you bring me some of that lily-of-the-valley soap?" she said. Lizzie promised to try and asked if she could borrow a bag.

The ceilidh gave her an excuse to pack her nice dress and good shoes. She put in extra underwear. Otherwise, she left her room as if she would be back in a couple of days, the picture of her parents on the wall, the weather house sitting on the chest of drawers, her shawl on the back of the chair. After her grandparents retired, she sat by the fire, staring at the glowing embers, longing for a storm, or an earthquake, anything to stop the machinery she had set in motion. She carried the candle to her room and knelt down beside the cradle where Barbara slept, her cheeks faintly chapped, her breath a gentle sigh. What madness had made her think she could leave her? She would go to Glasgow for two nights, remind Louis she wasn't far away, he had no need to go to the clubhouse with anyone else, and come home. She imagined herself on Monday, hanging out the washing with her grandmother, playing cribbage with her grandfather. She fell asleep to the sound of Barbara's breathing.

SHE HAD LAST BEEN TO THE TAM O' SHANTER ON THE night of Edith's wedding, when the pub was crowded with well-wishers. Now barely a dozen men were scattered throughout the wood-paneled room; a couple of greybeards puffed their pipes on the red banquette; four younger men were playing darts.

"Lizzie!" Edith emerged from behind the bar, voluminous in her pinafore. "Let me get Ralph to help with your box."

Was she always to be doomed by the presence, or absence, of a box? She explained she hadn't brought it. "Didn't Louis leave a bag for me?"

"He did." Given her belly, Edith could no longer lean forward, but her face leaned forward. "I shouldn't be telling you this," she went on, almost whispering, "but whenever he plays, the girls are all over him. He's a fine figure of a man, and he has a way of making a woman feel special. Ralph says he'll make a fortune as a tailor."

She called over to the darts players—she'd be back in five minutes—and led the way through a door and up a flight of stairs. Her and Ralph's room was at the far end of the corridor. "We've put you at the back where it's quieter."

"Thank you." She looked around appreciatively at the wallpaper patterned with violets, the bed wider than her bed at Lilac Cottage, the chest of drawers with a mirror, the blue-and-red hearth rug, the small armchair. As she stepped over to the window, her foot nudged something. Glancing down, she discovered her bag, a leaf from the hedge where she'd hidden it still caught in the handle.

Downstairs again, Edith introduced her to a girl with broad shoulders and stormy red hair who was rolling out pastry at the kitchen table. "Chrissie makes the best pies," she said.

"Edith says you know all about farming." Chrissie's tawny eyes glinted.

"I do, though there's not much call for that in Glasgow. Do you sell the pies?"

"At lunchtime. Oops." She plucked a long red hair out of the pastry.

"Careful," Edith scolded. "This evening you'll meet Frank. He helps Ralph behind the bar. You can work Friday and Saturday evenings until the music starts."

She was stammering her thanks as Edith continued. She had asked around about positions. There was a vacancy at a nearby office where girls drew engines. "I remembered you're good at drawing. I said you'd call round today before they close."

"I thought we were going to buy china?"

"Lizzie"—she patted her belly—"do I look like I'm going to be waltzing onto a tram? I wrote that for your granny."

I must tell her I'm not staying, she thought, but she couldn't, not until she told Louis. Edith was already giving her directions. As she walked down Grey Street, she told herself they wouldn't offer her a position; the idea of earning money by drawing was like a fairy tale. She passed a man wearing a dark suit Louis might have made, a group of schoolboys, ties loose, fingers inky. The address was on a side street, past the butcher's. At the top of the stairs, she stepped into a large room, one wall lined with windows. A dozen girls were sitting or standing at tables, drawing. As she hesitated in the doorway, a girl pointed to the desk in the corner where a man in grey overalls was moving papers from one pile to another. When he paused to frown at an envelope, she stepped forward.

"Excuse me. Mrs. Ogilvie said you might have a job."

Reaching for his spectacles, the man—he was almost her height—came out from behind the desk. "You must be Miss Craig. I'm Mr. Simpson. One of our girls left today. Have you studied drawing?"

"No, but people say I'm good at it."

Mr. Simpson nodded. The girls in the room, he told her, were locomotive tracers; they were tracing the drawings of draughtsmen and architects, or sometimes copying photographs, onto transparent cloth. The completed drawings were coloured to show the different materials and sent back to the factory or office. At a corner table, he handed her a sheet of paper clipped to a board and a photograph of a train engine. "Make a drawing of this," he said, "as like as possible."

She began to lightly mark the body of the engine, the chimney, the wheels, the pistons and valves. As she sketched in the details, carefully shading the chimney, she forgot that she did not want the job. She was drawing the rods between the wheels when Mr. Simpson loomed behind her. "Be here at eight thirty on Monday for a week's trial," he said. "Most girls bring a lunch."

Back in the street, she longed to tell Kate that she could earn money by drawing. But I'm not staying, she reminded herself. At a flower stall she bought a bunch of red roses so vivid that several people smiled at the sight of her carrying them down the street. In the kitchen of the Tam o' Shanter she found Edith at the table, her head buried in her hands. "Don't get up," Lizzie said, but she was already on her feet, filling the kettle, asking about the locomotive tracers. Lizzie explained they had offered her a week's trial and held out the flowers.

"Roses." Edith stroked a velvety petal. "I'm glad you've come back. We've always got on well, and with your nieces, you'll know what to do when the baby comes."

She let the steam from the kettle rise into her face.

They were still drinking tea, reminiscing about the Phelpses, when Ralph leaned through the door: Louis was here. Edith directed her to the mirror hanging in the corner and she patted her hair into place. At the sight of him standing at the end of the bar, his moustache neatly clipped, his shirt very white, she felt suddenly shy. "Good afternoon, Mr. Hunter," she said.

He gave a little bow. "Good afternoon, Miss Craig."

He was still smiling when Edith appeared. "Did she tell you she already has a job?"

Once again, she explained about the locomotive tracers—all due to Edith—and they both congratulated her. When they were settled at a corner table, her hands demurely in her lap, her feet secretly tucked between his, he said, "I've never heard of a tracers, but it sounds just the ticket, Lizzie. I invited Tom, the other apprentice, to the ceilidh so you'll have a partner."

She said she looked forward to meeting him, and Louis told her about the song he'd written, "Lizzie's Return"; he would sing it tonight. They ate at the chop house around the corner and by the time they came back, the pub was thronged with people. She scanned the crowd, wondering if she would recognise the girl in the dark dress. Louis and his fellow fiddler stood on a couple of boxes at one end. As they struck up their first tune, a voice said, "Are you Lizzie Craig?"

A lad barely her height, his forehead wrinkled, his eyes and mouth smiling, was standing before her. His hair, darker than Louis's but lighter than hers, grew in a sharp widow's peak that pointed to his long, straight nose. It would be interesting to draw him, she thought. "How did you find me?" she asked.

"He told me you'd be the prettiest girl in the room without a partner." Tom held out his hand. "Be warned, I have two left feet."

His claim proved true. Several times they had to stop until she could guide them back onto the floor, but he took her corrections in good humour. Between dances he told her he had grown up in Dundee and was still getting used to Glasgow and tailoring. "I never used to pay much mind to clothes," he said, "but the other day I stopped a man in the street because the lapels of his jacket were so elegant."

She was still smiling when she noticed Ralph gesturing from behind the bar. As she washed glasses, rinsing them carefully, a Gay Gordons began. She saw Tom being led into position by a woman with a tightly coiled bun; she marched him briskly one way, briskly the other until Lizzie lost sight of them. When the glasses were done, she returned to find him at their table. "Who was your partner?" she said.

He smiled and said he didn't know. "I saw her tapping her foot, so I asked if she wanted to dance. She wasn't as patient as you. Oh, this is Louis's new song."

She stood up so she could see him across the roomful of people. The other fiddler was playing and he was standing in his white shirt, watching her as he sang,

The lass from the land of the birches
Is the only one for me.
The winds may blow and the seas may rise
But she's the one for me.

When he finished, people applauded, Lizzie louder than anyone else.

The music ended and Louis joined them. He patted his shining forehead and took a long pull from his tankard. If you don't play hard, he had told her, people don't want to dance. She longed to put her hand on his arm, to feel the heat coming off him. If only the useful Tom would melt into the air.

"What did you think of my new song?" Louis asked.

"Beautiful," she said, trying to convey her delight.

"The lass from the land of the birches / Oh, how the birches dance in the breeze," Tom sang. "Most pleasing." Then, as if sensing her thoughts, he was on his feet, thanking her for the dancing lesson and heading for the door.

"Did Edith give you a nice room?" Louis said, eying her over his tankard.

For a few seconds she didn't understand his question; then she did.

AFTER THE SERVICE AT ST. CUTHBERT'S, EDITH INTRODUCED her to several women as a dear friend who had come to help at the Tam o' Shanter. Lizzie nodded and said hello, all the time thinking she must talk to Louis. If only she had spoken yesterday, when they went to her room, but how could she after his song? He arrived as they were finishing lunch and suggested a walk up the Necropolis.

"You get a nice view on a Sunday," he said, "without all the smoke." As they walked arm in arm among the elaborate graves and statues, he talked about how he was earning extra money mending clothes for the neighbours. "Flora gave me the idea," he said. "I don't charge much but it all helps. And you're nicely situated now, with your position and everything taken care of at the Tam o' Shanter."

"Louis." She stopped near a stone column; a delicately carved strand of ivy wound from top to bottom. "I can't stay."

"What do you mean?" He let go of her arm. "It's all settled."

"No. My grandparents are expecting me back. I can't leave Barbara with them."

"But you're going to pay for help. Lizzie, you have a job, you have a place to live. You can't let Edith and Ralph down."

She began to explain how she'd only gone to the locomotive tracers' to please Edith, but he interrupted. "You didn't tell them you were leaving, did you?"

Perched on a nearby gravestone a crow watched her sternly as she admitted that she hadn't. "I meant to, but I knew they wouldn't let me come. I've already done one very bad thing: having Barbara. Leaving her would be another. I'm sorry. I couldn't bear to tell you in a letter."

Beneath his moustache, his lips paled. He stepped over and seized her shoulders, not to pull her close but to hold her at arm's length. "I've been counting on your coming back for months." He gave her a little shake. "You promised."

She did not remember promising, but she said she had been counting on it too. "I still have Mrs. Phelps's money. I can come back and visit again soon. It's only a little over a year until you finish." Again and again she explained how she wanted to but she couldn't; Rab and Flora needed her; Barbara needed her. "But I need you," he said. She could have withstood his anger, but when his eyes grew wet with unshed tears, she found herself saying maybe she could stay until New Year's.

ON MONDAY SHE ROSE, WASHED, DRESSED AS IF FOLLOWING orders. Porridge was waiting on the stove; Edith had shown her where the bread and cheese were kept. In the street she came to a halt at the sight of the sign: Tam o' Shanter on his good grey mare. She remembered her grandfather reciting the poem, how he spoke the words

> But pleasures are like poppies spread,
> You seize the flow'r, it's bloom is shed;
> Or like the snow falls in the river,
> A moment white—then melts for ever

with particular emphasis. Barbara would be waking soon. It was not too late. She could tiptoe up to her room, pack her things, write a note and take a tram to the station. But what would Louis think? And Edith and Ralph, who had been so kind? She started walking only to be stopped again at the end of the street by the newspaper seller's cries: "*Glasgow Herald, Glasgow Herald.*" She had promised to bring her grandfather a paper.

At the locomotive tracers', Mr. Simpson asked Deirdre to get Lizzie started. "We've never had a girl as tall as you," Deirdre said admiringly. She chose an apron for Lizzie and something called sleeves to protect Lizzie's real sleeves and led her to a drawing board. "Everyone spends the first few days in a muddle," she warned. Lizzie did her best to pay attention as Deirdre demonstrated how to cut and stretch the transparent cloth. "You have to do it two or three times to get it as tight as possible. If you can, do the first stretching before lunch, or at the end of the day. Let me show you where we keep things."

She led Lizzie around the room, introducing her to the other girls and pointing out the shelves for paints, rulers, pencils, and shapes. Back at the board, she had Lizzie stretch the cloth again and pronounced it good enough. "Now rub in some chalk," she said, "so the ink will take."

ALMOST TWENTY MINUTES OF HER LUNCH HOUR WAS gone by the time she found the post office. She wrote out a telegram and handed it to the clerk: *Flora Craig, Lilac Cottage, Langmuir, Fife. Staying until New Year. Will send money. Very sorry. Love, Lizzie.*

"One, two, three, four . . ." The clerk counted as if this were the most ordinary of messages. "That will be a shilling and threepence."

As she left the post office a girl came in, a baby in her arms. Lizzie glimpsed pink cheeks, a tiny hand. On the pavement, she pressed her hands to her temples. Could she do this? Did she want to? Louis, Barbara, Louis, Barbara—each tried to claim her, each tried to push the other aside. Whichever way she turned, someone—her grandparents, Kate, Edith—was shouting at her.

Inside the post office the girl with the baby was waiting behind a man while another man stood at the counter. She stood behind the girl; she didn't care about getting her money back, only her words. Why had she let Edith send her to the locomotive tracers'? Stupid, stupid. The man at the counter was leaning forward, pointing at a piece of paper, when a church bell struck the hour. Once again she hurried out into the street.

Back at the locomotive tracers', the bolts she was drawing blurred as she imagined the telegram passing through the towns she had seen from the train, reaching the village shop, Mr. Ross's boy bicycling to Lilac Cottage, her grandmother, expecting news of a later train, opening the envelope. Deirdre reminded her to use the curved shapes that were stored in the corner cabinet. "Don't worry if you make mistakes today," she said.

That evening, feigning toothache, she asked Ralph for a dram to help her sleep. But sleep brought dreams: Barbara wedged in the branches of a tree; Flora rattling the stove; Rab, knife in hand, bending over a lamb. You can't pretend you don't have a daughter. The next night she stayed awake as long as possible. When at last she slept, Barbara was lying on top of a beehive.

All day as she drew, she wrote to her grandmother in her head. Finally, on Saturday, she bought a notepad and envelopes.

Louis begged me to stay until the end of the year. I knew I
would lose him if I didn't. I want Barbara to have a father.
Edith has found me a job. I'll send money to help pay Amy
and I'll be home for Hogmanay. I'm sorry. I'm sorry. I'm sorry.

Writing to Kate was easier. *I saw the picture again. It's only for seven weeks but it will make all the difference with Louis.* She carried the letters to the pillar box. Back at the Tam o' Shanter, Edith set her to help Chrissie, who was again making pies. They were a new thing, Chrissie explained. Men could eat them at the bar or carry them away for later. She showed Lizzie how to measure the filling, how to pinch the edges. "Smell them when they come out of the oven," she boasted, "and you can't say no." As they worked side by side, she told Lizzie she used to be a housemaid but it was too quiet. "Here there's always something going on. How's the drawing?"

"There's a lot to remember. I wouldn't want to do it forever."

"I don't expect you will"—Chrissie briskly cut more circles of pastry—"not with Mr. Malcolm around." Seeing Lizzie's look of surprise, she said she had stopped in at the ceilidh. "You were too busy twirling to notice."

"Mr. Malcolm is my dancing partner. Louis Hunter, he plays the fiddle, is my friend."

"Lucky you." Chrissie's red hair, as usual, was falling around her face. "They're both handsome lads."

She must, Lizzie thought, have seen Tom only from a distance.

KATE WROTE BACK AS IF SHE WERE SHOUTING. *HAVE YOU lost your mind? Some women do after having a baby. Your daughter is here, your home is here. Flora's too old to mind Barbara. Come back and we'll sort everything out.*

As for her grandmother, she did not reply, which at first was terrible but day by day made things easier. She did not write to her again, nor to Kate, only sent money every Saturday. What if Louis were to get the girl in the green dress in trouble? She told him her grandparents had agreed to mind Barbara until the new year and he said he'd been sure they'd come around. Every Saturday after the ceilidh, she waited until Edith was in bed and Ralph busy and led him up the stairs, trying to avoid the seventh, which creaked.

But of course Edith heard his comings and goings. They were hanging out the laundry, a line of sheets between them, when she said, "It's none of my business, but you're being careful, aren't you?"

"You told me how."

Last year her face would have grown hot at the question. Now she understood that Edith didn't disapprove, so long as Louis's visits were discreet. What she did disapprove of was Lizzie's plan to go home at Hogmanay. "You're sending money, aren't you?" she had said. "Ralph was saying only the other day what a help you are."

XII

❋

At the farm her days had begun with her grandparents, discussing the weather and the chores. At the Phelpses', Edith and Cook had planned menus and gossiped. Now she ate porridge alone in the dimly lit kitchen and tried not to think about Barbara. She was glad, as she sliced bread for lunch on her third Monday, to hear the tick of bare feet on floorboards: Edith still in her nightclothes, rosy with sleep, padded across the room to stand beside the stove.

"Please, Lizzie," she said, "can you put off going home? Ralph says Christmas and New Year are our busiest weeks and I'm sure my pains will come at the worst time."

"I can't. I'm sorry. My grandparents are expecting me." She busied herself with putting the loaf away, cutting the cheese, but as Edith, fair hair wisping around her face, kept gazing at her imploringly, she said she would write and see if she could stay a little longer.

Walking down Grey Street, beneath the flaring gaslights, she thought she would wait a week and then say she was sorry; her grandparents did need her at New Year's. For a few steps, the problem seemed solved. Then she recalled that Edith took in all the mail that came to the Tam o' Shanter; she would know there was no letter. Two men blocked her path, carrying a carcass into the butcher's. She was wondering where the cow came from, when she saw the postman round the corner. That was the answer; she would tell Edith she had met him in the street.

But a week later, she came into the kitchen to see Edith standing at the ironing board, crying over one of Ralph's shirts. Quickly she took the iron out of her hand and led her to a chair. Between sobs, Edith confessed how frightened she was. Her aunt had died having a baby, and what if something was wrong with the baby? "Please, Lizzie," she said, tears rolling down her cheeks, "can't you stay?"

AT CHRISTMAS, SHE SENT LILY-OF-THE-VALLEY SOAP FOR Kate and her grandmother, a doll for Barbara, and a note: *I have to stay and help Edith with her baby. I'll be back soon.* She heard nothing, nothing, and then four days after Christmas two sentences from Kate. *James was born on the 15th, a healthy boy. I hope one day you'll meet him.* No mention of her gifts, nor of her delayed return. She wrote back that she looked forward to meeting James at the end of January, and again heard nothing. Last year Louis had given her a book and a brooch. This year he was working night after night; she told herself he had no time to think of gifts. Not until New Year's Day, when they were sitting in the empty pub, their coats buttoned against the cold, did he produce a parcel wrapped in brown paper. Inside she discovered a blue blouse.

"Do you like it?" he said. "The colour reminded me of those flowers, and your eyes."

"Larkspur." After their first meeting at the clubhouse, he had bought her a bunch of the feathery blue flowers. "This is the nicest thing I've ever owned."

She ran upstairs to fetch her gifts for him: a drawing she had made of him playing the fiddle and a book of songs he had admired in a shop window. "Oh, this is grand, Lizzie," he said. He hummed a few bars of "The Lass from the Land of the Birches."

MOLLY ARRIVED, AFTER SIXTEEN HARROWING HOURS, ON the morning of January 4th. For days the household was in disarray. Ralph kept giving the wrong change, darting upstairs to see how Edith was doing. Each afternoon Lizzie hurried back from the locomotive tracers' to find Chrissie waiting to hand off tasks. She made supper and sat with Edith and Molly, reading aloud from *Alice in Wonderland*. Alice got bigger and smaller, drank potions and ate mushrooms, and met many talkative animals. She tried to keep her distance from Molly, but the tormenting dreams of her first weeks in Glasgow returned. By the end of the month, she swore, she would be back in Belhaven.

On Saturday she was minding the bar—Ralph and Frank were fetching a new barrel—when Chrissie stepped out of the kitchen, carrying a tray of pies. "Hot pies," she called. "Come and get 'em." Half a dozen men approached. Chrissie smiled—one cheek was smudged with flour—and handed the first man two pies. Taking his coins, she turned to the next customer. She's too busy to go to the till, Lizzie thought. Before she could see what Chrissie did next, Ralph was back, asking her to check on Edith.

That night, as they formed circles for an eightsome reel, she confided her suspicions to Tom. The frown he always wore grew serious. "You're sure you saw something?" he asked.

"Almost sure. She might have gone to the till later."

"Did you tell Ralph?"

When she said she hadn't, Tom shook his head. "Thieving is serious," he said. "You need to tell him so he can be on the lookout."

Before she could answer, the fiddlers struck up. As they began to dance, she remembered the day at the Phelpses' when Edith had caught Bert, the boy, with half a cake under his jacket. He had said he felt badly he got to eat so many nice things while his brothers and sisters never had any treats. Edith had cuffed him and handed back the cake. "Mrs. Phelps would have given it to him," she told Cook and Lizzie. But the Phelpses, Lizzie thought, as she twirled Tom round, could afford to lose many cakes.

She was still mulling over his advice when Louis came to her room. Sitting side by side on her bed, she told him what she'd told Tom. He put his hand on her thigh. "Forget it, Lizzie. You're not sure what you saw. Now close your eyes."

When she opened them, a parcel lay in her lap. He watched, smiling, as she undid the string and folded back the brown paper to reveal a small dress made of the same blue sprigged cotton as her Christmas blouse. "An early birthday present," he said.

He almost never mentioned Barbara, but now she held the proof; he did remember he had a daughter. Someday, some specific day next January, the three of them would be together, under the same roof. She posted the dress with a note—*Happy Birthday, Barbara. With love from your father*. The following week, she told him it fit perfectly, and on Wednesday, when a letter from Kate arrived, her first thought was that it contained those words. Perhaps the money she sent every week, the gifts, had finally convinced her sister she was not a terrible person. She opened the envelope, standing by the window in her room.

Sunday

Lizzie, I hate to tell you this—Grandmother has given Barbara to Miss Urquhart.

She had no idea how long she stood, forehead pressed to the cold glass, the letter lying on the floor, before she picked it up and read further.

Since you left, Miss Urquhart has been calling at Lilac Cottage once or twice a week, bringing little gifts and playing with Barbara. Finally, she got the minister to come with her and explain that she wanted to adopt Barbara. She'd inherited some money and could pay a girl to mind her while she was teaching. The next day they came back in Mr. Waugh's trap to fetch Barbara and the cradle.

The first I heard about it was when Amy arrived, saying the whole village was talking about Miss Urquhart taking in our niece. I went to Lilac Cottage straightaway. Flora was alone. I asked if it was true and she said last week she'd found Barbara trying to climb into the well. "Lizzie chose to give her away," she said. "I've made the same choice. The difference is Miss Urquhart asked."

Lizzie, I'm sorry to say she's right. Minding Barbara, now she's crawling, was too much for her, and the way you behaved—pretending you were coming back, sending a telegram, not coming back at New Year's—made her so cross, and so sad. Barbara has a good home. Now you can do what

you've wanted all along: start over. Come and visit soon. Rab
and Flora are much older.

Her mind was a house in flames with no way out. She left a
note on her door: *Feeling poorly. Early night.* In bed she piled her
coat on top of the quilt; still her teeth chattered. Faintly, from the
kitchen, she heard Molly crying. Barbara, too, must be crying, in
some strange room. I made a terrible, terrible mistake, she thought.
If only she could show the letter to Louis, but would he blame her?
Or be glad? Either would be awful, and perhaps he would do both.

On Saturday after work, she took a tram into the centre of town
and another out to the neighbourhood where Hugh and Beth
lived. A woman in the bakery by the tram stop directed her to their
street. Only as she climbed the stairs did it occur to her they might
not be home, but she was still knocking when she heard footsteps.
"What a nice surprise," Beth said. She ushered her into their single
room with its stove and sink and window. Hugh was sitting at the
table, a vase of daffodils beside him the brightest thing in the room.
"Lizzie, how are you?" he said, jumping up to embrace her.

She sank into a chair. Beth bent down to ask if she would like
Hugh to herself. That was what she had imagined, but she said
no, Beth needed to hear this too, and it was Beth whose face she
watched as she poured out the hidden history of the last year—
everything except the pictures—and waited for them to call her the
terrible things she called herself.

"Oh, Lizzie," said Beth, "I'm so sorry."

"You have a child," Hugh said wonderingly. "So that's why you
left Glasgow."

He began to pace the small room, three steps to the sink, eleven
to the bed. On the wall beside the bed was a drawing she'd done

of Belhaven, the house with the rowan tree beside the door. At last Beth said he was making her dizzy, and he stood holding the back of his chair, rocking it back and forth. "I can only think of two choices," he said. "One, you say nothing and let everything be."

She was staring at him, bewildered—how could this even be a choice?—when Beth said, "What did you put on the birth certificate?"

"Illegitimate," she whispered, hating the harsh word.

"Two," Hugh continued, "you go home, beg Flora and Rab's forgiveness, and ask Miss Urquhart to return your daughter. Or maybe"—he rocked the chair harder—"three, you throw yourself on Miss Urquhart's mercy. Ask her to keep Barbara until you're married."

Beth shook her head. "I can't imagine her agreeing to that."

What Lizzie couldn't imagine, as she gazed at the daffodils, was her grandparents forgiving her. Whenever she thought about going home, she remembered the long weeks before Barbara was born, when Rab had behaved as if she were invisible. "You mean"—she could barely utter the sentence—"I let them give away my daughter?"

"You already gave her away." Seeing her face, Hugh hurried on. "I know it isn't the same, but you gave up being her mother. Wouldn't it be easier to live here until Louis finishes?"

She was heading for the door when Beth said, "Forgive my asking, but are you sure you still want to marry Louis?"

That was the one thing she was sure of. "I've lost Barbara, and I've lost my grandparents. I can't lose him too."

"You haven't lost Rab and Flora," Hugh said. "You'll always be Lizzie Craig."

He said other things, so did Beth, but neither of them could suggest a fourth choice. Back on the pavement, surrounded by the unforgiving houses, she couldn't, at first, remember which way to turn. As she stood there, hesitating, a woman approached, grimy hand outstretched. "In the name of God," she said, "help me."

THEY WERE PAYING A SECOND VISIT TO THE TEAROOM— Louis had earned five shillings repairing a suit—when she handed him Kate's letter. "What's this?" he said, setting down his teacup. She could tell he expected good news. She watched his eyes follow a line, stop, follow it again.

"You told me they agreed to mind her," he said.

She had sometimes thought he knew about her lies. Now she saw he had had no notion. "Did you really think they'd let me leave her?"

"But you were sending money. Edith needed you."

The waitress whisked by, delivering a tray to another table. "If I'd gone home, I couldn't have come back until we got married. Louis, I never meant to leave her, but what with Edith finding me a job and you wanting me to stay, I let myself be persuaded. I forgot that Barbara would start crawling." She plunged on; what did she have to lose? "I know I wasn't the first girl you took to the club-house. I was afraid you might get another girl into trouble."

She expected protests and denials, but he was studying the table-cloth intently. "Lizzie"—she could barely hear him—"you know I'm no good on my own."

"Aren't you upset about Miss Urquhart taking Barbara?"

He raised his eyes and she saw, again, the shine of unshed tears. "I'm upset about the whole situation. About your going away, about having a baby early, leaving her with your grandparents. But we need to do what's best for her. What's best for us."

"I could bring her here," she said. "Even if we couldn't get married, we'd see you every week. Barbara and Molly would be sisters." Edith and Chrissie could mind them while she worked at the locomotive tracers'. Several of the girls had babies whom their mothers watched while they were at work.

Louis was looking at her incredulously. "Ralph isn't going to turn the Tam o' Shanter into a home for fallen women."

"I'm not fallen." When two women glanced over from the next table, she realised how loudly she had spoken. "My parents eloped," she went on more quietly. "We can do the same. Edith told me there's a train to Gretna Green." The prospect of following in Helen's footsteps had a kind of magical rightness, but Louis was still staring at her.

"You're not thinking straight," he said. "If Mr. Rintoull found out, I'd be in the street. We only have to wait until January."

"And then what? Miss Urquhart isn't going to want to give her up."

"You did."

Hugh had said the same, but from Louis it was unbearable. Somehow she was on her feet, making her way between the tables to the door. In the street she bumped into a man, swerved out of the path of a tram, bumped into another man, caught her elbow on a lamppost, as she tried to outrun the anger, the shame. Then Louis was beside her, saying stop, wait. He led her to the pillared doorway of a bank, closed for the day.

"None of this would have happened except for your clubhouse," she said.

"I thought you wanted to be there."

"Like the other girls."

"Lizzie, you're the one I want. We have to be patient."

He talked on and on, making himself feel better, but changing nothing. "I have to go home," she said at last.

She meant to Belhaven, to Barbara, but he misunderstood. He walked her to the back door of the pub and said he'd see her that evening. Inside, pleading a headache to Edith, she climbed the stairs. In her room she sat down on the bed and at once jumped up. There was something she needed to do, but what? What? She remembered her mother's gift for unravelling knots. If she could only find the first right action, that would lead her to the next, and the next. Barbara, she thought, shaping the words like an arrow, I am your only mother.

She tore up the first letter and the second. The third read:

Dear Grandmother,

I know it was wrong to leave Barbara without asking you. I'm very sorry and I'm very sorry I didn't come back at New Year's. Kate wrote and told me you've given her to Miss Urquhart. I have to find a way to get her back. There's no reason why you should believe me but I miss her every minute. I have her birth certificate.

Love, Lizzie.

SHE WOULD HAVE NO RECOLLECTION OF THAT SPRING. The days must have grown longer. The crocuses and daffodils and jasmine must have bloomed. She told Edith her grandparents were doing better; she could stay another month. She worked at the locomotive tracers'; she worked at the pub; she danced with Tom; she let Louis come to her room when it was safe. Lying down together was still her only reliable source of solace. During those days and weeks, she did her best to avoid Molly, but Edith would say, "Here, take her," and she would be holding that downy weight, listening to the gentle sough of her breathing. Kate had begun to write again: *We only lost one lamb. This year, we're planting a new kind of potato. I visited Miss Urquhart. Barbara is growing fast.*

She stopped sending money home and began to save every penny of her wages and the coins customers sometimes left. At night she would empty the tin onto her bed and pile up the pennies, threepences, and sixpences in comforting little towers. Somehow the money would help her get to Barbara. Then one afternoon, as she unpegged a shirt from the washing line, she heard above the rooftops the sweet call of a cuckoo. "Go home," it was saying. "Go home." That night in her room she made a plan. If she took a train after work and stayed the night in Cupar, she could be in Langmuir when the school opened. She could spend the morning with Barbara until Miss Urquhart returned for lunch. There was no reason she shouldn't visit her niece; no reason news of her visit should reach the farm.

It took a week to make a small stuffed bear for Barbara, to go to the station and enquire the times of trains, to tell Edith she was going home for her grandmother's birthday. On Tuesday she carried her bag to work and asked Mr. Simpson if she could have tomorrow off. She'd overheard another girl claim her sister was having a baby; now she offered the same excuse. He shook his head—"All these babies"—and said she'd have to make up the hours.

....

AT THE STATION IN CUPAR, SHE WAITED UNTIL THE other passengers had left the platform before she approached the guard. From a distance she had taken him for an older man, but as she asked if he could recommend a lodging for the night, she saw he was around her age; his long face was freckled like Sarah's. "I need to go to Langmuir in the morning," she added.

"My, you're a busy woman." Still swinging his green flag, he said his sister lived ten minutes away at 12 Queen's Wynd and let rooms much cheaper than the hotel. "Her husband's a baker. He'll know about a cart to the village."

The woman who answered the door had no freckles but the same long face. "Let me guess," she said, "Angus sent you. You can have an evening meal, a bed, and porridge for one and six."

In the kitchen two boys and a girl were doing their homework. The woman introduced herself as Irene and told the children to make room. Glancing at the girl's slate, Lizzie read 2 + 4 = 5 and offered help. They were on the last sum when a man who looked remarkably like Mr. Baker in Happy Families stepped into the room. Irene explained that Lizzie was on her way to Langmuir, and he said if she didn't mind an early start, the bakery cart was going there at seven. After supper she offered to read the children a story. "I should be paying you," Irene joked.

Lying on the shallow mattress, she counted the places she had slept: the farm, Lilac Cottage, the Phelpses', the Tam o' Shanter, and now here. That made five. No, she corrected, six. Once, although she did not remember, she had slept in her mother's house. Now that she was so close to seeing Barbara, she could allow the memories to return: how Barbara liked squeezing bread into balls; her love of wooden spoons; the way she frowned and tucked in her chin like a much older person; how she smiled when Lizzie sang "Row, row, row the boat" or made her fly through the air. Her daughter, banished for months, came rushing back.

In the morning she could scarcely eat the promised porridge; she pocketed two rolls for later. Irene and the children waved as the bakery cart clipped down the street. The boy who drove the cart was full of questions about Glasgow: Had she been to a football game? Was there a zoo? Did they really have a train that went underground? Half a dozen times he pulled over to allow a cart going to Cupar to pass and she drew her shawl close. She recognised Mr. McClaren and the miller's oldest son, but no one paid her any heed. The castle came into view. They passed the road to the mill, and she asked the boy to let her off at the church. Safely hidden from passersby, she wandered among the graves willing time to pass. Robert Strachan was still there beneath his flat stone. Here was the grave of her great-grandparents, Andrew and Margaret wife of, marked by a tall grey stone. Next to them was her grandfather's brother, also Andrew, who'd been gored by a bull when he was nineteen. Here was Miss Renfrew. And Frances McEwen, who had died having a baby when she was sixteen.

At ten to nine, she slipped out of the churchyard and walked towards the school. Standing beneath a leafy elm, she stared across the road at Miss Urquhart's house, with its neat windows. At last, the front door opened. The teacher, in her brown dress, stepped out, only to stop at the gate and turn back. Three minutes later she reappeared and, this time, continued to the school. As soon as the first notes of the morning hymn wafted through the window, Lizzie crossed the road and knocked twice. In the silence, she could hear crying. The door opened. A girl stood there, but all she saw was Barbara.

"Let me take her," she said. "I'm her aunt."

Lifting Barbara into her arms, she explained she was passing and wanted to see how her niece was doing. Meanwhile, Barbara only cried more loudly. Lizzie bounced her up and down, said, "What's the matter?" kissed the top of her head. In all her imaginings, it had never occurred to her that Barbara might forget her.

"She's gey vexed when Miss Urquhart leaves," said the girl.

There was something familiar about her beaky nose, the way she stood, helplessly, until Lizzie suggested they go to the kitchen. Following her down the hall, it came to her: she was one of the MacDonalds, Elspeth? Lillian? Since the feud over the cow, they had never spoken. In the kitchen she put Barbara in her high chair. At once she stopped crying, seized a wooden spoon, and began to hit the table with wild enthusiasm.

She and Kate had used to wonder what the teacher's house was like. Now she took in the pleasing golden colour of the walls, the settle holding blue-and-white plates like the ones the Phelpses used for ordinary dinners, a calendar showing Loch Lomond on the wall, a sampler she couldn't read. "It's a fine day," she said over Barbara's banging.

"It is." The girl set a bowl of stewed apples, a bowl of porridge, and a jug of milk on the table. Lizzie shaped a spoonful and offered it. Barbara stared at her wide-eyed. At last, tentatively, she opened her mouth.

Lizzie asked the girl how long she'd been working for Miss Urquhart and she said since last summer. At first, she'd been able to read but now all she did was clean and mind the bairn. "I'll mind her this morning," Lizzie said.

When Barbara was fed and changed, Lizzie carried her to the sitting room. Setting her down on the hearth rug, she noted with relief the clock on the mantelpiece. Barbara toddled towards one of the armchairs and reached for the book, a novel by Trollope, lying on the nearby table. Moving it out of reach, Lizzie imagined Miss Urquhart sitting here in the evenings, wishing someone were sitting in the other armchair. Barbara was still eying her warily, but after Lizzie gave her the bear and told her the story of Goldilocks, she seemed to remember the many days they'd spent together. She laughed and tucked in her double chin and made sounds like words in some other language.

When the clock showed quarter to noon, Lizzie went in search of the girl and found her with a book at the kitchen table. "I have to be on my way," she said. She gave Barbara a final kiss. Smiling, Barbara patted her cheek. She was crossing the road when the school door opened. Quickly she turned down the first road she came to. Soon she was back on the road to Cupar. The day was fine; her bag was not heavy. If no cart stopped, she could walk the whole way. She had seen Barbara, held her, fed her, breathed her. Soon there were no more houses, only Mr. Wright's fields, already greening. That "baa" sound Barbara made, was it a version of her name? Or an attempt to say "ball"?

EDITH TEASED HER ABOUT BEING ABSENT-MINDED, Mr. Simpson chided her for doing the drawings in the wrong order, Deirdre asked if she was dreaming about her tailor, Louis asked if she felt poorly, but all that mattered was she had seen Barbara. On Monday she came home from the locomotive tracers' to find a letter, the envelope larger and whiter than the ones Kate used, lying on the kitchen table. The bold C of *Craig*, the neat Gs of *Glasgow* looked familiar. As soon as she opened it, she understood why.

Dear Lizzie,

I am sorry I missed you on Wednesday. Lucy told me how much Barbara enjoyed your company. As she described your visit, it occurred to me that the situation is not quite as I understood. Barbara is your daughter, isn't she? I remember wondering that time I met you and your young man picnicking by the lochan. For reasons I can only guess, you left her with your grandparents to return to Glasgow. I am sure it was a hard decision.

In the last months I have come to consider Barbara as my beloved daughter so I can understand you must miss her. If you ask in advance, you are welcome to visit occasionally. If that isn't acceptable, then my door is closed.

I am going to find an older woman to mind Barbara, someone to whom I can explain the situation. If you try to visit again without my permission, she will know what to do.

Kind regards,

Isabel Urquhart

P.S. I've decided to let Barbara keep the bear, for now.

She read the letter again and again, her anger rising. A *hard decision*, as if three words could contain her anguish. And for Miss Urquhart to say she had come to regard Barbara as her daughter. She remembered Barbara patting her cheek.

The following day brought another letter.

There's a story you were loitering near the school, Kate wrote. *I didn't believe it until Miss Urquhart asked for your address. I've told Amy not to say anything to Rab and Flora. If they knew you'd been here and not come to see them, it would break their hearts.*

That night as she poured herself a dram in the empty pub, her own heart jolted. Instead of the shadowy room there was Chrissie in her grey pinafore, bending over an open drawer. Red cheeks smiling, she reached among the clothes and straightened, holding something Lizzie couldn't quite see; her face wore the pleased expression with which she regarded a freshly baked batch of pies. The chest of drawers was like the one in Lizzie's room, but each of the four bedrooms at the Tam o' Shanter had the same furnishings. Before she could search for other clues, the picture vanished. She was standing at the bar, holding a bottle of whisky.

XIII

*

She had thought seeing Barbara would slake her yearning but it was the reverse. Sometimes, for a few minutes, while working on a complicated tracing, or dancing with Tom, or lying with Louis, she forgot her daughter, but never for long. Now, when she counted the weeks until Louis finished his apprenticeship, she was also counting the time that separated her from Barbara, and from her grandparents. She was coming down the steps of the library, carrying her books, when she heard her name. Marie was darting towards her, closely followed by Celia. She bent to hug them, exclaiming how they'd grown, what nice hats they were wearing.

"Girls," Mrs. Phelps called, "come and stand where we won't be in people's way. Lizzie, I didn't know you were back in town. How are your grandparents?"

Beneath Mrs. Phelps's calm brown eyes, she stammered they were fine. "I'm visiting Edith and her husband. Their little girl was born at New Year's."

"What nice news. Please give her my kind regards." Her glance strayed to Lizzie's books, as if checking the titles, then back to her face as she said they'd been to the Botanic Gardens. "There's a greenhouse with ferns taller than a person. We pretended lions and tigers were hiding behind them, didn't we, girls?"

"How's Hamlet?" Marie said.

Before she could answer, Mrs. Phelps was saying they must be on their way. In the next street, Lizzie's pace slowed. What must Mrs. Phelps have thought, seeing her carrying her library books, as if she lived here? Perhaps—she recalled the small stones in the churchyard—that the baby had died. Surely that was more likely than a mother leaving her daughter. In her distraction, she realised she had turned in the direction of the tailor's. During her first months at the Phelpses', she had often walked by the shop, but since Louis told her Mr. Rintoull didn't like visitors, she hadn't been in over a year. If she could see him, even for five minutes, she would feel better.

Standing beside the lamppost near the shop, she had a clear view. Tom was at the table by the window, measuring a piece of material; Louis was seated at a sewing machine, holding a pair of scissors. Behind them she could make out the cutting tables, the bolts of fabric, and the stove they used to heat the irons. Of Mr. Rintoull there was no sign. She was about to step forward and knock on the window, when a door at the back of the shop opened and a woman appeared with a tea tray. No, not a woman, a girl. wearing an apron over her dark dress; she must be the maid. She poured the tea and carried a cup to Tom, another to Louis. Louis said something that made her laugh and pat his shoulder. When she had left by the same door, Lizzie thought again about knocking on the glass, but all she could imagine was Louis's face, wide with merriment as he spoke to the maid, snapping tight, like a pair of scissors, at the sight of her.

....

ON SATURDAY, AS THEY WERE WALTZING, SHE CONFESSED
to Tom she had walked by the shop. "A maid was bringing you cups
of tea."

"A maid?" he said. "Oh, you must mean Ivy. Why didn't you say
hello?"

"Ivy?"

"Ivy Rintoull. She makes the neatest buttonholes and she can
mend almost anything. If she were a boy, she'd inherit the shop."

She steered him between two couples and said she thought the
Rintoull children were all at school and he said no, Ivy had left
last summer; she helped with the women customers. Before she
could question him further, the waltz ended and he went to fetch
her a glass of lemonade. At ceilidh after ceilidh, she had searched
for the girl she had seen in the clubhouse and gradually—no one
resembled her—forgotten her fears; now they rushed back. Why
had Louis never mentioned that there was a girl, almost his age,
in the household, a pretty, accomplished girl who happened to be
Mr. Rintoull's daughter?

That night in her room as he reached for her blouse, she said,
"Tom was telling me what grand buttonholes Ivy makes."

"She does indeed."

"I didn't know the Rintoulls had an older girl." She tried to
sound mildly curious.

He untucked her camisole. "You're turning Tom into quite the
dancer. I saw the two of you waltzing away."

"Do you not get on with her? You never speak of her."

"We get on fine. How often do you speak of Frank?"

She was saying Frank was older, married, the father of twins, when he kissed her. Even on the hardest days, his touch had driven out despair. But now, as his hands slid around her waist, she could think only of Ivy.

SHE ARRIVED HOME EARLY—SHE'D FINISHED A DRAWING half an hour before the locomotive tracers' closed—to find the kitchen empty save for the smells of meat and pastry baking. Opening the door into the pub, she saw Chrissie standing at the bar; over her shoulder, she glimpsed a tray of pies. A man approached. Chrissie handed him four pies; then her hand moved to her pocket. Quietly Lizzie let the door close and walked twice around the kitchen table before making a noisier entrance.

She waited until Sunday, when Ralph went to wash the floor of the pub, and Molly was asleep, to speak to Edith. A moment ago, the three of them had been laughing at Ralph's story about a dog who loved sausages. Now even the little wisps of hair around Edith's face grew sharp as she scrutinised Lizzie. "Have you seen her take money before?" she demanded.

"Maybe once. I wasn't sure."

She rose to clear the plates, but Edith stopped her. "Is there more you're not saying?"

Seeing her frown, Lizzie suddenly understood; Chrissie's guilt cast a shadow on her too. How stupid she had been to ignore Tom's advice and jeopardize her only place of safety: her room at the Tam o' Shanter. "No," she said firmly. "The time I wasn't sure Ralph was right there. Yesterday I saw her put the money in her pocket. Maybe she put it in the till later."

"We've been short a few times," Edith said, "but I thought Ralph had muddled the change. Lizzie, if you see anything amiss, you must tell us right away."

"I will." As she carried the dishes to the sink, she recalled the day Flora had reached behind the flour bin and pulled out the pieces of the broken plate: a lie will always find you out.

SHE WAS IN THE DOORWAY OF THE LOCOMOTIVE TRACERS', buttoning her coat against the chill, when someone seized her arm; Chrissie was beside her. "What are you doing here?" Lizzie demanded. She tried to pull free, but Chrissie only tightened her grip. As she steered them down the street, weaving between other pedestrians, Lizzie smelled the fragrance of boiled potatoes wafting off her coat. "You put the wind up Edith," Chrissie said. "She's standing over me every minute, counting pies, counting money."

"Edith always keeps track. Right after Molly, she let things go. Now she's herself again." But even as she spoke, she knew it was hopeless. Chrissie was guilty, and by virtue of her guilt she guessed the cause of Edith's vigilance. They passed a chimney sweep and his boy, the whites of their eyes shining in their sooty faces, their black brushes over their shoulders.

"You've made her think I'm stealing," Chrissie continued.

"Aren't you?"

"None of your business"—she led them around the flower stall—"which is just as well because you already have plenty of business, Miss Lizzie Craig. You have a bairn, don't you, back on that farm. I'll warrant Edith knows nothing about her. All this nonsense about nieces. Anyone could tell watching you with Molly, you've one of your own."

So it was her chest of drawers she had seen Chrissie search. "You were in my room."

Her accusation rolled off Chrissie like water off Hamlet's back. "I knew there was something amiss with you," she said smugly. "I couldn't put my finger on what it was."

"Edith and Ralph treat you well. You shouldn't steal from them."

"Miss Goody Two-Shoes. Aren't you stealing their good opinion, pretending to be a good girl, pretending to visit your granny?"

For a moment she was so stricken, she could not speak. "What do you want me to do?" she said at last. "Tell Edith I was mistaken?"

"That won't help," Chrissie said. At the entrance to the church, her grip slackened. "What I was thinking," she said, "is if she sees you being friendly, if she catches the two of us having a blether, she'll begin to forget whatever you put in her head. You can tell me about the farm and I can tell you Glasgow stories." Standing a step above Lizzie, she was face-to-face with her. "Mind you," she went on cheerfully, "I don't think there's anything wrong with having a bairn before you have a ring, but plenty do. The Tam o' Shanter is a respectable place. Edith and Ralph are very keen on that."

You stupid, ungrateful girl, Lizzie said silently. Who do you think you are? Taking advantage of Edith, snooping, stealing? But as her eyes fell on the list of Sunday services, she understood that Chrissie was not stupid—quite the contrary. She knew people sometimes thought so, and she made use of their mistake. Pulling her coat close, Lizzie met Chrissie's tawny gaze. "I look forward to a good Glasgow story," she said.

That evening when she checked her savings, only a single shilling was gone, but Chrissie might not be so kind next time. All the hiding places she could think of—under her mattress, on top of the curtain rail, in one of her boots—seemed obvious. Chrissie had all day to search while she was at work. She was examining the floorboards, trying to find a loose one, when she recalled a poem she had read at school; a woman had buried her lover's head in a pot of basil. The next day she bought a geranium for her windowsill and put the tin beneath the roots. Barbara's birth certificate she sewed into the lining of her bag. At the locomotive tracers', she asked Mr. Simpson for a large envelope he was throwing out. She put her letters inside and sealed it with candle wax.

Edith took over selling the pies. "Chrissie's too busy making them," she told the men who enquired. Meanwhile, Lizzie did her best to keep her part of their bargain. She remarked how Chrissie got the stove to draw. "Oh, she's smiling," she said when Chrissie bent over Molly. She asked her which starch to use and where to buy pencils.

Gradually Edith relaxed her vigilance. In the mornings she often kept Lizzie company, nursing Molly beside the stove while Lizzie ate her porridge and made her lunch. One morning Edith was describing the new dress Ralph had promised her, green cotton with a lace collar, when a knock sounded at the door of the pub. "Oh, that'll be the beer delivery," she said. "Can you let them in on your way out?"

She pocketed her bread and cheese, opened the door into the pub and made her way between the empty tables. The key Ralph turned every night yielded at the second attempt. On the doorstep a boy in uniform, much smaller than his knock suggested, was holding a bicycle in one hand, an envelope in the other. "Elizabeth Craig?" he said, making each syllable separate as he handed her the envelope, then pedaled away.

She stared at her name with only one thought: Barbara. She was ill—or worse. Heedless of the schoolboys jostling along the pavement, she tore open the envelope and drew out the strip of paper.

Grandfather died Wednesday. Funeral Monday 11. Kate.

She felt an overwhelming wave of gratitude. Then the wave receded, leaving only bitter grief.

Faintly, she heard Edith calling, "Lizzie, what is it?"

Her legs carried her back across the pub to the kitchen, where Edith had set Molly in her cradle and was standing at the table, breaking eggs into a bowl. Wordless, she offered the telegram. Edith put down the egg she was holding. "Oh, Lizzie, I'm—"

As she spoke, the egg rolled off the table and splattered, the yolk golden against the floor. While she went to fetch a cloth, Lizzie retrieved the telegram and hurried back, past the tables and chairs, into the street. If she kept moving, maybe she could leave the words behind. Above the rooftops was a patch of blue sky, enough, her grandfather would have said, to make a pair of sailor's trousers. She was at the corner when the newspaperman's cries stopped her. She stood staring at the stack of *Glasgow Heralds*, remembering her empty promise, until the man called, "Are you all right, lassie?"

Turning down the next street, she remembered Kate had warned her—they were much older—but fear of her grandfather's anger had kept her away. Now she had missed seeing him one last time. On the stairs at the locomotive tracers', several girls said good morning; she heard herself reply. Mr. Simpson was standing by his desk, as he did every morning to greet them. Again, she held out the telegram.

While he adjusted his glasses, she watched the clock on the wall; the minute hand quivered and jumped forward. A whole day had passed since her grandfather died. How was it possible she had not sensed the change? Then Mr. Simpson was offering condolences and asking how long she would be gone.

She said a week, her grandmother was alone, and he said she could make up the hours when she returned. "Have a wee rest before you go home." He waved at the bench where the girls sat when they were taking a break, or feeling poorly, but she went directly to her drawing board, longing to put even a small barrier between herself and the awful facts: her last words to her grandfather had been a lie; his last thoughts about her had been hard ones. She remembered lingering in the churchyard, waiting for Miss Urquhart to go to school. If only she had taken him a newspaper.

THE PATH TO LILAC COTTAGE WAS THICK WITH DANDELIONS, some in flower, many already gone to seed: another sign of her grandfather's infirmity. As she stepped into the garden, a blackbird, perched a few yards away on the hedge, opened its yellow beak and launched into melodious song. So long as she stood listening, so long as she didn't step through the door, he was still alive. Suddenly the bird took flight. Her grandmother was in the doorway in her white blouse and grey skirt. Lizzie stepped into her arms. Everything else had changed, but here was the familiar fragrance of green soap and tea.

"Kate said you wouldn't come," she said, "but I knew you would."

Soon tea was poured; they each had a scone with butter and raspberry jam. But where to sit? Her chair was gone. Her grandfather's chair was out of the question. She turned a wooden chair from the table to face the hearth. "Why did he die?" she said. "He wasn't ill."

"He was old, Lizzie. Worn out. We were sitting here after supper on Wednesday night, the wind was wuthering around the chimney, when he looked up from his book. 'Remember,' he said, 'how we used to lie in bed on nights like this and say the trees were talking. We've had a good life, Flora. Not an easy one, but a good one, and now we're safe here.' He went back to his book. I thought if the wind kept up, I'd do the washing in the morning.

"But in the morning, everything was quiet. I went to put coal on the fire, warming the room for him as he so often did for me. When I came back to the bedroom, I heard the silence. I should have known, when he spoke about the wind, he was saying goodbye. These last months he kept saying he'd had his three score and ten. I miss him, but I can't wish him back."

Her grandmother went to lie down, and she set to work. She scrubbed the table, she scrubbed the floor, she blacked the stove, she polished the grandfather clock and cleaned the sink. She was outside, beating the hearth rug, watching the dust swirl away in the breeze, when the picture came: Flora, dressed as she was today, sitting in her chair by the fire, her eyes closed, her hands idle. I must talk to her, she thought, before it's too late.

As soon as supper was on the table, she began. "Something happened when I was May's age," she said. She described her first picture, Rab's accident with the scythe, and some of the later ones: Hugh, Acorn, Michael.

She had expected disapproval, and doubt, but her grandmother was nodding as if she already knew. "Rab's mother was the same," she said. "She saw the Crimean War, the riots. The week before our wedding, she told me I'd lose something precious and find it again. A month later I lost my wedding ring. I'd given up hope of finding it when it turned up in one of my shoes. Rab told me she was afraid if people knew she saw the future, they'd call her a witch. She got his father to plant the rowan tree beside the farmhouse door. You didn't have a picture of Rab's death, did you?"

"If I had, I would have been here. I wanted to come and see you but I was afraid of what he'd say."

Flora reached to clasp her hand. "If there was one thing I would have changed about Rab, it was his temper. Tell me"—she waited for the clock to strike—"when you went to Glasgow that Saturday, were you planning to stay? Rab said you were. I said no, you meant to come back—you'd left most of your clothes—but Louis had talked you into staying."

"You were right." She explained how Edith had found her a job and Louis had begged her to stay. "I had a picture of him with another girl. I was afraid I'd lose him if I came back." She felt a hot wash of shame as she described how she had written the telegram and tried to retrieve it.

"That telegram—" Her grandmother broke off, lips trembling. When she could speak again, she said she'd stopped by Miss Urquhart's last Sunday. Barbara was growing fast.

"Why did you give her away? You knew I'd take her as soon as we got married." They had both given up any pretense of eating.

Flora straightened in her chair. "Like we knew you were coming back from Glasgow," she said tartly. "Miss Urquhart dotes on Barbara. Another person like her, who can give Barbara a good home, wasn't going to come along any time soon."

Her mind seethed with angry questions; she managed to ask the one that mattered. "I'd give anything not to have left, but what can I do now?"

Across the table she had scrubbed so often, her grandmother's eyes—once the colour of bluebells now faded to that of forget-me-nots—held hers. "God willing, you'll have other children," she said. "What you can do now is endure."

"You mean"—she could hardly bear to say it—"leave Barbara with Miss Urquhart? How can growing up with a stranger be better than growing up with her parents?"

"What parents? Louis could be run over by a tram tomorrow. Or marry that other girl. When Helen asked me to take you, she made me bring you back to Belhaven that very day. She wanted to keep you, she lived three more months, but she did what was best for you. Promise me, you won't try to get Barbara back."

She was on her feet, her chair clattering to the floor. "I can't promise that," she said.

Her grandmother too, more slowly, stood. For a moment her gaze was as fierce as Rab's. "Lizzie Craig, if you meddle with Miss Urquhart, you're no granddaughter of mine."

In the silence she heard her heart beating, saying, No, no, no. "I promise," she whispered.

AT THE FARMHOUSE, KATE LED HER TO THE CRADLE, where James was waking from a nap. She introduced herself—"I'm your auntie Lizzie"—and he gave a froglike kick and a loud cry. Here, at last, was Callum's son. "What a strong boy," she said.

"He is," Kate said, "but I can't help worrying. That's what we thought about Michael."

"Michael was different all along; we didn't want to see it. James is like May, a good, healthy baby." Stepping back from the cradle, so James wouldn't hear the bad news, she described her picture of Flora.

Kate smiled ruefully. "Lizzie, I told you they were getting older. No one needs a picture to know Flora won't stay long now Rab is gone. You came to visit Barbara, didn't you?"

She admitted she had. "I wanted to go to Lilac Cottage, to come and see you, but I was afraid. You know what Grandfather was like. On the train yesterday, I decided to come home until I get married, but last night Grandmother made me promise to leave Barbara with Miss Urquhart. I don't know if I can bear living here and not seeing her."

Kate seized her wrist. "Nothing would make Flora happier than to have you home, but you'd have to stay until Louis is ready to marry you. You couldn't run off again because of a picture. If you swear to do that"—she gave Lizzie's wrist a little shake—"then I'll do my best to help you get Barbara back. We can ask the minister to find Miss Urquhart another baby."

She thought of Ivy bending over Louis, patting his shoulder. Kate let go of her wrist. "Don't say anything," she said. "I can see from your face. A word from Louis and you'd be off to Glasgow."

"Barbara is part of me. I miss her every minute."

"You miss her," Kate corrected, "but not every minute. If you did, you'd never have left. You like your Glasgow life with Louis, earning money, going to the shops. I don't blame you, but don't promise something you can't do."

Before she could explain how her feelings had changed, James began to whimper; Annie hit her knee. Between soothing one and telling the other to be a big girl, Kate asked if she could gather the eggs. It was a relief to be in the farmyard, doing a familiar task. Her hands moved so briskly the hens didn't have time to peck; twice her fingers encountered the soft mass of a shell-less egg. As she carried the eggs to the dairy, she thought Kate had forgotten how she used to threaten to run away if she couldn't see Callum. But her sister was lucky. Everything had fitted together; the children were part of the beams of light that passed between her and Callum. Perhaps that was possible only within the gated field of marriage.

AT THE FUNERAL THEY SANG "O GOD, OUR HELP IN AGES Past." Mr. Waugh preached about the one lost sheep, more cherished than the many gathered in the fold, and how Rab had tended his sheep and been a good neighbour and a pillar of the church. She thought of him out in all weathers, bringing home the early lambs, drenching a cow, ploughing a field, scouring a ditch, repairing a wall, his hands busy all day long and at night turning the pages of a book. In the graveyard, as they lowered the coffin into the grave, she longed to shout, "Stop! You're making a mistake." But she was the one who had made a mistake.

In the village hall the mourners ate the food Kate and the other women had brought and reminisced about Rab; the whisky bottle passed from hand to hand. Back at the farmhouse the family gathered for the reading of the will. She had given no thought to this moment, but as the minister produced a sheet of paper, folded and sealed with red wax, she was seized with apprehension. She beckoned Annie over and lifted the small girl onto her knee, a shield against whatever was about to happen.

"This is a sad day," the minister said, "but we give thanks Rab is in a better place. I will now read the will.

"*I, Rab Craig of Belhaven Farm, being in sound mind and judge-*

ment, do this day, Tuesday, November 30th, 1892, hereby make my last will and testament. . . .'" The farm, land and house, went to Callum and Kate on the understanding that they take care of Flora for the remainder of her life. To his friend Neil, he left his books. To his beloved wife, Flora, everything else: *"'I only wish it were more.'"* There was a letter for his brother, James in Aberdeen. She kept waiting for her name—"my beloved granddaughter Elizabeth"— but as the minister folded the paper away, she understood she was not to be mentioned. She buried her face in Annie's hair.

Back at Lilac Cottage, Flora was flushed, almost giddy. They had given Rab a good send-off. "Mr. Brown told me how he'd saved one of his ewes, and Douglas said the summer of '74, they'd never have got the oats in without him."

"How old were you when your parents died?"

Her grandmother smiled. "You've had a picture of me, haven't you? I hope to see the harvest in, but I doubt I'll see you wed."

"Do you think you and Rab will meet again?"

"I know the minister says so—'In my father's house there are many mansions'—but it doesn't seem likely. He and I, we had our lives together. The person I long to see is your mother, but that doesn't seem likely either. Lizzie, he changed his will after you left. I couldn't stop him. Neil won't mind if you take two or three books, and you should have the cribbage set." She fetched the scarred wooden box from the cupboard and set it on the table.

IN THE FIELD, A BROWN-AND-WHITE CALF STARTED towards her and fell back as she began to walk along the hawthorn hedge where she and Kate had searched first for the ducks and then the wild garlic. The birds, chirping in the trees, fell silent at her approach. She would do it, she thought; she would prove Kate wrong: she would stay with Flora. Louis would visit for the harvest, and in the new year they would marry and make a home for Barbara; she would take care not to have another baby too soon. But it was one thing to miss Barbara in Glasgow, quite another to live at Lilac Cottage, to meet her and Miss Urquhart in the village and pretend to be a mere acquaintance. Could she do this, even for Flora? She sat down on one of the fallen standing stones. At the bottom of the field the cows gathered around the gate, waiting to be milked.

Her grandmother had fed and clothed her, had taught her her letters, had let her keep Alice, had given her a sister, had helped her go to Glasgow, had cared for her during those days after Barbara was born when even to brush her hair was a struggle. And if she suffered, if she paid for her wrongdoing, didn't that mean she would get Barbara back? The brown-and-white calf was making its way over the tufted grass towards her. But she had promised to leave Barbara with Miss Urquhart. Only death, or marriage, could release her from that promise.

She remembered how solemnly Barbara had regarded her when they played peek-a-boo at Miss Urquhart's. The game had used to make her laugh; perhaps now it was too like life, her mother mysteriously appearing and disappearing. I'll come for you, she thought, as soon as I can. For now, she would go back to Glasgow, explain to Louis and Edith that her grandmother needed her, give notice at the locomotive tracers'. Then she would return to Lilac Cottage. The calf stood before her. She held out her hand for its rough tongue.

As she came through the door, her grandmother took one look at her and rose to meet her. "No, no, Lizzie. You stick to the furrow you've started. Things will only be more of a muddle if you turn around, and I won't be here to help. It's not many months until Louis finishes. You and he can sort things out when you're married. That'll be the way of it."

"I hate to leave you here alone."

"I'm not alone. Kate and the girls come every day. Amy stops by on her way to the farm, Callum has a cup of tea when he's passing, Neil comes over for a gossip. You go back to Glasgow and write to me often. I'll visit Barbara every Sunday."

In her relief she sat down in the nearest chair.

XIV

*

She was walking along Grey Street, nearly at the pub, when she saw a woman coming towards her glance down. Following her gaze, Lizzie discovered her boots still covered with the mud of Belhaven. She remembered Edith saying how the Irish immigrants carried a pocketful of soil to their new country. Cupar was less than two hours away by train, but she was like an immigrant, she thought, a part of her always left behind. Through the door of the pub she heard music and the stamp of feet. They were playing a Gay Gordons.

"Go in," called a man lurching by. "Go in and have a dance, lassie."

But it was beyond her to enter a room full of people enjoying themselves. She headed down the alley to the back door and, leaving a note on the kitchen table, climbed the stairs. In her room she unpacked the cribbage set and the weather house and set them on the chest of drawers beside the picture of her parents: her mother, lips slightly parted, her father, shoulders back, looking forward to their nonexistent future. Sitting on the bed, she tried to ignore the sounds of music and mirth. Would Louis sing "Lizzie's Return" tonight? I must stick to my furrow, she thought: getting Barbara back, getting her a father.

The next afternoon the empty pub was so quiet that every creak of Louis's chair was audible as he offered his condolences. "I remember Rab working in the fields all day," he said, "and then telling stories over supper. I thought he would live forever."

"What I can't bear"—she stared at the wooden table with its many ring marks—"is that he died thinking the worst of me."

"That's not true," Louis said. "Maybe he was angry when you left, but he was very fond of you."

From the kitchen came the singsong sounds of Edith talking to Molly. When she could speak again, she told him about the books she'd brought back: *Tristram Shandy, Persuasion, The Mill on the Floss, Kidnapped.*

"What else did he leave you?" The chair creaked again.

"Nothing."

"Nothing?" He sat straighter. "How could he leave you nothing?"

"The house and the land went to Kate and Callum. Everything else went to my grandmother."

In the dim light, she could see the little blond hairs in his eyebrows moving as he frowned. "He can't leave Kate the farm and you a few books," he said. "You have to talk to them. They should give you half the land, or what it's worth."

She remembered the day they had visited the sheep, how he had marveled that her family owned almost everything they could see. He must have thought it would be hers someday; she had too. Now she tried to distract him by asking about the bowling, but he refused to be lured away. "It's wrong, Lizzie. You're as much his granddaughter as Kate, more so. I understand not wanting to divide the farm, but that doesn't mean you get nothing."

Only when she agreed to write to Flora did he turn to other topics.

AT THE LOCOMOTIVE TRACERS' SHE TOOK ON ALL THE overtime she could; at the Tam o' Shanter she helped Ralph behind the bar. When there was no more work, she went for walks in the long, light evenings, not caring about a destination, seeking only the distraction of new streets, new sights. One night she walked all the way to the Necropolis. As she headed up the main path, two men, one thin as a rope, the other like a beer barrel, appeared from behind a gravestone. "Here's a pretty one. How much, dearie?" She picked up her skirts and ran towards the gate. The next day when she described her escape, Chrissie laughed. "You don't have the brains you were born with," she said. "A woman visits the Necroplis at dusk for only one reason."

"But it's a cemetery," Lizzie protested.

"With lots of hiding places and nice flat stones." Chrissie winked.

When Saturday came around again, she helped Ralph get ready for the ceilidh, moving the tables and washing the glasses, but as soon as people started to arrive, she wanted to flee. She was standing at the bar about to slip away when Tom, cap in hand, appeared. "Louis told me about your grandfather," he said. "I'm very sorry for your loss."

They were the words everyone offered, but his firm voice, his steadfast gaze, made her feel he understood some part of what she'd lost; he was not afraid of her pain. She saw how his shirt collar had been skillfully turned, how his trousers were neatly belted but a little too large; his shoes were shining in a way even Kate would have approved. When he asked if she would like company, she heard herself say "For a few minutes." He led her to a table near the door into the kitchen and went to fetch drinks. Once they were seated, with a beer and a lemonade, he remarked that the tune the fiddlers were playing was a favourite of his grandfather's. "He's the one who got me in with Mr. Rintoull. I never expected to be a tailor."

"What did you expect?" She remembered Flora telling her you could choose a path without knowing you were doing so.

"Och, I was never a practical lad." He smiled his earnest smile. "I used to tell my parents I was going to Africa, to ride an elephant and discover a secret kingdom. I'd read a book about Dr. Livingstone and Mary Kingsley."

"I wanted to be an archeologist," she said. "To discover Troy, or Xanadu."

"I could have helped you with my elephant. Louis has a drawing you made of him on the wall by his bed. Did you never think of studying drawing?"

When she said she hadn't known you could study it until Mr. Simpson had asked her, he told her about the School of Art on Sauchiehall Street. "I'm sure you're as talented as the students."

"Maybe someday," she said, "I'll draw pictures for a book. What happened when you couldn't be an explorer?"

"We used to put on plays at school. I liked that fine, but acting's no way to make a living. Hopefully some tailor will take me into his shop."

"Won't Mr. Rintoull help you?"

He looked at her askance. "You know Louis's his favourite."

She thought of Kate, her sister, her dearest friend, who had unwittingly pushed her out of Belhaven. "Don't you mind?" she said.

"He pays for it," Tom said. "Mr. R. always has his eye on him.

But here I am going on about myself. Forgive me, Lizzie. Will you tell me about your grandfather?" He nodded towards a grey-haired couple circling the room. "Would he be dancing tonight?"

"Until the last note." She told him about the village ceilidhs, after the harvesting and the sheep shearing, and then found herself describing the shearing, what a day of commotion it was, how her grandfather worked so swiftly the sheep scarcely knew what had happened; how they emerged from the dip so much smaller and whiter. "One year, after we finished, Grandfather and I lay down on a pile of fleeces—it was like lying on a cloud that smelled of sheep—and he told me about the time he'd been in an earthquake as a boy. He'd gone to fetch the ducks when the earth started shaking and suddenly the pond was almost empty."

Remembering that day, she wanted only to be back in her room. Before Tom could speak, she pushed back her chair, apologising.

"If you want company next week," he said, "let Louis know."

From her window, she watched a woman in the house across the drying green, carry a lamp from room to room, the windows lightening and darkening until the last room turned dark. She remembered her grandfather saying, "It was the most curious thing, Lizzie. For a few seconds, everything that is normally still—the ground, the buildings, the tree trunks—was moving."

THE NEXT AFTERNOON, WHEN THE WOMAN CAME OUT OF the weather house, she went in search of Louis at the bowling green. She had not been there since she left the Phelpses'. As she drew near the privet hedge, she heard the unmistakable clack of bowl meeting bowl. Inside the hedge, several women were seated on the benches around the green; she chose an empty one near the gate. Louis was standing among the dozen men gathered in front of the clubhouse. His cap was pulled low, as it often was on sunny days, and he was talking to an older man, wearing spectacles.

"Well done," someone called.

A bowl had grazed the jack. Louis was walking with the older man to inspect it. She raised her hand, not a wave but a gesture that could become a wave if only he would glance in her direction, but he passed within a few yards, still deep in conversation. As he and the man walked back, each carrying a bowl, she knew from the way he stared straight ahead that he had seen her. When a woman rose from a nearby bench and headed to the gate, she followed.

ONCE AGAIN ONLY RAIN WOULD ALLOW THEM TO MEET. She sent a note, *If there's no bowling on Saturday, meet me at the Botanic Gardens*, and was glad to wake that day to overcast skies. He grumbled about paying a penny to see some plants, but once inside the Palm House he looked around with interest at the glossy foliage and dazzling flowers. "Maybe they have flowers like this in North America," he said.

"I came to watch the bowling the other night."

"I saw you. Lizzie, I wish you wouldn't. When we're practicing, the green's not open to the public. You don't want to make things awkward."

A beautiful white vine grew beside the path, the black-and-yellow stamens like question marks. They passed a palm tree and a bush covered with waxy, golden flowers. "Why would it be awkward?" she said. "We're engaged."

"I've told you over and over. I'm a good tailor, the customers like me, Mr. Rintoull talks of taking me into the business, but nothing's certain. Did you not see him at the bowls? He would've been upset to see you there, on your own."

"Was he the older man with spectacles?"

Louis nodded.

"There were other women watching."

"Wives," he said flatly.

"So, when will you tell him we're getting married at New Year?" Beside her, she sensed him biting his lip. Would he at last speak of Ivy?

As they approached the palm tree for the second time, he blurted out, "But everything's changed. You have a nice situation: getting your keep at the Tam o' Shanter, working at the tracing. You're not sending money home, so you can save. We can afford to wait until I'm settled."

If she kept staring at the waxy flowers, she might be able to contain herself. "What about our daughter?"

"She's Miss Urquhart's daughter now." His voice was low and forceful. "Lizzie, we don't have to keep being punished for one mistake. I want my own shop and Mr. Rintoull can help. I'm not going to ruin everything by getting on his bad side."

The phrase "Miss Urquhart's daughter" was like a knife in her side. "You made her a dress," she whispered. "You said you felt badly."

"Lizzie, she has a good home. We'll have children, when we're ready." He did not say "more children."

Two small green birds were flitting among the fronds of the palm tree. "You talk as if Mr. Rintoull wouldn't understand," she said. "Tom doesn't talk like that. He said I should have said hello when I came by the shop the other day."

This only seemed to anger him in a new way. "Tom thinks if he tries to be a good tailor, everything else will follow. But that's not enough. You need to scheme. Look how Callum was able to get the farm by marrying Kate."

She stopped walking. "What did you say?"

He repeated his claim.

"Callum didn't scheme." Her anger rose. "He and Kate were in love before either of them knew about Belhaven. Then he liked farming better than joinery. They were lucky she was the older sister."

"Pardon me." A man in a gardener's apron stepped briskly around them.

"I'd like to get lucky enough to own a house and land by the time I'm twenty-five," Louis said. "But you have to meet luck halfway. We're lucky the teacher took a liking to Barbara."

She could feel the blood leaving her face. Behind him the palm trees were spinning, lifting off, circling; the sky was turning dark. He glanced over and at once took her arm and guided her to a bench near the door. He dipped his handkerchief in a little pool of water under one of the trees and pressed it into her hand. She closed her eyes and patted her forehead. "You think," she whispered, "we should leave her with Miss Urquhart?"

"Lizzie, everyone thinks that: your grandmother, Kate. She has a good home. We can start again." As he talked on about how Mr. Rintoull would help him, maybe take him on at the shop, she remembered Barbara playing with her new bear, saying "Baa, baa."

In the kitchen of the Tam o' Shanter, he told Edith the heat of the Palm House had been too much for her. Edith helped her upstairs and returned with a glass of water, a plate of oatcakes, and a bell. "Ring and I'll hear you," she promised. Alone in bed, she studied the faint web of cracks on the ceiling. One April day, Miss Renfrew had led the school into the playground and given each pupil a piece of smoky glass through which to watch the sun. As a dark sphere crept across the lower part, stealing the light, several of the smaller children burst into tears. Her feelings for Barbara had grown, like that sphere, stealthily eclipsing even her passion for Louis. But his, she could no longer deny, had dwindled.

And his feelings for her had dwindled too. He still liked her, still wanted her, but he wanted other things more: money, security, a home. Surely he would not risk getting Ivy into trouble. Or maybe he would. Then Mr. Rintoull would have no choice but to bless their marriage.

A pigeon flew past the window, clapping its wings. As she followed its clumsy flight, her heart jolted. She was looking at an elm tree. Beyond the tree, across the road, she recognised Miss Urquhart's house. In one of the downstairs windows a lamp shone, but there was no sign of whoever had lit it. As she watched, a wisp of smoke escaped the window. Perhaps something was burning on the stove. More wisps, a cloud. Still the front door stayed shut. Still no one shouted "Help!" or "Fire!" Flames flickered at one downstairs window, then another. A pane of glass exploded, fragments flying into the garden. The flames leapt higher.

AS SOON AS EDITH COULD SPARE HER, SHE HEADED FOR the tailor's. Whatever Louis had said or failed to say in the greenhouse was irrelevant now that Barbara was in danger. The elm tree had been in full leaf, green but not yet dusty, which meant high summer. The shop was shuttered for Sunday. She knocked at the door once, then again. If there was no answer, she would leave a note asking him to come by the pub as soon as possible. But the door opened and a woman, her dark hair escaping in little wisps like Edith's, regarded her brightly. "Good afternoon. What can I do for you?"

"I was hoping to have a word with Louis Hunter."

"Let me fetch him." Showing no sign of disapproval, Mrs. Rintoull—surely it must be she—ushered Lizzie into the shop and urged her to take a seat. Finally, she was inside the place she had seen so often from the street, but all she could do was wander from sewing machine to sewing machine. At last she heard footsteps on the stairs.

"Louis isn't here. Is everything all right?"

Tom, in his shirtsleeves, stood before her, forehead furrowed, mouth smiling. He had no idea, she thought, of how he'd dashed her hopes.

"I'll write him a note," she said. "Have you time for a walk?" Anything was better than being alone in her room.

He took a step back and she thought he was going to refuse. Perhaps he had other plans. Then he said, "Give me a moment." He left the shop and after a few minutes returned with his cap and jacket. Outside he led her past the new greengrocer's and the water pump, down one street, then another, to a square where, he told her, he sometimes took the Rintoull children to play hide-and-seek. In the middle was a statue of a man on horseback, surrounded by grass and flowerbeds. Around the edge of the grass, screened from the road by trees and bushes, ran a path. They fell in behind two women walking a copper-coloured Pekinese. "Is everything all right?" he said again.

She caught the sweet smell of azaleas. "Promise not to tell Louis," she said.

"I promise."

"You may not like me once I've told you." Through the thin soles of her shoes, she could feel the pebbles of the path.

"I can't think of anything you could say that would make me not like you." He spoke as if he had given the matter some thought.

She began by describing the pictures and, when he said nothing, hurried to tell him the rest. He walked beside her, his pace matching hers, not interrupting, not exclaiming, even at the news of Barbara. When she finished, he led her to a bench beneath a sycamore tree. Across the grass, the bronze man held a sword in one upraised hand, a shield in the other.

"Barbara is in danger," he said. "You need to rescue her."

"Aren't you—?" She did not know how to finish the sentence.

"Of course I'm surprised," he said slowly, "but I knew there was something Louis wasn't telling me. He was so glad when you came to Glasgow, so miserable when you went back to the farm."

She recounted their conversation in the Palm House. "He wants to pretend Barbara is no longer our daughter."

"When you tell him about the fire, he'll help."

A winged seed glided down from the sycamore. That was why she had come to the tailor's, to ask Louis for help; but watching the seed spiral down, she was sure he would find a way to refuse. "No," she said. "He'll say I'm imagining things. That she's better off with Miss Urquhart. He changed while I was away."

She hoped Tom would contradict her, but he said, "He did. At night in our room we used to joke about the customers, make up little stories. Now all he wants is to please Mr. R. If I make a cheeky comment about someone's waistcoat, he cuts me off. And," he added, "there's Ivy."

The two women passed again, the Pekinese lagging.

"Tell me."

"She likes him." He was looking across the grass towards the statue. "When he and I started, she was still a child—we used to play hide-and-seek, Happy Families. Now she's seventeen and she makes no secret of her affections."

"And he likes her?" Again, she felt him hesitate.

"She's a nice girl," he said. "Clever, full of spirit. He likes being part of the family. I told him several times he ought to write to you about her, but he said there was no need. Then you came back and I thought maybe it would be all right."

Nearby two sparrows spread their wings and scuffled in the dust.

"But wouldn't it be best," Tom went on, "to tell the teacher so she can take precautions?"

In all her imaginings of how to save Barbara, this had never occurred to her. She recalled Miss Urquhart telling her pupils the pathetic fallacy existed only in poetry. "I don't think she'd believe in my pictures," she said slowly, "and the precautions might not work." She described her efforts to save Acorn.

"What if your grandmother fetched Barbara?" Tom said. "Or your sister."

"Grandmother is too frail. As for Kate"—she understood only as she spoke—"she wouldn't dare upset her husband, and everyone in the village, by crossing the teacher."

"So you—" he began, but she interrupted.

"There's no point in going on my own. They won't let me have Barbara."

Again he started to speak and again she cut him off. "Will you help me? My daughter's life is in danger. Miss Urquhart is an adult. She can save herself."

"How can I?" he said. "What would Louis say?"

Above them in the sycamore a bird shrilled. "We don't have to tell him," she said.

"Lizzie, I share a room with him. I spend all day with him." For the first time he sounded angry.

"I'll give you everything I have," she said, conscious of how little this was. "Do anything you want. I wouldn't ask you if there was anyone else."

He leaned forward, his elbows on his knees, his head in his hands. Above them the leaves of the sycamore rustled. "If I help you," he said, "I'm not saying I will, how would we save her?"

While the clouds gathered above the statue, she repeated the plans she'd rehearsed. "But you'd have to be the one to go to the house and ask for Barbara. Maybe say Flora Craig needed to see her."

He stood up and raised his hand. She watched him, puzzled, and then understood. She stood and mimed opening the door. "Good morning," she said. "What can I do for you?"

"How do you do?" He gave a little bow. "I'm sorry to trouble you. I'm Callum's brother. Flora Craig has pneumonia. She's asking to see her great-granddaughter—"

She interrupted to explain that Barbara was known as Callum's niece. As he adjusted his lines, she smelled tobacco; a man with a pipe ambled by. "The doctor says Flora doesn't have long." His expression was so serious that for a moment she almost believed him.

"You'll have her home this afternoon." She tried to sound stern.

"I swear. You'll be making an old woman very happy." He broke off. "I'm sorry. Please know, I don't wish Flora a minute of poor health."

"No, you're very convincing." For a moment it was as if the three of them were already on the train, heading back to Glasgow. Across the square a clock began to chime.

"I need to get back." Tom stood there, looking at her soberly. "Lizzie, I understand you're worried about Barbara, but I don't think I can do this. It's one thing to play-act beside a bench, another to lie to Louis day after day. He should be helping you."

"Please." She held on to his sleeve. "Please don't say no. Usually my pictures come a few weeks before things happen. The elm was still in full leaf." She would not let him go until he agreed to meet her at the library on Tuesday.

That night, washing the supper dishes, she tried to think what she would do when Tom said no. She could not ask the girls at the locomotive tracers'. As she rinsed a plate, Chrissie came to mind. She was strong, she was cunning. If only she would agree, she would make a good ally. And what—Lizzie reached for another plate—would make her agree? At once she knew the answer: her tin box, hidden beneath the geranium. She could pay her a pound, more if necessary. Even to imagine Chrissie arguing about her fee made her feel better.

AS SOON AS HE WALKED INTO THE LIBRARY, HIS EYES searching the room, his faded satchel slung from one shoulder, she was certain he was going to refuse. Why would he help her when even Louis wouldn't? Any offer of payment would only insult him. She led the way to the alcove with her favourite bookcase, the shelves filled with novels bound in blue and green, black and maroon. Together they stood as if studying the books.

Tom reached to straighten *Lady Audley's Secret*. "I woke up this morning," he said quietly, "determined to tell you I couldn't go to Langmuir. Then at breakfast Mr. R. announced he was closing the shop next Wednesday so he could visit a woolen mill. Louis and I were welcome to come too, or do what we please. I've never known him to take a day off."

Before she could ask what this had to do with saving Barbara, he went on. "It means I don't have to lie. I said I wanted to visit my grandfather in Burntisland. I'll go there after we get Barbara."

The floor was trembling—or perhaps her knees. She wanted to throw her arms around him, shout her gratitude. She seized his hand and kissed it.

"Stop," he whispered. The blood rose and fell in his cheeks so quickly, it was as if she had imagined it.

Chrissie would have helped, but Tom, with his deft acting and kind face, would persuade whoever minded Barbara to surrender her. Doing her best to speak calmly, she said the trains went every hour. They could hire a cart at the Royal Hotel in Cupar and, with luck, stay at the place she'd stayed on her last visit.

"And you'll write a letter warning the teacher," he said. "Even if she doesn't believe you, she'll be on her guard."

"Excuse me." A woman reached past them for *Dombey and Son*.

"I will," Lizzie said, "as soon as we have Barbara. Do you know any cheap boardinghouses?"

Beside her, she felt Tom startle. Why was she asking, he said, when she had her room at the Tam o' Shanter? Now she was the one to blush as she explained that Edith and Ralph didn't know about Barbara. "They would think I'm a fallen woman."

"But what kind of life will that be," Tom said, "living alone, caring for a baby? How will you manage for money?" His gaze was almost accusing.

"I can mind other people's babies. Or find a place as a maid." She tried to sound cheerful. "Several of the girls at work have babies. I'll ask them."

"I didn't realise," he said slowly, "that you don't have a place to go."

Something had shifted; she did not dare ask what. On the steps of the library, she tried, again, to thank him, but he cut her short. "I'll see you at the station," he said, "four on Tuesday." She hurried away before he could change his mind.

XV

*

The hours until Tuesday lay before her like endless rows of corn waiting to be cut. She worked overtime at the locomotive tracers' and asked Edith what needed doing. After Kate's weekly letter, she broke the news. Her grandmother was failing; she could no longer delay her return to Belhaven.

"Thank you for staying," Edith said. "We'll miss you, won't we, Molly?"

By way of answer, Molly dropped her rattle. Stooping to retrieve it, Lizzie caught sight of her friend's neat ankles. If only she had taken Edith into her confidence back at the Phelpses'. A lie might not always find you out, but it did make it hard to get back to the truth. "I'll miss you too," she said, offering the rattle.

"Not for long, though." Edith smiled knowingly. "You'll be back when you get married. Let's hope Louis finds a shop near here. Can you bring in the washing?"

She nodded dumbly. Ever since the picture of the fire she had avoided Louis in her thoughts, and when he stopped by the pub, she had asked Edith to say she was poorly. Once she had Barbara, she would write to him. In the drying green she bent to smell the sweet William Edith had planted beside the path—the small red flowers smelled faintly of cloves—and turned to the washing. She was unpegging a sheet when Chrissie appeared.

"I hope it's not me that's making you go," she said, reaching for another peg.

As they stood, each holding two corners of the sheet, she heard herself say, "No, it's my daughter. She's in danger."

Chrissie's tawny eyes softened. "I wondered," she said. They each brought their hands together, quartering the sheet. "When all's said and done, you're her mother."

"I thought of asking you for help."

"And I would have if I could." She gave a firm nod.

"You won't tell Edith."

"Cross my heart." As they finished folding the sheet, Chrissie confided that she too would soon be leaving the Tam o' Shanter. "My husband is due home at the end of July."

Lizzie nearly dropped the folded sheet. "But you're not married."

"Going on three years," Chrissie said. "He's a sailor. Sometimes people are funny about hiring a married woman, so I don't talk about him, but I need to work, like everyone else."

"How do you bear him being away for months, years?"

Chrissie's red hair flickered in the breeze. "The same way everyone bears things. Some days I hardly think of him. Others, it's like he left yesterday, and I can't stand one more minute. Don't tell Edith," she added.

So they each had their secret, Lizzie thought, but they were the opposite.

....

ON HER LAST DAY AT THE LOCOMOTIVE TRACERS', SHE
was working on the interior of a Boiler, three inches scale. She had
stretched the cloth the night before. Now she stretched it again,
as Deirdre had taught her, and rubbed in the chalk. She took special care drawing the wooden fittings, which someone else would
paint burnt sienna. At three o'clock Mr. Simpson paid her, adding a day extra. Deirdre and the other girls clustered around, wishing her goodbye, good luck. Then she was out in the street, where
the pavements were wet but the clouds were scudding over the
rooftops. As she walked to the tram stop, her bags knocked against
her skirts. Between the one she had brought with her and the one
Louis had delivered months ago, she had managed to pack her
clothes, her books, and her sketchpad. On top, carefully wrapped
in a shawl, were the picture of her parents and the weather house.
At the tram stop she stared at the worn cap of the man ahead of her
in the queue. What if Tom had had an accident? Or changed his
mind, and decided to go to the mill?

When she stepped into the ticket office, her fears were con-
firmed; a dozen people were waiting but not him. She set her bags
on the floor by a pillar and forced herself to confront what she must
do next: buy a ticket, catch the train. Even as she got out her purse,
she imagined herself struggling with some burly woman over Barbara; Miss Urquhart running from the school to bar her way.

"Lizzie, I didn't see you."

He was standing before her, his jacket over his arm, his shirt collar dragged askew by the strap of his satchel, holding their tickets.
"Are you all right?" he asked, reaching for her bags.

"The tram was slow." Any mention of her fears would, she knew,
be an insult.

On the train, they shared a compartment with two grey-haired men, each reading the newspaper, the identical front pages of advertisements side by side. Once the train was moving, when the noise of the engine muffled conversation, Tom said he had something for her. He held out a leather box, a little bigger than a postage stamp. Inside was a plain gold ring. "My grandmother's," he said. "My mother gave it to me in case I needed it, though this"—the colour rose and fell in his face—"wasn't what she had in mind."

The one time she had tried on Flora's ring, she had been nine or ten, it had fallen off her finger. This ring fit perfectly. As she raised her hand to show Tom—the men were still hidden behind their papers—she was struck by how the gold band changed everything. All at once she was respectable; she belonged to someone. Reluctantly she slipped it off and returned it to the box. "I can't be a widow," she whispered, "until we have Barbara."

Again his face changed, but he said nothing. He reached into his satchel and pulled out a book. She couldn't see the title. She got out *Kidnapped* and tried to interest herself in David Balfour's flight across the heather, but mostly she stared, unseeing, out of the window. She was an immigrant in Glasgow, and what they did tomorrow would make her an outlaw in Belhaven. Where would she find a home again? The men folded their newspapers and left the train at Stirling. An hour and forty minutes later they pulled into Cupar. She was glad to see that Angus, with his guard's flag, was at the far end of the platform. The fewer people who knew about her visit, the better. As she led the way across the bridge over the river Eden, towards the High Street, she told Tom about Irene, her three children and jolly husband.

"Who am I going to be?" he said, as they passed the greengrocer's.

"What do you mean?"

"When we ask for rooms. Maybe I could be your brother. We have the same colouring."

She hadn't noticed before but it was true: his hair was the same shade of brown, his eyes almost the same larkspur blue; his nose was longer and straighter but his skin, like hers, was neither fair nor dark. She said that was a good idea, and when Irene answered the door, that was how she introduced him. They were visiting their niece and hoped she might have rooms.

"I can sleep anywhere," Tom added.

"No need for that," Irene said. "Why don't you take a stroll while I get things ready?"

Lizzie left her bags and they retraced their steps. At the Royal Hotel Tom enquired about hiring a cart and was directed to Mr. Dodd, a couple of streets away. No one was home. Back at the hotel, the clerk suggested he try the Station Arms on the next corner. She was waiting outside the greengrocer's, thinking once the cart was arranged, she would show Tom the old church, when a voice said, "Lizzie, fancy seeing you here."

Mrs. Waugh, the minister's wife, was standing before her, wearing a blouse familiar from many Sunday schools, and a new hat. "You'll have been visiting Flora," she said, her little upturned nose quivering.

She let herself nod. "I hope you and Mr. Waugh are keeping well," she managed. Over Mrs. Waugh's shoulder, she saw Tom, studying the apothecary's window.

"We're grand," said Mrs. Waugh. "And how did you find Flora?"

"As well as could be expected. I'm sorry." She gave a little wave. "I have a train to catch." Stupid, stupid, she thought, as she hurried towards the station. She had forgotten she was not in Glasgow anymore, anonymous among a crowd.

On the platform Tom caught up with her. "She went the other way," he said quietly.

"I've ruined everything. Everyone will know I'm here."

"Lizzie, it's past six. She won't be gossiping until tomorrow. Let's wait by the river."

As he led the way, he told her Mr. Dodd would meet them at eight, drive them to the village, and bring them back for the ten thirty train. When they were seated on a wall beside the slow-moving green water, he said, "I hope you won't be upset. I wrote to my grandfather in Burntisland, asking if he'd like a housekeeper."

Every day since they met at the library, she had planned to go after work to Govan, the neighbourhood Deirdre had recommended for cheap boardinghouses, and every day, unable to contemplate whatever dingy room awaited her and Barbara, she had ended up walking back to the Tam o' Shanter. Now she asked what his grandfather had said, and Tom said there hadn't been time for a reply. But tomorrow, instead of going straight back to Glasgow, she could go there with him, to Burntisland. If Mr. Malcolm said no, she'd have lost only the price of a train ticket.

On the other bank a wren bobbed along a branch. Flora had always claimed the small brown birds, with their jaunty tails, brought good luck. "What is he like?" she said.

"Curmudgeonly but kind. He might say out of the question; he might be glad of the company. My grandmother died two years ago, and he has three bedrooms and a garden."

She remembered her grandfather holding Barbara on his knee, rocking her gently while he sang "Comin' Thro' the Rye." "Let's go to Burntisland," she said.

....

OUTSIDE THE ROYAL HOTEL, TOM LED THE WAY TO A
cart with a lively chestnut gelding between the shafts. While he and
Mr. Dodd discussed football and fishing, she kept her shawl over
her head, looking down when they passed other travelers. In the
fields the corn and barley were already knee-high, and the chestnut
trees were in bloom. When they reached the village, she directed
Mr. Dodd to turn the cart around and wait at the end of the road.
Tom had explained the urgency of their errand: taking their niece
for a last hour with her grandmother. Holding her shawl close, she
led him to the elm tree. As they passed the school, a hymn wafted
through the open windows. He hummed a few bars. She stared,
amazed that he could hum at such a time. She herself felt as if she
had run all the way from Cupar, as if she were still running. She
pointed out the house and hurried back to the cart.

She could not speak, she could not pray, all she could do was
silently recite the kings and queens—Henry VIII, Edward VI,
Mary I—while Mr. Dodd talked about the dovecot he was building. He hoped to breed some of his favourite pigeons, but who
knew what went on in their feathery heads? Elizabeth, James I
and VI. The horse whisked his tail. Charles I, Charles II. She tried
to imagine herself riding to safety, the wind in her hair, tried to
imagine being the wind, going effortlessly from place to place. But
all she could hear was the woman shouting, "Stop, thief," see her
running to the school to summon Miss Urquhart.

There was a sharp cry. Tom was pushing Barbara into her arms,
scrambling up himself. "If we move along," he said, "maybe we
can catch the earlier train." And they were clip-clopping down the
street, back past the castle and Mr. Wright's fields, past the grove
of chestnuts and more fields, and all the while Barbara kicked and
cried. Lizzie sang "Row, row, row the boat" and "My Nut-Brown

Maiden," bounced her up and down, wiped the tears from her hot cheeks.

"Och, the wee girl's worried about her granny," said Mr. Dodd.

Tom kept looking over his shoulder.

Only when she thought to offer one of Irene's rolls did Barbara's cries begin to fade. She squeezed a piece of bread into a ball. "Bird, bird," she said, pointing at a crow.

They were at the station with fifteen minutes to spare. Mr. Dodd thanked Tom for the sixpence extra and said he hoped the train was on time. While Tom bought their tickets, she carried Barbara to the far end of the station and stood in the shadow of the eaves.

"You should put on the ring," Tom said when he joined them.

She found the box in her pocket and slid on the gold band. In less than twenty-four hours, she had gone from being a spinster to being a widow.

Several people were waiting—all, as far as she could tell, strangers—but she stood as still as possible, holding Barbara, feeding her the roll piece by piece. Since they left Glasgow, Tom's calmness had surprised and steadied her. Now, watching him scan the platform, she realised he too was afraid. They stood waiting, silently, for the approaching train. Still there were no pursuers, no one who seemed interested in them. The train, only two carriages, puffed to a halt; doors opened. They moved swiftly to the edge of the platform. Carrying Barbara, she climbed the steps, Tom followed with her bags. The doors closed; Angus blew his whistle and waved his flag. The train pulled out of the station.

The compartment was already occupied by a woman dressed entirely in black. For a moment Lizzie feared it was an omen, but the woman said cheerfully that her great-uncle had been ninety-six; no one had regretted his passing. Tom said they were taking their daughter to visit her grandfather. Oh, she thought, remembering how his face had flushed when he gave her the ring. I'm not a widow. I'm a wife. She was glad that the noise of the train, as it gathered speed, made further conversation hard. Beside her, she could feel Tom leaning forward, urging the engine faster, faster. She was doing the same.

ON THE PLATFORM AT BURNTISLAND, THEY STOOD watching the train pull away, the puffs of steam vanishing in the breeze, until it disappeared behind a stand of trees. "I've never been so hungry in my life," she said.

Tom smiled and said he was hungry too. While he went to buy food, she chose the bench in front of the station with the best view over the Firth of Forth and sat down with Barbara, still asleep, on her lap. She was looking across the choppy water to Arthur's Seat—she had last seen the hill from Lower Largo with her grandmother—when an engine creaked by, pulling a line of wagons filled with coal towards the firth. As the last wagon disappeared, she was struck by the thought: no one knows I'm here. All her life she had been tied to her family, to Louis, to Edith, bound, like Gulliver by the Lilliputians, with many tiny bonds. Today she had severed them.

Another train of coal was creaking by when Tom reappeared. As he cut slices of bread and cheese, he told her the coal wagons were going on a ferry to Edinburgh. For several minutes they were both too busy eating to speak. Presently she felt him watching her. "Are you sorry?" he said.

"A part of me is. I've broken my promise to my grandmother. I've made difficulties for you. I can't go back to Belhaven, and my life in Glasgow is gone. But if Barbara were hurt, I would never forgive myself." Taking another piece of cheese, she repeated the thought she'd had while he was gone. "No one knows where I am."

"I do," he said. "And you'll let Kate and your grandmother know when you're settled."

"What about you? Are you sorry?"

"I don't know." He looked down at the bread and cheese, suddenly sombre.

"If I live to be a hundred, I can never thank you enough."

The colour rose in his face. After a long moment, he reached to stroke Barbara's back. "You have your daughter," he said. "That's the main thing."

"What will you tell your grandfather about us?"

"That you're a friend who needs help." He regarded her quizzically.

"Please," she said, "don't tell him that Louis abandoned us."

"Lizzie, he's my grandfather. I'll tell him what I see fit."

Leaving them on the bench, he headed off again; his grandfather's house was twenty minutes from the station. She got out *Kidnapped*, but David Balfour's adventures still seemed much less exciting than her own. With Barbara lying in her lap, she was able to contemplate the possibilities with equanimity: they would stay here, or they would return to Glasgow and she would find a room. The sun came out and she closed her eyes.

She heard footsteps on the cobbles; Tom was back. "Grandpa wants to meet you," he said. "I told him you're a widow. There's some difficulty with your husband's family."

Still drowsy, she lifted Barbara into her arms. "Did you know," she said, "that the Kingdom of Fife used to be called the Kingdom of Fib?"

"You mustn't think I like doing this," he said sharply. "You never know who you'll meet. You ran into that woman in Cupar. Last week a man came in to order a jacket and recognised me from a play at school." Not waiting for a reply, he picked up her bags and set off up the hill, away from the station.

She followed as quickly as she could. "I'm sorry," she said when she drew level. "I know you're only trying to help me."

He nodded and pointed out an oddly shaped building. It was called the Octagonal Church; the steep hill at the back of the town was called the Binn. They turned in to the High Street and walked past the shops and businesses, towards an expanse of grass. "The links," Tom said. "There's a tunnel under the railway to the beach. At low tide you can wade out to the Black Rocks."

As they headed up Cromwell Street, she tried to memorise their route so she could find the station again. What was she thinking, putting herself and Barbara at the mercy of some strange man? But perhaps, she thought, taking in the pleasant houses they were passing, she could rent a room here. Maybe that would be better than living in Glasgow, the people she knew nearby but forbidden.

The man who opened the door filled the hallway. His grey eyes stared at her, fiercely, from beneath shaggy grey brows, and his white beard billowed over his barrel chest. "Good afternoon," he said. "I'm Andrew Malcolm." He offered a hand that resembled her grandfather's, nicked and scarred and then, seeing Barbara asleep, withdrew it.

"I'm Lizzie Craig, and this is my daughter, Barbara." A sentence she had never uttered before.

"You can put the bairn in here." He opened the door to a room off the hall and gestured towards a bed covered with a quilt the colour of roses.

"She might roll off," Lizzie said, and laid Barbara on the hearth rug. As she stepped back, Mr. Malcolm picked up the quilt and carefully folded it over her.

In the kitchen a dark shape rose from an armchair. Mr. Malcolm introduced Oscar. She hadn't seen a cat indoors before. What if he scratched Barbara, or knocked her down? But Oscar was pressing against her legs, purring.

"He's taken a fancy to you," Mr. Malcolm said, and she could tell it was a point in her favour.

While he and Tom exchanged news about Tom's mother, she looked around the kitchen. Flora had often remarked on Neil's bachelor housekeeping: the piles of dishes, the crusty pots, the ash around the stove. Here the sink was empty, the dishes on the shelves, the stove newly blacked, the floor swept. Mr. Malcolm poured the tea and set a cup before her. "Tom said you and the bairn need a room." He was again studying her fiercely.

"I can clean and cook, do the messages, the washing, the mending. If you have a garden, I can take care of that too. Barbara won't be much trouble." She stopped, realising how much she wanted to stay here, where a man laid a quilt over her sleeping daughter.

"A bairn is always trouble," he said. "I manage fine on my own."

"I can see that." She met his gaze. "We've nowhere else to go."

He said nothing; Tom said nothing; the coals flared and chinked in the stove. She was preparing to pick up Barbara and walk back to the station when Mr. Malcolm set down his cup. "There's something amiss in your life, lass," he said. "I trust my grandson that it's nothing shameful. Let's try how we get on for a fortnight."

She was still thanking him when he asked Tom to go to the grocer's. He wrote a list; she added apples and milk for Barbara. As the door closed behind Tom, Mr. Malcolm said something about the garden. "I'm sorry," she said. "I think I need to lie down."

....

SHE WOKE TO THE CRIES OF SEAGULLS AND, FROM THE hearth rug, the small sounds that meant Barbara too was awake. There was water in the jug on the night stand. After she'd washed and straightened herself, she turned to her daughter. Her only provision for their flight had been to take a couple of Molly's nappies. She had changed Barbara in Stirling; now she changed her again. Perhaps Mr. Malcolm would have an old shirt, or a sheet, she could use to make more nappies, even make a dress. If he didn't, the days were mild; she could wash Barbara's clothes at night and hang them on the stove to dry, wrap her in a shawl when the wind blew.

In the kitchen she introduced Barbara to Mr. Malcolm. When he bent to greet her, she reached for his beard. "No. Naughty." She snatched back Barbara's hand.

"Och, I doubt she's seen a beard like mine," he said. "Come and admire my garden."

The back door opened onto grass, surrounded on two sides by flowers and on the third by a vegetable bed. She was noting how well his onions were doing when Tom returned.

XVI

✳

In front of his grandfather, she had to pretend this was an ordinary farewell. "Good luck, Lizzie," Tom said, clasping her hand. Perhaps he too was pretending? During their day and a half together, she had come to count on his company and kindness. Now the sound of the door closing behind him was the sound of her old life leaving. But there was no time to think of that; she must figure out her duties in this strange house. She installed Barbara beneath the kitchen table and asked Mr. Malcolm what she should do.

"Do?" His shaggy eyebrows rose.

"I'm your housekeeper."

"Well . . . why don't you bake a cake? My cooking's tolerable but my baking is wretched." He settled down in his armchair with the newspaper. She asked where the eggs and flour were kept, and he pointed to a cupboard. She discovered the larder.

While she beat the eggs, Barbara tugged at her skirt. "Up, up." Ignored, she crawled towards the stove. Lizzie retrieved her and set her back beneath the table. She headed once more for the stove. The third time, Lizzie gave her a little shake and whispered, "Please, be a good girl." She could hear the newspaper rustling.

Any moment, she thought, Mr. Malcolm would ask them to leave. She began to mix flour, sugar, salt, and baking powder.

"Up, up."

Mr. Malcolm lowered the paper and pushed himself out of his chair. "Don't bother your mother," he said gruffly. "Come and have a wee look at my garden." He leaned down, holding out a large, scarred hand. Barbara pursed her lips. "Come," he said again. Cautiously she reached for his hand and took a faltering step.

The Victoria sponge was almost as good as one of Kate's. They ate slices after lunch, while it was still warm, and again at tea. Mr. Malcolm told her to call him Andrew. He showed Barbara how to stroke Oscar, gently, from head to tail. Using a clothes peg and a duster, he made a small figure wearing a dress. Carefully he drew on a face, glued on strands of brown wool for hair. "Leave it long," Lizzie suggested, "and I'll braid it." Soon the doll had two neat pigtails. That evening, after Andrew went to bed, she wrote to Kate, just two lines to say she and Barbara were safe; she would write and explain soon. She addressed a second envelope to Miss Urquhart and then sat, staring at the sheet of paper, all the words she couldn't write cascading through her head. At last she dipped her pen in the ink: *I'm sorry I took Barbara without telling you. Soon there's going to be a fire at your house. Please be very careful.* A blot pooled around the final *l*. They would know, from the postmarks, that she was not far away.

She cleaned and cooked, she made clothes for Barbara and tried to keep her from crying, she mended Andrew's clothes and trimmed his splendid beard. When he chided her—the plates were in the wrong place, she left the bread out—she learned to say nothing and wait for his ire to pass. After watching him sit over a chessboard, she asked him to teach her. She liked that it was more complicated than cribbage, that the pieces moved according to different rules. Soon the three of them had their routines and small jokes; soon Barbara grew more at ease with her and with Andrew. But she missed the locomotive tracers', the busyness of the Tam o' Shanter, Edith and Molly and Ralph. And sometimes, inadvertently, she missed Louis. "She's Miss Urquhart's daughter," he had said in the Palm House. But she imagined the three of them living in a small flat, like Hugh and Beth's, the idea there in her head before she could shut it out. She abandoned half a dozen letters to him. At night, in the empty kitchen, she sat by the stove, wondering if this was the rest of her life: her only company an elderly man, a small girl and a cat?

Dear Lizzie,

I was back at the shop for lunch. Louis and Mr. R. had a grand time at the mill. There was lots of chat about wool and tweed which I didn't entirely follow. Thankfully Mr. R. set me to some simple hemming. I pleaded a busy day, helping Grandpa, and went to bed after supper.

This morning we had a dozen customers. Nice weather brings people out. It was past two when Mr. R. and Louis headed to the bowls. Now I'm here at the cutting table, thinking about you and Barbara and Grandpa. Have you warned the teacher? Louis still thinks you're at the Tam o' Shanter. Please write to him. And please write to me so I'll know how you are. Get Grandpa to address your letter. I think about our amazing journey.

Yours,

Tom

She was still trying, and failing, to write to Louis, when another letter came. Andrew remarked that his grandson was turning into a fine correspondent.

Dear Lizzie,

Yesterday Louis went to meet you at the Tam o' Shanter and Edith told him you'd gone back to Belhaven. He came home smelling of beer. Why would she leave without telling me? he kept saying. I had to tell him to keep his voice down.

I asked if you'd quarreled and he said no. Then I asked— forgive me, Lizzie—if you knew about Ivy. He said you knew the Rintoulls had four children. I said he'd been paying Ivy a lot of attention. He insisted you understood he was keeping in Mr. R.'s good books.

I feel like a spy, writing secretly, knowing where you are when he doesn't. Please write to him.

Yours,

Tom

She wrote back: *I haven't written to Louis because I don't know what to say but I will soon, I promise.* How could she admit she still had the smallest ember of hope that Louis would appear in Burntisland?

ANDREW DID NOT MENTION THEIR FORTNIGHT'S TRIAL, but, as the days passed she watched him keenly for signs. After he borrowed a cradle from a neighbour, and sat beside it reading to Barbara, she wrote a proper letter to Kate, giving her Andrew's address, telling her about the fire. *I wrote to Miss Urquhart but*

I doubt she believed me. If you tell her too at least she'll be on her guard. Please show this letter to Grandmother so she'll know why I had to break my promise. She could not bear to write to Flora directly, but every morning, she hoped for a reply. Four days in a row, the postman walked by. On the fifth, soon after Andrew had headed out to the dairy, she heard the sound of the letter box.

Lizzie,

I know you believe your pictures always come true but how could you steal Barbara from Miss Urquhart? She came to Lilac Cottage and the farm in such a state. We didn't know what to say. And now you're in Burntisland, keeping house for the grandfather of Louis's fellow apprentice. Are you still going to marry Louis?

Grandmother is beside herself. I worry this might be the end of her. I'm almost ashamed to be your sister.

Kate

When Andrew returned, he took one look at her, set the milk in the larder, and moved the kettle onto the hob. Once the tea was made, he said he'd run into the minister outside the bakery. "I don't know how to heal what ails you, lass, but Mr. Nicholson is a kindly man. He has three bairns and he used to live in Edinburgh. Maybe you could talk to him."

She could only imagine a minister like Mr. Waugh, who if he had known the truth of Barbara's existence would have thundered about sin; but beneath Andrew's grey eyes, she agreed to meet Mr. Nicholson. Perhaps he could tell her how to make amends to Flora.

....

AS SHE CLIMBED THE STEPS TO THE CHURCH, THE SUN slid from behind a cloud. Inside, the stained-glass windows above the altar were so radiant that, momentarily, she forgot why she was there. She recognised the first two windows: the Sermon on the Mount and Christ expelling the moneylenders from the temple. She was staring at the third, Christ walking across stormy blue water, when a man several inches taller than her, his domed head quite bald, emerged from a door near the altar. Mr. Nicholson introduced himself and, gesturing for her to join him, sat down in the front pew. "Whatever you choose to tell me," he said, "will stay here."

Haltingly, doubling back to include forgotten details, she described growing up in Belhaven, meeting Louis, moving to Glasgow, going home to have her daughter, and then—Mr. Nicholson sat quietly beside her—all that had happened since. When she finished, she slid her hands under her thighs and, watching the light shift behind the windows, waited for him to call her sinful, or worse.

"What a time of it you've had," he said. "Jesus said, 'Suffer the little children to come unto me.' I'm sure that includes your daughter. What baffles me is why you were so sure there'd be a fire."

"I'm afraid you'll think I'm wicked." The Sea of Galilee was so much bluer than the Firth of Forth.

"I have days," said Mr. Nicholson, "when I don't believe in any of this." He waved towards the pulpit. "God, Jesus, heaven, hell, it's a fairy tale for children. I believe in helping the poor, in turning the other cheek. On Sundays I have to mention God, but mostly I tell people to be kind. Now you know one of my secrets."

"Nothing leaves the church?" she said. When he put his finger to his lips, she told him about the pictures.

"Some people would envy you," he said thoughtfully. "We all want to know the future. You didn't think of warning the teacher?"

As she explained how she'd written to her and to Kate, there came a faint rustling.

"I hope you're not afraid of mice. I meant warning her rather than stealing Barbara. I believe your intentions were good, but"— now he sounded more like Mr. Waugh—"you lied, you deceived people, and, if I understand correctly, you caused a woman who has shown your daughter nothing but kindness considerable anguish."

She did not try to explain, as she had to Tom, that Miss Urquhart would not have believed her. It was a relief, at last, to be blamed. "I made a terrible mistake," she said, "going back to Glasgow. Since then everything has been a tangle. I never meant to hurt Miss Urquhart, but what can I do now? I can't give up my daughter." Out of the corner of her eye, she glimpsed a small grey mouse.

As if he were proposing something quite ordinary, Mr. Nicholson said, that if the weather held, he could go to the village on Thursday and visit her grandmother and Miss Urquhart. In the notebook he handed her, she marked the road to Cupar, made X's for the church, the school, Miss Urquhart's house, Lilac Cottage, and Belhaven.

"Now go home and read your daughter a story," he said. "I'll call as soon as I have news."

THAT EVENING, AFTER BARBARA WAS ASLEEP, SHE TOLD Andrew what she had told the minister. He too listened quietly,

Oscar on his lap. The lamp was not yet lit and the gathering shadows eased her confession. "Tom wanted to tell you the truth," she said, "but I was afraid you'd throw us out." In the silence she heard the rumble of Oscar purring.

"Lizzie," he said, "you're not the first to have a bairn before you have a husband. I hoped Tom was the father, but it's to his credit that he helped you out of the goodness of his heart. Let me tell you how I ended up here alone, with Oscar."

Growing up in Dunkeld, he had spent hours exploring the town's medieval cathedral, and as soon as he was old enough he had apprenticed himself to a stonemason. When he finished his training, he found work with a mason in Stirling; Douglas was the kindest of men.

In the near-dark she could see only his grey eyes and his billowing white beard.

"If we were working on a building outside town," he went on, "Douglas and I often stayed over during the week so as not to waste the daylight coming and going. In town, I rented a room, but I took my meals at his table. His wife, Rosie, made me welcome, and her sister, Claire, was often there too. Who can say why one woman's step makes your heart leap while another's, she may even be prettier, leaves you unmoved?

"One Saturday, Claire and I visited Bannockburn. She told me where the English and Scottish armies stood, and how the fighting went. She waved a stick, pretending it was a sword, and when I tried to put my arms around her, she waved it at me. Douglas kept urging me to ask for her hand, but I saw how Rosie was with him, the little touches, the fond glances; I knew Claire didn't care for me that way. Then one Sunday in kirk, I saw the expression I'd been hoping for. She was looking at Marcus Kennedy; his family owned the big shop in town.

"You can guess what happened. Claire was in need of a husband; Marcus couldn't marry a carter's daughter. Douglas and I were sitting by the fire in the house we were building when he asked me. 'She's fond of you,' he insisted, 'and she'll grow fonder.' Tom's father was born four months after the wedding. Two years later we had our daughter, Isabel; but Claire didn't grow fonder, and I didn't like to impose. Then Douglas fell off a roof. He died in my arms. Rosie and her girls moved in with us. She helped me, as she'd helped Douglas, and I got more work, took on more apprentices. One day Claire started coughing. My darling was dead within a month. I waited a year to ask Rosie if she'd have me. We moved here, and we did well for ourselves. But two winters ago, she caught a chill."

Now only his beard glimmered in the darkness. "You must miss her," she said.

"Every day." He reached for the lamp. Suddenly they were both blinking in the circle of light.

"What happened to Tom's father?" She had never asked him.

"An accident at the shipyard. It's a strange thing: of all my grandchildren, Tom's the one I'm closest to. He doesn't know any of this. I'm only telling you because I'm an old man who can't hold his tongue. And"—he put Oscar on the floor and stood up—"so you'll know you're not alone on your winding road."

He went to his room and she stepped into the garden. The bats were flittering back and forth, small dark shapes against the dark sky. Flora used to urge her to listen for their high-pitched cries: "When you're my age," she said, "you won't be able to hear them."

Andrew's feelings for Claire, she thought, were like hers for Louis. But he had felt something else for Rosie, something he valued. Or had his feelings for her changed? A bat darted by, almost grazing her hair. Once she had made her thoughts into arrows to send to Louis, then to Barbara. Now she sent them winging towards her grandmother: Forgive me.

AS SOON AS MR. NICHOLSON STEPPED INTO THE KITCHEN, she knew, from the way he held his hat, something was amiss. Andrew came to stand beside her.

"I'm very sorry—"

He was still talking when she opened the back door, ran outside, and flung herself down on the grass. She pressed her cheek against the tiny blades. Beneath the earth, not many miles away, her grandfather was lying in his good suit. Now, soon, her grandmother would join him. She would never again hear her voice, never again watch her stroke Acorn's neck, or peel an apple, or gather the corn into stooks, never again feel her hand straightening a collar, or see her blue eyes, laughing or stern. "I hope you and Rab are enjoying an evening stroll by the lochan," she whispered. "I hope you found Helen."

Someone patted her arm. Barbara was sitting beside her. "Ball," she said.

Back in the kitchen Mr. Nicholson offered his condolences. "The funeral is tomorrow," he said. "We give thanks that she's at peace with God, but I know how much you wanted to see her one more time. Your sister sent this." He held out a folded sheet of paper and an envelope.

Unfolding the paper, she read:

Dearest Lizzie,

Forgive my last letter. I wrote in haste. It must have been terrible to see Miss Urquhart's house on fire. As soon as we could, Flora and I went to warn her. When we got back to Lilac Cottage, she said, 'Tell Lizzie I forgive her everything. I'm very sorry I gave Barbara away.' She died a few hours later in her armchair, like your picture.

I wrote to you about the funeral but I worry it might not reach you in time. The minister promised to deliver this today. Please come.

Love, Kate

P.S. This arrived from Louis.

She thrust his envelope, unopened, into her pocket.

"When I called on Miss Urquhart," Mr. Nicholson said, "she told me she's keeping a pail of water in every room."

Barbara had toddled inside and was talking to her peg doll beneath the table. "Is she very angry with me?"

"I wouldn't presume"—his domed head caught the light—"to know her feelings."

When he returned from showing the minister out, Andrew came and stood before her. "Lizzie," he said, "you have my heartfelt condolences. I know your grandmother was a fine woman." Seeing that she couldn't speak, he busied himself at the stove, adding coal. Watching each lump send up a shower of sparks, she remembered her grandfather, standing over a dead ewe, saying, "Man is born unto trouble as the sparks fly upward." And she, she thought, had been part of that trouble.

"If you trust me," Andrew said, "I can mind the bairn while you go to the funeral."

"I'm afraid I'll shame my grandmother. Everyone must hate me."

"I doubt that's true." He put down the tongs and, still not looking at her, went to rinse his hands. "You only get the one chance to be there."

Before Mr. Nicholson knocked, she had been about to wash the windows. Now she returned to the garden and her pail of water. As she rubbed each pane, working from top to bottom, scrubbing at the bird droppings, she remembered her grandmother in the barn, years ago, telling her they would die; she would be left alone with Kate. Through the glass she saw Andrew stoop to talk to Barbara and then Barbara, over his shoulder, catching sight of her. She waved her arms until he carried her to the window.

Later, when she was alone, she opened Louis's envelope.

Dear Lizzie,

   I went to meet you at the Tam o' Shanter and Edith told me you'd gone back to the farm. We agreed you must have been very worried to go without telling me. Have I done something to vex you?

   I hope your grandmother is keeping well. Please write and tell me what's happening.

   Love, Louis

In the fire the paper blackened, crinkled, burned. It took barely a minute to write the only reply she could think of: her address.

THE FOLLOWING WEEK SHE STARTED WORK AT THE bakery on the High Street. She left the house at six and came home at eleven with a loaf of warm bread. She helped Jean, the baker's wife, unload the ovens, wait on customers, make change, sweep the shop. Meanwhile, Andrew gave Barbara breakfast, read to her from Walter Scott, played with her ball or her doll. He even — she had shown him reluctantly before going to Flora's funeral — changed her nappie. "I did this for my own bairns," he said. "Not often, I'll admit."

Her first morning at the bakery she caught Jean wincing as she lifted a tray. She had hurt her shoulder and didn't want her husband to fuss. "Leave the trays to me," Lizzie had said. "I'm a strong farm girl." The little conspiracy began their friendship. Within hours, Jean was telling her about her older sister, who still ordered her around, and her four daughters, whom her mother minded while she was at the shop. They filled the shelves with loaves. Then they had a cup of tea before they hung up the Open sign and Miss Lawson, always their first customer, stepped in, saying, "My, it smells good in here." Within a few days Lizzie knew most of the regulars. From the women's kindly expressions, she guessed Jean had spread the word about her dead husband; Tom's gold ring was keeping her safe.

Farming, her grandfather used to say, was about waiting: for the weather to change; for the crops to ripen, or rot; for the lambs and calves to be weaned, or sicken. Now, despite her best intentions, she was waiting for Louis. But when the postman brought a letter, it was again from Kate, asking her to visit Belhaven to go through Flora's possessions. That evening, after Barbara was asleep, she walked down to the beach. The sun was still above the hills, and people were strolling on the sand, watching the last coal ferry make its way to Edinburgh. A few hundred yards from shore the Black Rocks rose sharply out of the water. A flock of small grey birds was running along the tide line. When she came too close, they took flight, their white bellies flashing over the waves, only to land a few yards farther along the shore.

A woman she recognised from the bakery was kneeling at the waterline beside two girls. "We're collecting shells," she said. "If you find any special ones, can you save them for us?"

She promised she would and walked on. The birds once again took to the air as several boys ran into the sea, water spraying around them. A hundred feet from shore, they were barely knee-deep. She remembered Tom telling her how he and Andrew used to wade out to the Black Rocks. If Louis didn't come soon, she would take the train to Glasgow. What could be worse than his silence?

Back in the kitchen, as Andrew lined up their pawns, she asked, "If you'd had to choose between Rosie and Claire, who would you have chosen?"

He gave her a look. "Rosie was married when I met her. As for Claire, I thought the sun came out when she entered a room, but she didn't feel the same about me." He set his rook in position, then his knight. "If you're asking did Rosie feel like second-best, no, never, and she never made me feel like that either."

She moved her white pawn two squares and wished she could ask about those feelings no one spoke of, that did not necessarily have to do with goodness, or kindness, but a glint in the eye, the curve of a lip; those feelings that led to lying down and which lying down only deepened.

"I can't help you, lass," Andrew said. "I've known Tom all his life and I'd trust him with mine." He moved his pawn towards her.

He must think Tom is courting me, she thought; she did not correct him.

....

SHE CARRIED BARBARA PAST THE DANDELIONS, PAST THE lilac bushes, through the gate, and set her down on the doorstep. Standing before the faded green door, she imagined stepping into the kitchen, filling the kettle, telling her grandparents that George had said they were planting both Achilles turnips and Mungoswell giants. Her grandfather would say the Achilles were sturdier; her grandmother that the giants were tastier. Slowly, as if one of the goblins of her childhood might leap out, she opened the door. Even from the threshold, the cottage smelled different: not of the mice and mould of their first visit with Callum, nor of Kate's baking, nor of her grandfather's pipe. But when she stepped inside, the familiar furnishings—the table, the armchairs, the settle—were just the same. For a moment it was as if her grandmother had stepped out to visit Neil or walk beside the lochan.

"This is where you were born," she told Barbara.

"Bird."

A blackbird, a dark brown female, was standing in the doorway. The bird watched while she opened the door of her grandparents' bedroom, then her own. In theirs, the bed was tightly made, the clothes put away. In hers, a shawl hung crooked over the chair, a pair of shoes lay askew beneath the bed. Back in the kitchen, she set the clock to what she guessed was the time and wound it, glad to hear the reassuring tick-tock. When she turned around, the bird was gone.

That evening she and Kate left the sleeping children in Callum's care and carried a blanket up to the orchard. The blossom was almost over, but as Kate described the visit to Miss Urquhart, a few petals drifted down, catching in her hair. "I wish you could have seen Flora," she said. "She was like her old self. She told Miss Urquhart that second sight runs in our family and you'd seen her house on fire. Then she said she owed her an apology: Barbara wasn't hers to give away. Miss Urquhart looked so sad. She said all she wanted was to give Barbara a good home.

"Afterwards I tried to get Flora to come to the farm, but she insisted on going back to Lilac Cottage. She wanted to be alone."

Above them, the leaves murmured. From nearby came the scream of an owl, hunting. "Do you remember," Kate went on, "how when I first came to Belhaven, I was frightened of everything, including you. You were so tall."

"We'd been waiting all day and you shut yourself in your bedroom and wouldn't speak to us."

Kate laughed. "What a beast I was! I thought I'd never see Callum or Grandpa John again. Lizzie, won't you come back? Neil would gladly let you have the cottage. Barbara could be with her cousins. We'd be together every day until you get married."

The owl screamed again, farther away. She imagined Barbara playing in the garden with May and Annie, learning to feed the ducks. Then she imagined her own life: not the owner of Belhaven but the penniless, unwed sister, milking the cows, churning the butter, washing the clothes. "Louis wants to marry Mr. Rintoull's daughter," she said, "the girl I saw in the clubhouse."

"But he's devoted to you!" Kate sat up. "All that harvesting and mending. I remember how he wrote when Barbara was born. Maybe his fancy wandered for a few weeks, but he'll come around."

"I don't think so." Beyond the trees were a few dull stars. "He's afraid of being poor again. With Ivy, he won't have to worry."

"Why aren't you angry?"

"I was angry, furious, but I know Louis didn't mean to betray me. He was just being nice to Mr. Rintoull's daughter, the way he's nice to women, and one thing led to another."

"So has he said he's marrying her?" Kate pressed. When Lizzie admitted he hadn't, she said, "Don't give up now. You've caused everyone so much trouble. In six months Louis will have finished his apprenticeship. Maybe he can't marry you on New Year's Eve, but once he finds a situation, he can."

She did not admit that she was still waiting for him; that if he didn't come in a fortnight, or by the end of the month, or soon, she would go to Glasgow. Instead she said, "Do you still remember things the way you used to? I've never met anyone else who can remember what happened when they were two."

She sensed rather than saw Kate nod. "Yes," she said slowly, "I remember you as a baby, and our mother playing games with me. Maybe it's because Granny Agnes talked about you both all the time. I talk to May and Annie about Rab and Flora every day so they won't forget them."

As they walked back to the farmhouse, it was Kate who guided Lizzie around a fallen branch, reminded her to latch the gate. "I'll visit you soon," she said. "I'd like to bring the girls to the seaside."

THE NEXT DAY, BOTH HOLDING BACK TEARS, THEY sorted through Flora's possessions. They each took a shawl and a necklace. Kate took the plate depicting Robert Burns; Lizzie took the Toby jug. Afterwards she picked a bunch of cornflowers, put Barbara in the wagon, and set off for the village. She would visit the churchyard while Miss Urquhart was safely in school. On the outskirts of Langmuir she met Dr. Murray coming home from splinting a broken leg, and at the horse trough, Miss Dawson and Mrs. McClaren. Each offered condolences and each asked Barbara if she was being a good girl. They know, Lizzie thought, but no one is going to say anything. She left the wagon at the churchyard gate and carried Barbara and the flowers inside. On her grandfather's grey granite stone, a space waited for *Flora, wife of.*

"Remember Grandfather reading to you?" she asked Barbara as she knelt to set the cornflowers in a jar before the stone. "And Grandmother playing Pat-a-cake."

But Barbara was walking away from the grave, crowing. Turning, Lizzie saw Miss Urquhart, face alight, arms outstretched. As she kissed Barbara, her blue hat fell to the ground. She retrieved it and, bending to hold Barbara's hand, walked towards the grave. Lizzie leapt to her feet.

"I was very sorry to hear about Flora," said Miss Urquhart. "She was a remarkable woman."

She had always thought the teacher's eyes were brown. Now, as Miss Urquhart knelt beside Barbara, she saw they were that greenish brown called hazel. "Lizzie Craig," she said, "you've treated me worse than your worst enemy. I didn't steal Barbara. Flora was glad to let me have her and I gave her a good home where she was happy. Then you came and stole her like a thief, not even a note. Do you know how terrible it was to come back from the school and be told some strange man had taken her?"

She was looking down at the teacher kneeling on the grass, but it was as if she were back in the classroom, Miss Urquhart standing over her, scolding her French verbs, her untidiness. "I'm sorry," she said. "Barbara was in danger."

"All you had to do was tell me so I could be careful. What kind of mother will you be? That ring you're wearing"—she pointed—"is a lie. You've no husband. Even your grandparents despaired of you. You just do whatever suits you: run off to Glasgow, run back. You don't deserve to have Barbara."

"She is my daughter."

"No," said Miss Urquhart firmly. "You gave her up. If you'd come a week later, the paper making her my ward would have been signed."

So she had had not one narrow escape, but two. From the road came the sounds of a cart rolling along, someone shouting, "Come on." When she could speak again, Lizzie said, "Lots of children in Glasgow need a good home. Why can't you find another daughter?"

"Why can't you?" Beneath Miss Urquhart's hazel eyes, she felt herself growing smaller and smaller. At last, as if she had her answer, the teacher turned away. She bent to pick several daisies, offered them to Barbara, and rose gracefully to her feet. Above them the church bell began to chime. When the air stopped vibrating, she spoke again. "Flora told me you have second sight. That must be a big responsibility."

She had never thought of her pictures in that way. "But I can't stop what I see," she said. "Or change it." They both watched as Barbara placed the daisies beside the jar of cornflowers.

"I'm being careful," said Miss Urquhart, "but if you really see the future, then I suppose there will be a fire. At school you were so quick and you had a fine gift for drawing. I used to think you might be a teacher."

For a moment Lizzie considered telling her about the locomotive tracers'—how she had made money by her drawing—but from the road came the sound of bleating; someone, probably Mr. Wright, was driving a flock through the village. By the time the sheep had passed, she had come to her senses. "Sometimes," she said, "I wish I'd gone to one of those homes for fallen women in Glasgow. I never meant to cause so much trouble and be a bad person."

A little cry made them both turn. Barbara had left the flowers and was trying to climb onto Robert Strachan's stone. Miss Urquhart reached her first. With Barbara in her arms, she walked back to Lizzie. "Try to take good care of her," she said. She kissed Barbara, set her down, and walked away.

XVII

*

In Burntisland it rained, it stopped raining, she hung out the washing, Andrew borrowed a little chair for Barbara, Jean passed on
two of her daughters' dresses and Lizzie drew their portraits, she
almost beat Andrew at chess, Oscar brought home a dead starling.
When the woman came out of the weather house three days in a
row, Andrew suggested he teach her to play golf. He led the way
down Cromwell Road, past the old links, to the new course that
lay beside the road to the east. On the first hole, while Barbara
examined the grass, he showed Lizzie how to set the ball on a tus-
sock and swing the club not just with her arms but with her whole
body. She practiced a few times. Then she put her head down and
swung. She was still holding the club over her shoulder as the ball
landed in the middle of the fairway and bounced twice.

"I knew you'd have the knack," Andrew said.

His own ball was only a few yards ahead of hers. "Ball, ball," said
Barbara. She had found a worm in the damp grass and was holding
it tenderly.

They started walking down the fairway. To their right the Firth of Forth, beneath cloudy skies, was grey as flint. To their left the Binn rose up. Andrew had told her that, like Largo Law, it was an extinct volcano. What a fiery place the Kingdom of Fife used to be, she thought. Again, her ball landed a few yards behind his. They played five holes and she lost by nine shots. "It's your putting that lets you down," Andrew said. "You hit the ball too hard."

That evening, when Barbara was asleep, she carried a club and a ball out to the garden. While Oscar sat on the doorstep, and the swifts and swallows wheeled overhead, she set four saucers on different parts of the lawn and tried to hit them. Andrew had told her to keep her head down, her arms close to her body. The ball swerved at invisible dips and hummocks, overshot or fell short, as she tapped and retrieved it, tapped and retrieved. The bats came out. She had hit two saucers when she felt the familiar jolt.

A woman was walking towards a building with a row of pillars in front. She recognised the station at Burntisland and then, with a sense of wonder, she recognised the woman. It's me, she thought. It was a sunny day, and she was walking fast, almost running, her larkspur-blue blouse pulling loose, strands of hair falling around her shoulders. On the platform, too impatient to stay still, she walked up and down, devouring the minutes until she heard the train approach. The engine was one she had drawn at the locomotive tracers'. It ground to a halt; the carriages lined up along the platform; the doors flung open . . .

She was alone again with the bats and the saucers. Bending to pick up the latter, she heard the high-pitched cries of the former. Louis was coming, she thought, but why had she, finally, seen herself?

....

IN THE MORNING ALL ANYONE COULD TALK ABOUT WAS the heat; how close it was, how airless. Despite propping open the bakery door, she and Jean were constantly patting their foreheads, wiping their hands. After lunch she left Andrew in the garden, a wet handkerchief over his head, and took Barbara down to the shore. Even there the air was still, but the water was pleasingly cool. She envied Barbara sitting down in the waves. Other children were doing the same, splashing and laughing. Back at the house, she put together a cold supper. They had just sat down to pork pie and salad when a jagged seam of lightning split the sky. Oscar fled to the bedroom and the three of them stood in the doorway, listening to the thunder roll around the Binn. Lightning lit their faces, and a peal of thunder rang overhead. Barbara cried out. As Lizzie bent to pick her up, fat drops of rain began to fall.

After Andrew retired, she sat at the table and, while the rain drummed on the roof, wrote to Tom. She told him about the bakery and Barbara and that Andrew was teaching her golf and chess.

He still beats me at both but I'm improving. Today was very warm and this evening a thunderstorm broke. The noise was deafening. I keep wondering if there will be a fire at the teacher's house. In the past my pictures have always come true, even when I tried to stop them, but maybe, if Miss Urquhart is careful, the fire won't happen. I know I've caused problems for you and I hope you won't be angry. Andrew said you usually visit in the summer. We could take Barbara out to the Black Rocks.

She could not decide how to sign the letter and finally settled on *Yours, Lizzie.* Quickly she sealed it in an envelope and, not caring whether Louis saw, wrote the address.

SHE WAS LEAVING THE BAKERY, CARRYING HER LOAF, planning to buy apples, when she heard her name said in the way only he did. He was wearing a brown jacket she hadn't seen before, dark trousers, and his usual shoes, the laces neatly knotted. "Mr. Malcolm told me where you worked. He said to tell you he and Barbara are fine."

For a few seconds, at the sight of his blue eyes, she forgot everything.

"Why did you leave Glasgow without telling me?" he said. "Why aren't you at Belhaven?"

Anxious to escape the curious glances of the High Street, she began to walk towards the links. He fell in beside her. "This seems like a nice town," he said. "Is there a tailor's?"

After a dozen steps on the links, she could feel the dampness seeping into her shoes as it had that day at the farm when they walked to the old bridge in the rain and, later, she had left Barbara for the first time. On the beach the tide was low, the sea ruffled beneath swift clouds. She kept walking, heading away from the town. If only she could walk to Lower Largo and meet Flora on the beach.

"Lizzie, stop. Let's sit here."

He was gesturing towards a tree trunk. Reluctantly she sat at one end, setting the loaf beside her. Without looking, she knew he was biting his lip. "Why did you leave like that?" he said again. "I felt like a fool when I found out Tom knew where you were all along."

Two women walked by, arm in arm, each using her free hand to hold up her skirt. She and Kate could walk like that if they didn't have five children between them. Briefly she told him about the pictures, the fire, Barbara being in danger.

"You're telling me"—his voice was ripe with indignation—"you gave up your job and your room at the Tam o' Shanter because of some daydream? Lizzie, you're not a child. Has there been a fire?"

"Not yet."

"So you see—" He broke off. "What's that?"

He was pointing at the ring, which nowadays she wore unthinkingly; the gold was dull with flour. "People here think I'm a widow," she said.

"A widow?"

Again, she realised, he had given her circumstances no thought. She remembered Tom, shyly presenting her with the leather box. How his face had changed when she took it as a sign of widowhood. A boy ran by, chasing a ball. "Does Ivy know you're here?" she said.

"No one knows I'm here. Lizzie, I never meant for anything to happen with her. You have to believe me. I didn't see how you and I could ever be together."

"People wait," she said. "People wait all the time. Edith and Ralph waited three years."

"They knew what they were waiting for: Ralph's father to hand over the pub."

"We were waiting for you to finish your apprenticeship." How often had he reminded her of that? "You took her to the clubhouse, didn't you? Did you use the blanket?"

She had been sure she already knew. Now, in some hidden part of herself, she discovered she was still hoping he would say, "No, all we did was talk about tailoring, drink lemonade." With his silence, the hope vanished as swiftly as his letter in the fire.

"How could you?" she said. "How could you replace me after everything I did for you? I remember the morning I knew I was in the family way, I was so glad. I was sure you would be glad too, that we'd get married. Instead I had to go home and tell my grandparents and hide from everyone in the village. All those months I wanted the baby to go away, but after she arrived, I began to have new feelings. Not at first. At first, all she did was cry and need things. I came back to Glasgow because I wanted her to have a father. I didn't know how much I'd miss her. But I was too late. If anyone's a child, it's you, thinking you can have both of us, me and Ivy."

"I don't want to lose you." He was drumming his feet on the sand.

"And Barbara?"

Sand spurted from beneath his heels. "She came to the door with Mr. Malcolm. I didn't recognise her."

"You are her father."

"Not on the birth certificate."

She jumped up and shoved him, hard, off the tree trunk, into the sand. While he lay there, sprawling, she unlaced her shoes, peeled off her damp stockings, and ran towards the sea. The water was cold but not perishing. It covered her feet, her ankles. Behind her he cried, "Lizzie, stop. Lizzie." She raised her skirts higher, took another step. If he wanted to talk, let him follow. Overhead a seagull, its wings two perfect arcs, flew towards Edinburgh.

The rocks were still a hundred feet away, the water only up to her knees. Next year, she thought, she would teach Barbara to swim. Behind her, she could hear splashing. She stood waiting, not looking back, until he was beside her, a few feet away.

"How can you think of leaving Barbara," she said, "after your father left you?"

"Lizzie, she doesn't know me. I saw my father every day for nine years. His last words were 'Be ready to play me a tune in April.'"

"Tom lost his father," she said. "So did I." She had never noticed the coincidence.

A drop of water—a tear? the sea?—rolled down his cheek. "Tom's father died in an accident," he said. "You never knew yours. I'll be a good father when I'm ready."

"Barbara's here now. My grandfather put 'illegitimate' on the birth certificate to save you."

Wind zigzagged across the water, turning it light and dark. A coal ferry steamed towards Edinburgh. He began to recite the familiar details—the importance of Mr. Rintoull's goodwill, working at the shop—until she interrupted. "Why would he help you if you break things off with Ivy?"

"There's nothing to be broken."

She could see he believed his own words; he was still the boy who had waited, month after month, for his father to write. "Tom told me Ivy is a nice girl," she said. "She wouldn't have gone to the clubhouse if she didn't believe you were going to marry her." No need to add "like I did."

The water rippled around them. "But," he said, "I want to marry you."

Here were the words she had waited for, for so long, but uttered in a tone of such despair. He took a step towards her and gasped. He must have stepped on something sharp: a stone or a shell. His shirt was open a couple of buttons and she glimpsed the faint freckles on his chest that she had thought of as their private constellation. She remembered Miss Urquhart's accusation: she just did whatever suited her.

"No," she said. "No, you don't, not really. And"—she clenched her hands; it took all her determination—"I don't want to marry you."

If he had looked at her, he would have seen what the words cost her, that she was throwing down a gauntlet. Or if he had kissed her. If he had awoken those feelings which began and ended with him. But he was reaching into the water, examining his foot. For the first time she noticed a bare spot, the size of a shilling, on the crown of his head. In a few years, he might be as bald as the minister.

He was still bending down when she began to walk, slowly, towards the shore. She kept waiting for him to run after her. To tell her she was wrong, to kneel down, to say he was sorry, to beg her, over and over, to marry him. She let her skirts fall so that the fabric clung to her legs and dragged with every step.

Come, she thought. Come to me. You have only to ask.

Through her tears she could make out the little seabirds skimming the waves.

XVIII

＊

On Monday they were drinking tea, surrounded by warm loaves, when Jean asked about the lad she'd seen waiting outside the shop. Was he a friend, she said, her round face shining with curiosity.

"A friend of my husband's."

Jean nodded, curly hair bobbing. "Did you see me lifting the trays today? My shoulder's healed. Forgive me if I'm prying, but you never said how he died."

"In a fire."

The words came to her unbidden, and at once seemed true. The picture of the fire had changed everything. Only by thinking about Barbara had she managed to walk away from Louis, to return to the tree trunk and put on her shoes and pick up her loaf of bread and walk across the links and up Cromwell Road to Andrew's house. Jean was still saying how terrible as she went to hang up the Open sign and Miss Lawson, with her customary greeting, stepped into the shop.

When she got home, Barbara was saying "Och"—her version of "Oscar," Andrew claimed. Sensing her restlessness, he suggested a round of golf and, after supper, a game of chess. She lost both.

After he went to bed, she fetched her sketch pad and settled to drawing Louis as she had last seen him, standing in the water, staring past the Black Rocks towards Edinburgh. For the first time, she thought, a picture was wrong; she hadn't met him at the station. She had drawn him before, sometimes forgetting the small bump on his nose. Now she included that and every other detail, his slightly large ears, his too-long moustache; she tried to suggest the wind lifting his hair. From memory she drew his jacket with its four buttonholes. She made his expression calm and serious, as if he were contemplating the spires of Edinburgh rather than how to please both her and Ivy. At the bottom she wrote: *Your father, Louis Hunter, August 10th. 1893.*

SHE WAS SERVING FRANCES, THE WOMAN WHOSE DAUGHTERS were collecting seashells, when Andrew, still in his shirtsleeves, came into the bakery, carrying Barbara. She gave Frances her change and he held out a small, pale envelope. Who else, she thought, as she stepped from behind the counter and followed him into the street, who else could be ill, or dead? The coalman's wagon, piled high with sacks of coal, lumbered by.

"Open it," said Andrew, and she did.

Fire at Miss Urquhart's Sunday. Safe. Staying at Lilac Cottage.

Ten words, ten words that vindicated everything.

"Is someone ill?" He was standing beside her, still holding Barbara.

She handed him the telegram. He read it aloud, stumbling over the teacher's name. "This was the fire you saw," he said.

When she told him about the pictures, he had nodded as if he believed her. Now, from the way his grey eyes regarded her, she knew he believed her in a different way. She stepped back into the bakery to ask Jean if she could leave early. As they walked home, swinging Barbara between them, she told him about Lilac Cottage, how first Kate and Callum had lived there, then her grandparents, she and Barbara. "It's strange," she said, "to think of Miss Urquhart sleeping in my bed."

After lunch, when Barbara was sleeping and they were drinking a second cup of tea, he questioned her about the pictures. What kinds of things did she see? Were they always bad? How much warning did she have before something happened? Yesterday the newspaper had reported a mining accident in Yorkshire; a hundred and thirty-five men had been killed. Did her pictures ever show her that kind of thing?

"They don't," she said, "but my great-grandmother saw the outbreak of the Crimean War."

"So, you come from a family of seers," he said.

She had not thought of it that way before, but yes, that must be true, a gift passed down, sometimes skipping a generation. The idea made her feel a little less alone.

"Maybe Barbara will see pictures," he suggested.

"I wouldn't wish it on her," she said, "but I have no choice."

When Barbara and Andrew were both in bed, she fetched the drawing of her parents and studied it in the lamplight. Through all the changes in her life they had remained the same: her mother in her good dress, her lips slightly parted, her father in his Sunday suit, looking straight ahead, eager for whatever came next. Surely they had known—what else could explain their elopement?— the pleasures of the clubhouse. I hope you enjoyed your nights together, she thought. Soon she would be older than they had ever been.

ON SATURDAY AS SHE GOT READY TO GO TO THE BAKERY, Andrew said he needed a favour. "When you finish work, will you meet the train that arrives at eleven fifteen?"

"Why?" She was washing Barbara's face.

"I'm only the messenger," he said. "Meet the train and come back and tell Barbara and me about it. We'll be waiting for you."

As she brushed her hair, she thought Kate must have written to Andrew, wanting to surprise her. She slipped on her grandmother's necklace and tucked it under her blouse for safekeeping. All morning as she sold bread and talked to the regular customers, she thought about seeing Kate. She hoped she would bring May and Annie but not the younger boys. They would meet Andrew; then she could take them down to the shore. Kate would tell her about the fire, and they would make a plan to help Miss Urquhart find another daughter.

By eleven the bakery shelves were almost empty, everyone stocking up for the weekend. She put an extra loaf in her bag and hurried up the slope, past the Octagonal Church, and down towards the station. As she approached, a coal wagon creaked by, heading for the ferry. A white butterfly hovered over a spray of purple flowers. This is my picture, she thought: me meeting a train. She stopped to tuck in her blouse before she walked onto the platform. Other people, none she knew, were waiting patiently, but she could not contain herself; she walked swiftly from one end of the platform to the other. At last, in the distance, puffs of steam rose above the trees, and the whistle sounded. The engine came into view—it was a kind she had drawn at the locomotive tracers'—and hissed to a halt. Everyone else on the platform stepped forward, ready to board. She stepped back so she could see the doors opening the length of the train. There was a woman, not Kate. There were two families. A man in a suit with a suitcase. A man wearing a clerical collar. From the last door of the train a young man stepped down, a faded satchel swinging from his shoulder. As he came towards her, the colour rose in his cheeks, he reached out his hand, and she reached out her own hand, the one not already wearing his ring, to greet him.

Acknowledgements

In 2001 I published *Eva Moves the Furniture*, a novel that contained almost everything I knew about my mother, Eva McEwen, and her gift of second sight. At that time I believed Eva's only living relatives were the great aunts who, after her early death, took care of me. But in 2016, thanks to Irene Connelly and Ancestry.com, I received an email from Australia. It turned out Eva had many relatives. When Gayle Phipps kindly welcomed me to Brisbane, I met dozens of cousins once, twice, three times removed. I am especially grateful to Gayle, John Strickland, and Gwen McCown for telling me about Eva's mother and grandmother. Heather Baldwin gave me a lock of my grandmother Barbara's hair.

In March 2020, when I understood that the pandemic meant I couldn't go to Scotland, I sat down to write about those stories: a way of visiting the landscapes I loved every day.

One of the pleasures of writing *The Road from Belhaven* was rereading the books of my youth in the guise of research: *Mansfield Park* by Jane Austen, *Wuthering Heights* by Emily Brontë, *Alice's Adventures in Wonderland* by Lewis Carroll, *Great Expectations* by Charles Dickens, *Sylvia's Lovers* by Elizabeth Gaskell, *Tess of the D'Urbervilles*, A

Pair of Blue Eyes, and *The Mayor of Casterbridge* by Thomas Hardy, *The Water Babies* by Charles Kingsley, *The Princess and the Goblin* and *The Princess and Curdie* by George MacDonald, *Imagined Corners* by Willa Muir, *The Quarry Wood* by Nan Shepherd, *Kidnapped* by Robert Louis Stevenson, *The Small House at Allington* by Anthony Trollope.

For a sense of more factual details about weather, work, and place, I am indebted to the following: *Joseph Ashby of Tysoe* by M. K. Ashby, *The Ballad and the Plough* by David Kerr Cameron, *Scottish Folk and Fairy Tales*, edited by Gordon Jarvie, *Night Falls on Ardnamurchan* by Alasdair Maclean, *An Autobiography* by Edwin Muir, *Kilvert's Diary*, edited by William Plomer, *Hedingham Harvest* by Geoffrey Robinson, *Life Among the Scots* by Janet Adam Smith, *The Yellow on the Broom* by Betsy Whyte. I owe several crucial insights to Diane Johnson's marvellous biography, *The True History of the First Mrs. Meredith and Other Lesser Lives*.

Thomas Graham Bonar kept a meticulous diary of Greigston Farm near St. Andrews from 1824 to 1833. I am grateful to Marie Robinson for transcribing the diary and to the University of St. Andrews library for making it available.

My gratitude to "Edelweiss," who in 1897 won the Girl's Own Paper competition for the best essay on the topic "My Daily Round: A Competition for all Girls who work with their hands." Her eloquent description of locomotive tracers delighted me and gave my heroine Lizzie Craig a job.

My deep thanks, once again, to the amazing Amanda Urban and to Jennifer Barth, who entered into this story so fully—we discussed how Louis would knot his shoelaces—and responded with fierce intelligence and unfailing patience to my many cris de coeur. I am glad to be back at the wonderful Knopf. Thank you, Reagan Arthur, Jordan Pavlin, Vanessa Haughton, Kelly Shi, and Morgan Fenton for giving my work a home and for putting me in such excellent company. My gratitude to Nicholas Latimer for taking my author photograph.

I have the good fortune to teach at the Iowa Writers' Workshop. My gratitude to the incomparable Lan Samantha Chang, Sasha Khmelnik, Deb West, and Jan Zenisek for inspiration, companionship, and help, and to my excellent colleagues: Jamel Brinkley, Ethan Canin, and Charles D'Ambrosio. Thank you to my students, past and present, who every day teach me something new.

It is a pleasure to thank the friends and fellow writers who keep me company in Boston and our brilliant local booksellers. Thank you, Kim Cooper, for watching over me. Thank you, Kathleen Hill, for smiling when I said I'd been reading Proust. Susan Brison read the novel in the final stages and offered vital comments. I am so grateful for her keen eyes and her devoted friendship. After more than thirty years, I am running out of ways to thank Andrea Barrett for sharing her excellent brain and for helping me, in conversation and by stellar example, to write about the past.

I am lucky to be part of a family of readers. Sally and Keith Rose, Janet Sylvester, and Richard Shorter were particularly generous in helping with research. Emma Shorter lent me her lovely flat. Chris Forrest and Rich Sylvester provided a desk and delicious meals. Eric Garnick kept me company on and off the page.

My wonderful nieces and nephew, their partners and their children, make my life larger in the best way. My beloved adopted mother Merril Sylvester taught me to read many years ago and has been guiding me ever since. Her knowledge of Victorian Scotland was unparalleled, and she was always happy to discuss details of history, manners, and mores. "Just write the book, darling," she said in one of our last conversations, "and I'll tell you what's wrong with it." I am very sorry that she is no longer here to do so.

A NOTE ABOUT THE AUTHOR

Margot Livesey was born and grew up on the edge
of the Scottish Highlands. She is the author of a
collection of stories and nine other novels, including
Eva Moves the Furniture, *The Flight of Gemma
Hardy*, and *The Boy in the Field*. She has received
awards from the National Endowment for the Arts, the
Guggenheim Foundation, and the Radcliffe Institute.
She lives in Cambridge, Massachusetts, and is on the
faculty of the Iowa Writers' Workshop.

A NOTE ON THE TYPE

The text of this book was set in Electra, a typeface
designed by W. A. Dwiggins (1880–1956). This face
cannot be classified as either modern or old style. It
is not based on any historical model, nor does it echo
any particular period or style. It avoids the extreme
contrasts between thick and thin elements that mark
most modern faces, and it attempts to give a feeling of
fluidity, power, and speed.

Typeset by Scribe
Philadelphia, Pennsylvania

Printed and bound by Berryville Graphics
Berryville, Virginia

Designed by Anna B. Knighton